THE SEVEN SORROWS

GREGG KUEHN

DIVERTIR
PUBLISHING
Salem, NH

THE SEVEN SORROWS

Gregg Kuehn

Copyright © 2017 by Gregg Kuehn

Cover design by Kenneth Tupper

Published by Divertir Publishing LLC
PO Box 232
North Salem, NH 03073
http://www.divertirpublishing.com/

ISBN-13: 978-1-938888-19-9
ISBN-10: 1-938888-19-7

Library of Congress Control Number: 2017950855

Printed in the United States of America

DEDICATION

Dedicated to my mom M.M, wife Kathy, sons Charlie and Andy, and daughter-in-law Jane whose deep love of a far-away island inspired me to never give up.

CONTENTS

"This government, as promised, has maintained the closest surveillance of the Soviet Military buildup on the island of Cuba. Within the past week, unmistakable evidence has established the fact that a series of offensive missile sites is now in preparation on that imprisoned island. The purpose of these bases can be none other than to provide a nuclear strike capability against the Western Hemisphere."

Address to the nation by President John F. Kennedy
October 22, 1962

"I thought I might never live to see another day."

Robert S. McNamara, U.S. Secretary of State
Reflecting on the Cuban Missile Crisis, 1962

"The Soviet government has ordered the dismantling of bases and the dispatch of equipment to the U.S.S.R."

Letter to President Kennedy from Nikita Khrushchev,
Premier of the U.S.S.R.
October 28, 1962

CHAPTER 1

Skornyazhny Lane, Moscow, Russia

The man who had less than one hour to live raised himself up on an elbow, craned his neck, and peered out of his filthy window. The smattering of rain blurred his view of the street below, and he fell back with a grunt. Alexei Baranov stiffened, leaned over the edge of his threadbare cot, and retched into his handkerchief. He pulled it away from his mouth, wiped his lips, and crushed the cloth into a ball. Reddish spittle oozed onto his fingers. The soiled handkerchief slipped from his hand and fell to the floor.

Alexei fell back onto the cot and groaned. His long snow-white hair lay in stark contrast to the dirty yellowed pillow. The pain was worse today, but he would not give in to it. He would not die before the boy arrived. Everything depended on Pyotr.

The pains in his stomach had increased to the point where it was nearly impossible for him to hobble down the dim hallway to the toilet he shared with another tenant of the aging apartment building. The three story brick structure sat on a narrow lane in a northeast section of Moscow not far from several metro stations, the busy "B-Ring" road that circled Moscow, and a few restaurants. On warm sunny days children played in a small playground just across the street from Alexei's second floor window. But today his windows were fully shut and the street outside stood silent in response to the cold and rain. Alexei stared at the water-stained ceiling and drew a thin blanket over his frail body. The slight movement sent a stabbing pain deep into his belly. His body convulsed. The pain shot up into his chest and he grunted again. He lifted his head a few inches off the pillow and studied the door, hoping for Pyotr's arrival. The hallway remained silent.

Panic gripped Alexei as he stared at the empty doorway. What if Pyotr hadn't received the letter he'd sent nearly two weeks ago? Would his secret die with him? He closed his eyes, laid his head back on the pillow, and tried to smile, ignoring the rancid stench of his dim room. Pyotr will come soon, he told himself.

Alexei sighed, recalling those glorious days long ago when Khrushchev had challenged the West, when the real glory of Soviet Communism reached its peak. He'd never been as proud of Mother Russia as he'd been during those October days of 1962 when the Soviets had challenged the power and influence of the capitalist pigs in America. Damn that arrogant Kennedy and his smug little brother, Bobby. They had ruined everything. A chuckle escaped his lips as he considered that he outlived them both. Another cough wracked his frail body. He felt each of his eighty one years, and they had been hard ones. The long years of running and hiding had taken their toll.

He flinched, and then smiled as he caught the sound of a distant door creaking open and then closed a moment later. Hurried footsteps pounded up the stairway and echoed from the hallway as Pyotr Asimov swept into the room. He was young, not yet thirty, with short sandy hair and brown eyes. His thin muscular body complemented his five foot eleven inch height. If not conventionally handsome, many women his age found him attractive. Something about the way his eyes smiled interested them. Pyotr stopped in mid stride as he took in the sick old man lying on the filthy cot. His eyes opened wide at the sight of Alexei's shriveled body, hollow eyes, and blood-spattered chin. He stared at the old man for a brief moment, taking in his crooked yellow teeth and dirty stringy beard, then hurried to the window and peeked out to the street below. It was empty. He took a step toward Alexei.

"Thank heaven, Uncle Alexei. I am so happy to see you. I'm sorry I couldn't get here sooner, but I only received your letter this morning. My mother sent it to me. The letter was unopened. Neither she nor my father knows where I am. But why am I here? What's going on? Why did you tell me to be careful?" Pyotr said as he sidled back to the window and glanced out again. In spite of the chill he raised the window an inch to allow fresh air into the stinking room. He studied the street below for a moment, but it was quiet. He was certain he hadn't been followed.

"Yes, my boy. I am happy you are finally here. It is good to see you after so many years. You have your mother's eyes. Is she well? I am dying and have something important to tell you. And something you must do. For the glory of old Russia. I don't have much time. Sit down and listen.

"Our entire nation was so proud, so excited, in 1962 when the thug Castro agreed to take our missiles in Cuba. But soon our joy turned to bitterness and despair when Kennedy outsmarted Khrushchev and forced him to send the nuclear weapons back to Russia. I was right there, in Cuba. We had the capitalist pigs cowering in a corner but we lost. Yes, later Khrushchev got what he deserved when the Presidium threw him out of office in disgrace, but by then the damage was done."

Pyotr leaned forward, his face just inches from Alexei's. "I am aware of the history of the Cuban Missile Crisis. But that is ancient history. Why am I here? What am I to do?"

"I will get to that, but I must tell you other things first. Only a few of us soldiers knew what truly happened. We stole some of the nuclear weapons and a launcher, hoping some day to return them to Cuba or to use them ourselves against America. Not the big ones. Those came back to Russia. The small hand-held ones that the Russians stole from the Americans when they were in Germany in 1957. We stole them from the shipment returning to Russia and then hid them. But not in Cuba. They were in a few small trunks and we were able to steal them without anybody noticing. We took them out by boat. I am the last who knows where they are hidden." Another hacking cough interrupted his story.

Pyotr fell back in his chair, shocked by what he was hearing. His mind reeled and he blinked hard. Was this finally his opportunity to get to America? The weapons could be his ticket to freedom and a better life.

"Yes, Alexei. How may I help you?"

"I must tell you where to find the nuclear weapons. You will be in danger, but you are young and can protect yourself."

Pyotr glanced at the window again, and then turned to Alexei. He had to get this information to Colin Farthington in America. It had been a long time since he'd communicated with him, but he still had the phone number for Colin's niece, here in Moscow. He hoped she hadn't returned to America.

"OK. I will help you. Now tell me: where are the weapons hidden. What do you want me to do?"

Alexei wiped his mouth with his sleeve. It came away with thick bloody phlegm. He rested on the pillow and closed his eyes, his breath shallow and labored.

"Soon everything went to hell," he continued, ignoring Pyotr's plea. "Captain Karmov had us posted to Siberia where we changed our names; eventually every one of my comrades disappeared or died under mysterious circumstances. I fled and imagined I was safe after Karmov himself died in a car wreck, but I was wrong. Somehow others found out and have hunted me all these years. If they caught me I would face a horrible death. I moved like the wind: here one moment and gone the next. Those who chased me are bad men who have no love of Russia. I, alone, had no power to bring the weapons back home, and those who ruled after Khrushchev were weak old men. Too weak. They were all a disgrace to the Party. I was poor scum in their eyes, and nobody would listen to someone like me. I had no choice but to flee for my life." Alexei paused, coughed, and took several raspy breaths.

"Enough of this history, Alexei. Tell me where the weapons are hidden. I need the information. Tell me while you still can." Pyotr glanced at the clock and turned to the window. The building and street below were quiet.

"You must do what is right to restore the glory and honor of our Motherland. There are now men in the government who can help. Good men like our President. Old KGB. They are standing up to America again. You must find them. Tell them to get the nuclear weapons. They are called Davy Crockett."

"Yes, yes! I will do as you ask," said Pyotr. "Please hurry."

A minute passed in silence. In spite of the chill in the room, sweat trickled down Pyotr's forehead. He couldn't fully process what this information might do for him, but he knew he must get it to the American. He peeked out the window and watched a small blue sedan creep past Alexei's building. The driver turned his head, gazed directly toward Alexei's room and then turned toward a man sitting next to him. Pyotr flinched in surprise, leaned away from the window and waited until the car disappeared from sight.

Alexei let out an agonizing grunt then opened his eyes and stared at the boy. His vision blurred and his lower lip trembled as spittle dribbled down his chin. A new intense pain stabbed into the back of his head, confusing his thoughts.

"Alexei! Cuba! Nuclear weapons! Tell me where they are hidden!" Pyotr said as he grabbed the old man's shoulders with both hands.

"Yes, for Russia," Alexei croaked.

Pyotr released his grip and let out his breath.

"Baranov! Tell me!" Pyotr nearly screamed as panic began to take hold. He must learn the truth. He grabbed a small flask of vodka from his pack and forced some into the old man's mouth. A long minute passed in agonizing silence.

The old man jerked. His eyes opened and he tried to speak, but only a hoarse wheezing sound escaped his lips. Another shot of vodka made him shudder. Alexei closed his eyes, shivered in the damp cold and tried again. Slowly.

"Pyotr…go…Kremlin…secret…tower…tunnel…" he stuttered.

This time the cough brought blood from his nose. Pyotr tore off a small corner of Alexei's blanket and, with shaking hands, shoved it into Alexei's nostril.

"Go on," Pyotr urged.

"Map…nuclear…Davy Crockett…" the old man gurgled as blood began to trickle from his mouth. A deep hacking cough brought another horrid stench as his bowels failed him. Gasping in pain, he tried again, his trembling hands clutching his belly under the thin blanket.

"Yes, you told me about Davy Crockett. Tell me the rest," Pyotr said. Bile rose in the back of his throat and his heart pounded.

"Bonny...on island eh...fortune...in cave..." his voice failed as he stared wide-eyed into the horror of Pyotr's face. He smiled weakly taking another shallow breath, "not Cuba...near..."

Finally he sighed and fell back on his pillow. Bloody spittle dripped from his chin and he spoke no more.

"Alexei! Who, what is bonnie? What island? Do you mean fortune?" Pyotr said in a hoarse whisper. Then he understood. Alexei Baranov would tell him nothing more. A moment later the old man's eyes became dull marbles staring at the ceiling. The weak smile, more like a grimace, remained on his face.

Pyotr Asimov scanned the room for something to cover the old man. He would have to leave the body but couldn't leave the corpse for the rats. He rushed out into the hall and into an open apartment. Yellow light filtered through a dirty window, providing enough light for Pyotr to see an old green metal desk, a rusty cot with no mattress, and a filthy gray military trunk. He grasped the handle of the trunk and found the latch still worked. This will do, he sighed.

Moments later he stepped out of the building and pulled his collar up around his neck. A young woman wearing a long gray coat and a black knit hat pushed a baby stroller on the sidewalk across from Alexei's building. She hesitated for a moment and glanced at Pyotr. He turned toward her and she quickly bent over and reached into the stroller, cooing softly. A moment later she rose up and hurried down the sidewalk, ignoring Pyotr. He, however, watched until she disappeared behind a tall clipped hedge.

As soon as she turned the corner she checked her surroundings and then pulled a cell phone from a deep pocket and punched a button.

CHAPTER 2

El Fortunato Island, British West Indies—Somewhere East of Cuba

KC Jameson woke to the sound of water cascading over a large waterfall. The roar filled his head with a throbbing echo. He rolled over, pried one eye open, and peeked at the other side of his king sized bed. Empty. There was no waterfall he knew, just the flushing of his toilet down the hall. He sighed, closed his eyes and tried to will away the headache pounding right behind his eyes. Slight nausea tickled at the back of his throat.

A moment later the bathroom door slid open and the sound of footsteps clicked down the hallway outside his room. Melinda Singleton, wearing the same red shorts and white sleeveless top she had worn last night, stuck her head through the bedroom doorway. She was young, about 24, with short brown hair framing a narrow face and a turned up nose. Her thin lips bore no trace of lipstick. She was a small woman with just enough curves in the right places. Her tanned face betrayed no ill effects from the revelry of the previous evening.

"Morning KC. I started the coffee for you. I know it's kinda early, but I have to go. Gotta change my clothes before work. Hey, I had a lot of fun last night. See ya around sometime. Soon I hope. Cheers," she said in a loud voice, forcing KC to shut his eyes even tighter. The back door slammed, the noise pounding deep into KC's skull. Minutes later he listened to the coffee machine finish its task, then struggled out of bed, hobbled to the bathroom, and downed two extra strength aspirins as he stood at the toilet. He felt much older than his thirty three years.

Half an hour later, after three cups of strong coffee and two glasses of mango juice, KC began to feel almost human again. At least physically.

Another meaningless fling, he thought, remembering the previous evening's festivities at the Pink Grouper Bar & Grill. This wasn't the first time he'd slept with Melinda, but he sensed that the next time, if there was one, would not be soon. There would be someone else, but probably not Melinda. At least for a while. Few of the young women on the island desired long-term relationships; they were all free spirits who enjoyed the wild lifestyle of the island. Women like Melinda always made him think of his little sister, Beth, and what she might have become. Their cheery optimism and enthusiasm for life was in stark contrast to the memory of the horrible night in Seattle when a stray bullet had smashed through Beth's bedroom window killing her instantly. KC and Beth, not yet teenagers, had only each other after their father deserted the family and their mother sought refuge in the bottle and a series of abusive men. Somehow KC and Beth survived in their gruesome and dangerous lower class neighborhood. Throughout most of his twenties KC had fallen in and out of many shallow relationships that satisfied his physical, but not emotional needs. He shrugged off the depressing memory of his sister's murder, the blood, and the screeching of runaway tires, and the unsympathetic police.

"Same-old-same-old, maybe my luck will change today," he muttered to himself as he peeked out the window as the sun began its slow rise over the low hills. The needle on his outdoor thermometer was already pushing 80. It would be a good day to go fishing. Better hurry, he mused. Gotta get in my skinny dip before the tourists get to the beach. That should clear my head.

Grabbing a bright green and white striped beach towel, he dropped his shorts on the floor, slipped into his flip-flops, and shuffled down a narrow sandy path. Far to the north a bank of gray clouds hung low in the sky. The easterly breeze blew gently, and the salt water lapped quietly on the beach. The tall grasses on the sand dune waved at him as he hurried past. He never failed to marvel at his luck in finding the small cottage located less than one hundred feet from the beach. Far from the tourist resorts, his stretch of beach was usually quiet and rarely crowded. However, weekends became busier, and quite often a jogger or two trotted past in the cool early morning air. He stopped and squinted up the beach as the rising sun peeked through a break in the clouds and paused when something flickered in the glaring sun light. He waited a moment, but whatever he might have seen had disappeared.

"Safe to take my swim, no little old lady to offend," he said, laughing to himself. His wavy brown hair was cut short, a concession to the salty humid air of the island. Green eyes complemented the shimmering aquamarine colors of the ocean. He dropped the towel from his well-tanned six foot one inch frame, waded naked to knee depth, and dove into the warm water. With powerful strokes he aimed for a distant buoy. He loved the ocean, from its beautiful blue-green hues to the wondrous mysteries that lay beneath the ever changing surface. He was happy he had been able to leave his troubled life in Seattle for the sun and salt water of El Fortunato Island. After his sister's death he had floundered for several years, caught up with the petty crimes and risks of gang life. But ten days in the county jail at age 17 opened his eyes and gave him a new perspective on life. In jail he'd been badgered by stinking drunks, ridiculed by haughty pickpockets, and pestered by heroin addicts. He'd retreated from them all, refusing to enter their dark world, and spent his time brooding in the corner of the large communal cell counting the hours until his release.

One of the local cops had kept his eye on KC and had suggested KC go and talk to Colin Farthington. The super-wealthy industrialist had immediately hired KC as a yard boy at his waterfront estate in an eastern suburb of Seattle. Colin had no family of his own and had taken an instant liking to the lad. For about a year KC performed a variety of menial tasks for Colin and then was promoted to his personal assistant. He learned basic self-defense tactics and began to travel with Colin. He saw the world in a different light, realizing there was much more to life than the back streets of Seattle. While the death of Beth still weighed heavily on him, he began to look at life in a more positive and confident way. During his off hours he worked on earning his high school equivalency. Studies in Environmental Science and Marine Biology at Western Washington University followed. For the past twelve years he'd moved around the world performing ocean related research for one of Colin's charitable foundations.

A sudden wave splashed over his head, bringing him back to the present.

Forty yards up the beach, a lone figure emerged from the glare of the early morning sun and eyed KC as he swam back toward the beach.

CHAPTER 3

El Fortunato, Up the Beach, East of KC's Cottage

Goddamn shit-hole." Nikki Colt said to herself as she stepped out of her room at the Blue Wave Bed and Breakfast. The turquoise water and silky white sand beaches of the world famous Secret Bay held little interest for her. She'd much prefer to be climbing craggy mountains and exploring dark caves. El Fortunato was very dry and dusty with scrubby vegetation; the highest point on the island less than two hundred feet above sea level. Postcard photos completely ignored the interior of the island, focusing on the pristine sand beaches and the tantalizing water. In spite of her distaste for the immediate surroundings she aimed for the water's edge. A brisk walk along the beach was an excellent way to stay in shape. She strolled past the swimming pool, hesitated, and studied the reflection of her face in the calm, clear water. She was aware that men found her attractive, intrigued by her natural beauty, and had learned to pay little attention to their stares.

A short walk later Nikki kicked off her flip-flops, stepped onto the cool sandy beach, and glided along the water's edge with her back to the rising sun. It was unfortunate that her work had led her to this island with its low flat-topped hills and uninteresting flora. Nothing like the magnificent mountains of the Virgin Islands or the sheer beauty of Iceland's glaciers.

Out to sea several fishing boats passed through the cut in the long barrier reef. The coral reef defining Secret Bay was one of the longest in the world and created a special place for tourists. The reef was miles long and protected the pristine white sand beaches from the ravages of strong wave action. Huge rollers only came ashore during the strongest gales. The generally calm waters were perfect for vacationers.

Nikki slowed when a small crab scurried inches from her bare feet and raced to the safety of the salty water. A few minutes later she turned her attention to the beach far ahead and stopped abruptly when a man dropped a towel and waded into the water.

"What the hell? Is that guy naked?" she said to herself. Shaking her head, she frowned when the man dove into the water. Silly, she thought, and turned her mind to the workday ahead.

Minutes later KC grazed the buoy, pivoted and began the return leg of his swim. His head was clear, his headache gone, and he felt terrific. Tiring of the crawl, he changed his stroke and swam like a dolphin, knifing through the waves. He knew the distance to the beach without looking; he sensed the gentle ocean current and adjusted his path to counteract the subtle forces and hit the shore exactly where he had dropped his towel. When his knees brushed the soft sandy bottom, he stopped and sank back on his heels and began to clear saltwater from his face and eyes.

He started to stand and wade out of the water when he glanced toward his beach towel. A pair of long, slim, and shapely female legs filled his view. KC quickly slumped in the water while his eyes traveled up the body of the owner of those beautiful legs. She wore short shorts and a light green T-shirt with a V neck. She wasn't wearing a bra, and the effect, while subtle, caused something to stir below the water line. The T shirt hung comfortably from her well-toned shoulders, exposing athletic arms that matched her legs. She had dark brown hair and wore it short. A simple pair of hoop silver earrings hung from her small lobes. Her lack of a deep tan told KC she had not been on the island for long. A pink hint of sunburn graced her round face. Standing with one hand on her hip, sunglasses propped on the top of her head, she stared at him and smiled.

"Hi," KC said from the relative safety of the water.

"Hello. Have a nice swim?" the woman replied with a grin.

"Yes, I do this almost every morning. Wakes me up. Say, I've never seen you around here before. Ah, what's your name?"

"I'm Nikki Colt."

"Are you on the island for long? Where are you staying?" KC said, running his fingers through his wavy hair.

"A little ways up the beach at the Blue Waves. Once my work is finished I'm out of here. A few weeks, maybe. Who are you?"

KC looked past her and pointed a finger.

"I'm KC Jameson. I live in the house over there and I do ocean research. I'm trying to get a handle on coral decline. What kind of work are you doing?"

"Oh, I'm here getting ready to install a new radar detection system for the island's government. I'm sort of the advance person. A larger team will be here soon. The system we're putting in will warn the government when unauthorized boats approach the island—I'm sure you're aware of the problems with illegal immigrants. We hope to have it up and running later this month," she replied.

"Cool. Say, would you mind turning your back for a bit so I can get my towel?" KC continued, looking first at her long legs and then at her large blue eyes.

"Why should I do that?"

KC scratched his neck with a forefinger and said, "Well, um, I'm in here without a suit. My daily tradition, you know, and I can't spend all morning sitting in the ocean."

"That's OK. I don't mind" the woman said slowly. Her blue eyes twinkled with humor and her lips curled with a smirk.

"Well, it matters to me," KC said with emphasis.

"Tsk, aren't you the modest one. And on a deserted beach to boot," she said.

"Wouldn't you be?"

"How would you know?"

KC hesitated. "Well, then I have an idea: why don't you strip down so we're on equal terms and then I'll come out." KC said.

"No, I'm sure my fiancé wouldn't approve," Nikki replied.

KC stared in disbelief and turned red. Another strike-out. Abruptly he rose to his feet, stormed out of the water, grabbed his towel and marched up the path toward the house, ignoring his flip-flops and sunglasses lying at the edge of the sand dune.

"See ya around, shorty!" Nikki hollered, and snorted as KC disappeared behind a large succulent flowering shrub. Her laughter followed him all the way to his private porch.

CHAPTER 4

Moscow, Russia

Pyotr Asimov huddled in the shadows outside the front door of the building that now served as Alexei's temporary tomb. Soon enough the body would begin to smell. The authorities would come and haul it away with little thought about how or why the trunk contained a stinking rotten corpse. Pyotr waited as a faded gray sedan rumbled down the street and a young couple hurried past him on foot, paying him little attention. In the dim light he headed down the narrow lane past several gated properties, keeping to the shadows as much as possible. He glanced at his watch and shivered in the cool afternoon breeze.

Pyotr pulled his cell phone from his pocket, scrolled down through his contact list, and pressed the call button. Three rings later a young woman answered.

"Yes?"

"Hello Kristen. This is Pyotr Asimov. Remember me?"

"Of course, Pyotr. Where have you been, stranger?" she said. "What's up?"

"Well, I don't want to say too much over the phone, but I need to speak with your uncle, Colin. It's about those things he collects. I have some information for him and need to talk to him. You still at the pub?" Pyotr said.

"Yes," she said slowly. "Why not stop over tomorrow night. I have a conference call scheduled at 8 pm."

"I don't think you understand. I need to talk to him right now. It's a matter of life and death." Pyotr said, speaking faster than usual.

Pyotr listened to silence on his phone for about fifteen seconds and for a moment thought she had hung up on him.

"Come over to the pub right now. I'll try to set it up, but I can't promise anything. Order a beer at the bar and wait for a signal from the bartender," Kristen said as she ended the call without letting Pyotr respond.

Pyotr closed his eyes and let out a deep breath. He had to reach the pub immediately but couldn't afford to get careless. Dangerous men might be anywhere. He crossed a small park where the mature trees silently marked his path and hurried across the street. Stopping in the shadow of a larger tree he kept his eyes on the entrance to the Metro station for nearly ten minutes. His thoughts turned to his dead relative and the difficult task ahead. He felt little regret, knowing Alexei's last dream would not be realized. The Davy Crockett weapons would not be returning to Russia.

Last year he'd come to the aid of an American named Colin who'd become lost in Moscow. Pyotr had guided the man and his niece, Kristen, around the city for three days, showing him the sights, especially the old weapons at the Museum of the Armed Forces, and getting him to his business appointments on time. Pyotr learned that Colin was an avid collector of unusual and rare weapons of all kinds. While Colin was working, Pyotr spent time with Kristen and they became good friends. Colin instructed Pyotr to contact him if he ever needed anything. Pyotr had long thought about moving to the United States—now he might have a chance. But first he had to reach Kristen's small office behind Flannigan's pub and contact Colin Farthington. With a sudden start he dashed across the street, sailed into the ornate Metro Station, and bought a ticket. He leaned against a stone pillar clenching his fists until the train began to move. His eyes darted from side to side searching the platform for anyone who might be watching him. At the last moment he leapt aboard the moving train.

Minutes later he emerged from the Biblioteka Metro Station near the Kremlin and hurried along Mokhovaya Street where he hoped to blend in with the University students who frequented the area. Massive brick buildings lined the street adding to the perpetual gloom of the neighborhood. He slipped around the corner and stepped inside Flannigan's Irish Pub. The dim tavern was crammed with young people, most of them smoking cigarettes and sipping Irish lager. He hurried to the bar, found an empty stool at the far end, and ordered a beer. The bartender filled the glass, looked Pyotr directly in the eye, and gave his head a small shake. Pyotr checked the time again and studied the interior of the pub. The dark wood typical of Irish pubs and the dim lighting gave him a sense of safety even as he scanned the room for anyone who might not fit. He found only a typical bar crowd with loud young men leering at smiling coeds. Pyotr played with the top button of his shirt and sipped his beer. Minutes later the bartender finished serving a pitcher to a table of young men and turned toward Pyotr. He didn't smile but cocked his head, shifted his eyes and nodded toward the back of the pub. Pyotr slid off the stool, left the remnants of his beer on the bar and waded through the sea of people until he reached a narrow door at the back wall. One last turn to survey the pub and he opened the door.

He passed into a dimly lit narrow corridor with worn walls and chipped flooring and hurried along the dusty hallway to a single door at the end. He knocked three times and waited. Moments later, Pyotr listened to the sound of several deadbolts opening. A young woman jerked the door open and signaled for him to enter. She was tall, about 25, with long red hair and a well-proportioned body. Long shiny earrings hung from her ears. She wore black pants, black shoes, and a gray sweatshirt with a yellow smiley face on the front. The room was bright and clean, without windows. She closed the door and reengaged the sophisticated locking mechanisms.

"Good to see you Pyotr. The bartender buzzed me when he saw you enter the Pub but had to make sure the coast was clear before sending you back," she said. "You're in luck. Uncle Colin will be on the secure video conference line at any moment. Quick, sit down and I'll log you in. Should I know what's going on?"

Pyotr took off his coat and hung it on the back of a chair. "No. It's very dangerous stuff," Pyotr replied as he eased into the chair in front of the computer monitor. Kristen stepped into an adjacent room and closed the door, understanding the conversation with Colin was private. The less she knew, the safer she'd be.

The computer screen flickered briefly. Then a high quality image of a middle aged man with graying hair cut to medium length flashed on the screen.

"Hello, Pyotr. Very good to see you. I hope to get back to Moscow in a few months. Kristen tells me you have some urgent news. I have several undercover operatives in Moscow keeping an eye on the mob and a number of the more corrupt government officials. My informants are becoming concerned that our financial interests may be at risk. At this point we don't know if it's the Russian Mafia, the government, or one of the subversive groups," Colin Farthington said. "Now tell me what is so urgent this early in the morning."

Pyotr repeated Alexei's stuttered references to nuclear weapons, a map, the Kremlin, a secret tunnel, bonnie, and an island near Cuba. He spoke slowly and accurately and finished by telling Colin of a fortune, a cave, and Davy Crockett.

"Now, Colin, I have a request. I want to come to America. I have little future here in Moscow. My job with the tour company is a dead end for me. And with what I know about the nuclear weapons, I fear for my life. I can't live like Alexei did. I want to come to Seattle and work for you. Do you think this is possible? Do you understand what Alexei meant?"

"Well, I know what he meant about Davy Crockett, but not the rest of it. I'm very interested in acquiring the weapons. They would be really cool to have for my collection. I'm sorry to hear Alexei passed away. I would have loved to meet him. Hold there for a few minutes. I'll get back to you," Colin said and the computer screen went blank.

Eight minutes later the screen brightened and Colin's face filled the screen.

"I've started people working on Alexei's clues. I don't think there will be too much of a problem in solving the mystery. But we'll forgo searching for a map that may be in the Kremlin because we prefer to keep a low profile in the city. We don't want the local bureaucrats snooping into our affairs. We'll get the information we need another way. And you'll be in America soon, my friend. You must leave Moscow immediately. No time to say goodbye to your parents. I have arranged to have you picked up, but not in Moscow. It's getting late, but I think you can catch the next train, if you hurry. Get to Bellorusskaya Station and take the 195 train to Minsk and get off at Smolensk. Better to avoid the Belarus border guards if you can. They are usually no problem, but why take the chance. Your contact will be a woman about 30, short blond hair. Wears wire-rimmed glasses. Her name is Gabrielle, and she'll be wearing a green sweater. Her father is a very close friend so you can trust her completely. When she asks what you are doing in Smolensk your response is 'I'm here to shop for my mother's birthday'. She'll get you past the border guards, and then my chief European operative, Tom Smithers, will get you to the US. OK boy, go for it. Be careful, we cannot let anyone find out about this. The weapons will be safe in my private collection, but I hate to think what might happen if the wrong people get their hands on them. Remember, tell no one about the Davy Crocketts. I'll see you in a few days. Colin out."

The screen went blank.

Pyotr leaned back in his chair, stared at the ceiling and let out a long breath. He had to be very careful. Getting to America would not be easy. He feared bad men had nearly found Alexei hiding in his tenement and now they might find him. Pyotr shivered, realizing he and Colin Farthington might be the only people on earth who had real information on the location of the missing nuclear weapons—even if he didn't understand everything Alexei had told him. He hoped his fears were unfounded, but the memory of the blue sedan creeping past Alexei's building gave him cause to worry. Kristen returned to the room, interrupting his thoughts. He explained he had to leave to catch a train. He was going to America.

"Good luck, Pyotr. I will try to send someone to collect your things from your apartment and ship them to Colin. Safe travels, and keep in touch," she said, leaning over and giving him a kiss on his cheek. A quick hug and he was gone.

At the end of the dirty hallway, Pyotr stopped at the closed door. Loud music pulsed on the other side. He opened the door and peered into the room. The pub crowd was louder than when he'd first stepped inside. Empty beer pitchers littered the tables. Young servers were replacing them with full ones.

Pyotr didn't find anything to give him reason to be concerned. He stepped into the main pub room and stationed himself in the shadows searching for something or someone that didn't look right to him. He froze in place when a drunken girl reeled toward him, smiled awkwardly, and spun off to the toilet. Two more followed, both stumbled into Pyotr, giggling and teetering after their friend. He had to hurry, but couldn't take unnecessary risks. He inched to the front door and surveyed the street outside the window. Curtains covered the lower half of the panes, providing a bit of protection as he eyed young couples stroll past, arm in arm. A few customers arrived, passing him without giving him a glance. He checked his watch yet again. I must hurry, he thought, only forty five minutes.

He rubbed his nose, opened the door, and hurried up the street toward the Metro station.

Half an hour later he marched down arched marble passageways to the train for Smolensk. He purchased his ticket then casually scanned the station. Nothing seemed to be out of the ordinary. He relaxed a little.

Pyotr failed to spot the lone man standing in the shadows with a cell phone to his ear. The man's eyes followed Pyotr until the doors of the train closed.

"He's on the train to Minsk. Place two men at each station on the route," the man spoke into the phone. Then he turned and strolled out of the station. His face held a satisfied smile.

CHAPTER 5

Train Station, Smolensk, Russia

Pyotr's train arrived on time at 2:20 am. He had slept well during the six hour journey, but his stomach growled from lack of food. He hoped the woman in green would have something for him to eat. The few passengers who disembarked with him clutched their cases and bags and scurried away from the train to waiting cars and a lone rusted public bus.

Pyotr stepped off the platform and searched for his contact. No one appeared to be waiting for him so he followed the last of the passengers hurrying toward a parking lot on the east side of the station. Outside the front door he spotted a small garden area planted with trees and shrubs. A young woman with short blond hair and wire-rimmed glasses was standing alone nearly hidden by a tall evergreen tree. Her leather coat hung open revealing a green sweater underneath. She had chosen the best location to monitor both the walkways and the main terminal door.

"I am Gabrielle. Why are you here?" she said when Pyotr stepped close to her.

Pyotr hesitated when he gazed into her beautiful large brown eyes. He caught himself and started to say, "I'm here to shop for my mother's birth-" but stopped when her body stiffened and she squinted over Pyotr's left shoulder.

"Oh, shit! Run now," she hissed in a high-pitched voice. "I have a car."

Gabrielle wheeled around, grabbed at Pyotr's sleeve and sprinted toward the parking lot. Confused, Pyotr hesitated until he sensed a figure racing toward him from the direction of the train tracks. He raced after the girl and reached the passenger door at the same time the car roared to life.

He lunged for the door handle when something stung him sharply on the side of his neck. He slapped at the pain as a strange warmth spread to his shoulder. His fingers grasped the hard object sticking out of his neck but he couldn't quite get a hold of it. Stumbling, he tried to pull the door open. His fingers slid off the handle. Gabrielle's horror stricken face became a blur.

"Come on, hurry! Get in!" she shouted, reaching over to help him open the door.

It was too late. Pyotr was unconscious before his head hit the pavement.

Footsteps pounded on the pavement as Gabrielle slammed the gearshift into drive and spun out of the parking lot. In her rear view mirror she saw two men, both dressed in dark clothing, leaning over Pyotr.

CHAPTER 6

Somewhere in Smolensk, Russia

Pyotr Asimov's head throbbed and he nearly vomited as a sour taste rose to the back of his throat. He opened his eyes and squinted immediately as bright lights shot painful darts in the back of his skull. He shivered involuntarily in the chilly room, but tried to ignore his pain and assess the situation. Confused, he opened his eyes wider and was shocked to discover that he was completely naked and strapped tightly to a large wood table. Leather straps gripped both legs and arms, another wrapped around his stomach. He felt a strap hanging loosely at his throat.

When his eyes adjusted to the bright lights he inspected the room. It was small, perhaps three meters square, with plain white walls and no windows. A white door loomed straight ahead of him. To his right, on the floor, lay a large wooden trunk, its lid closed. He couldn't see anything behind him. He struggled without success to free himself from the bindings, and then lay still when he detected a sound from the other side of the door. His heart pounded and stomach churned in fearful anticipation. The door opened slowly with an eerie creak. A tall man entered and dimmed the lights.

"Ah, my young friend is awake. Welcome Asimov. With your cooperation I trust we will have a fruitful conversation," said the man.

"Where am I? What did you do to me? Who are you and why am I tied up? Why am I here? I am cold. Where is the girl?" Pyotr said with growing fear.

"I ask the questions young man. It is most unfortunate that your woman friend eluded my best men. I think you would have spared her much pain and given me the information I desire without delay. If you cooperate, your discomfort will be brief," replied the tall man.

With the lights dimmed, the man's features became more pronounced. He was very tall, well over six feet, with gray skin and a face so gaunt he appeared to be anorexic. The cigarette hanging from his thin lips only increased the appearance of evil. His shaved head and long narrow beak of a nose reminded Pyotr of a vulture. When the man moved around the table, as if eying his prey, Pyotr's stomach tightened with fear and his heart hammered against his ribs.

23

"What are you talking about? Why am I here?" cried Pyotr.

"I am Nikolai Ivanovich Chuikov and you are in Smolensk. Nobody knows where you are. This room is fully soundproofed. When we track down the woman, and I guarantee we will, there will be no hope of rescue for you. No help from Belarus. I do not care how wealthy your American friend is. He won't find us. We are invisible. Now, I want you to give me the information you learned from Alexei Baranov," the tall man said as a sneer curled his upper lip.

"He-he died right after I arrived," Pyotr spoke rapidly. The effects of the poison dart had worn off and his mind was now clear. Fear gripped him as he stared at the creature that hovered over him. Cold sweat glistened on his naked chest.

"Hmmm, I do not think so. Why would you flee Moscow without any of your belongings?" Chuikov stated as he sidled to the foot of the table.

"I, I was in a hurry to meet my girlfriend," Pyotr stuttered.

"No, I don't think so. Here is something that might help to refresh your memory," Nikolai said coldly.

He took a slow drag from his unfiltered cigarette, tapped the ash off with a long forefinger, and pressed the glowing tip into the bottom of Pyotr's bare foot. Pyotr yelled and writhed but could not escape the pain. His feet remained strapped firmly on the table.

"Tell me what that pathetic old man told you," Nikolai said.

"He told me nothing!" Pyotr said as each burn seared deep into the sole of his foot.

Again and again the glowing tip of the cigarette pressed gently on Pyotr's exposed flesh. Nikolai Chuikov moved his cigarette up Pyotr's leg leaving small piles of glowing embers every few inches until he reached the groin. Each time he wielded the burning cigarette long enough to bring an agonizing scream from Pyotr. He lit a second cigarette.

"I will give you another chance, my young friend. Tell me, and your pain will end," the vulture-man pressed on. "These little burns are nothing."

Nikolai lit a third cigarette when the second was only half burned. When both glowed brightly he pressed them on each of Pyotr's exposed testicles. Pyotr screamed in pain as his stomach muscles cramped. Sharp pain raced like wildfire, and his lower body shook in waves of sharp spasms. Chuikov displayed his evil grin as the two cigarettes continued their slow singeing burn. Pyotr vomited and lost consciousness.

Sometime later, he woke, alone in the room, still strapped to the table. He shivered again as a frosty mist rose from his mouth. His burns throbbed in spite of the chill of the room and his mind reeled with fear and confusion. For a brief moment he wondered if he would be freed if he told the truth. He had made an oath to Colin Farthington, and telling everything he knew about the nuclear weapons would mean losing the only person who could get him to America.

The door swung open and Nikolai marched in with a scowl on his gray face, his eyes betraying no emotion. He wore a heavy fleece jacket, no hat, and tight leather gloves.

"Ah, you waken so soon. You are shivering, I see. If you help me, I will relieve your discomfort. Are you eager to tell me what the old man shared with you about the nuclear weapons? You see, Pyotr, it is unfortunate for you that Alexei eluded us for so long. His comrades were not so fortunate. But alas, they, too, were stubborn and only gave us a few pieces of valuable information before they left us. We know about the Davy Crockett nuclear weapon system stolen from the American pigs in Berlin and eventually shipped to Cuba. Not only warheads, but also a launcher. The whole works, ready to fire. We also know some of the warheads never reached the Soviet Union after the Cuban missile debacle. We have wealthy and dedicated associates, shall we say, in the Middle East who will pay dearly for them. We will once again turn the tables on the imperialist pigs in America. Now, tell me where they are hidden!"

"I can't tell you what I don't know," shouted Pyotr.

Nikolai rolled his eyes and said, "Oh, you don't lie very well."

Chuikov spun, reached into the trunk and extracted a strange looking wooden vice-like instrument. It was comprised of two thick spiked wood blocks, about 50 cm long, each with six sharply pointed eight to ten cm spikes on one side. Two long wooden screws connected the blocks, with the spikes facing each other. Chuikov lifted Pyotr's left knee and placed one of the blocks under it.

"Hey! I don't understand what you want from me. Please let me go," Pyotr stammered.

Chuikov ignored Pyotr's plea and reached under the table and pressed a button. Fifteen seconds later the door opened and a young woman, wearing olive drab military clothing entered the room. The chill of the room seemed to have no effect on her. She stood about five feet five inches and wore her dark brown hair cut short. She wore neither jewelry nor any obvious tattoos. She stalked toward Pyotr and studied him with narrow eyes, lingering for just a moment at his naked groin.

"Ha," she said, shaking her head. "And you call yourself a man?"

"Welcome, Lukova. Thank you for taking the time to assist me. I just need a little help with my device. Please just hold this block steady over his knee while I insert the screws."

Moments later the wooden device was snugly clamped in place above and below Pyotr's knee. Chuikov nodded and Lukova spun and marched from the room without uttering a sound.

"Enough of your lies. I will untie your head so you can have a better view," the vulture said in a flat monotone. He unlatched the loose strap around Pyotr's neck and pressed a small lever below him. The table creaked as the head lifted up a few inches so Pyotr had an unobstructed view of his knee and the ominous looking device. Nikolai checked to make sure the straps holding Pyotr to the table were snug then tightened the vice on his knee.

"Tell me, Asimov," he said.

"I-I can't," Pyotr said as the sharp spikes dug into the soft skin behind his knee. A spot of blood dribbled from a spot on his kneecap. "I know nothing."

"Oh, so that hurts, does it? But you don't really know pain yet," Chuikov said and tightened the screws a quarter turn. Pyotr's kneecap flattened and the spikes penetrated the skin on the underside of his knee. Sweat formed on his forehead and he groaned with pain.

"Pyotr, tell me about the nuclear weapons and your pain will cease."

"I don't know!"

One more slight turn of the screws sent shock waves of intense pain up Pyotr's leg and into his spine. Blood began to seep more freely from the wounds and into a small pool on the table. A wave of nausea swept over him and the room began to spin.

Chuikov looked on, his face betraying no emotion. Slowly he unscrewed the knee splitting device and removed it. Pyotr's pain subsided just a little and he took a deep breath.

"Tell me and I will give you something for your pain," Chuikov urged.

"He-he said something I didn't understand."

"I will," Chuikov said as he fumbled with the device. This time, working alone, he spent a long minute attaching the device to Pyotr's right knee. Pyotr could do nothing but watch Chuikov thread the two screws.

"No, no more please," gasped Pyotr as Chuikov roughly tightened the screws. "He said-something like—a bonnie fortune and an island. I do not understand what he meant. One moment he was alive and talking to me and the next he was dead."

"Now we are getting somewhere," Nikolai said as he loosened the screws one more time. "Tell me the rest."

"Believe me, that is all I know," Pyotr said trembling from pain and fear. He dared not betray Colin. He sealed his lips and glared at his captor. He struggled with the straps, only causing more agony for his knees and back.

Chuikov stared at his captive, eyes mere slits, face gray and thin lips closed tightly.

Pyotr, drenched in sweat, gulped for air, his head swimming. His left leg, now swollen to nearly twice its normal size and turning a deep purplish red throbbed as blood continued to drip onto the table.

Chuikov tightened the screws again and the spikes dug in deeply. Vomit welled in the back of Pyotr's throat and he tried without success to spit it at Chuikov. One more slight turn of the screw and Pyotr felt a sharp snap in the back of his knee as the sharp spikes severed tendons. Pain hammered his entire body.

"He said something about a secret in the Kremlin!" he whimpered, voice growing weak.

Nikolai paused and stared at the bare ceiling, a frown barely creasing his smooth forehead. He paced around the table once, a dull humming sound escaping his lips. A sudden jerk of his head displayed a huge grin, exposing crooked, brownish teeth. He smirked, nodded his head and relaxed. His body softened, but his beady vulture eyes maintained their evil stare.

"And you passed all this information on to your American friend?"

"No. No, we lost the internet connection. I had no time. I had to catch a train," Pyotr said, eyes darting from side to side searching the small chamber. His captor had disappeared from view.

"You disappoint me, boy," Chuikov said as he stepped back into Pyotr's view. He reached once more for the screws and turned them violently. Pyotr howled in pain as he felt his kneecap shatter into small pieces. Several shards of bone poked through the side of his knee.

"A map. And a tunnel," Pyotr squeaked, his voice a mere whisper, his eyes closed tightly.

Nikolai sighed and squeezed his nose with forefinger and thumb.

"Thank you, young man, but I'm afraid my patience has worn out. Our conversation is at an end."

Pyotr let out a long breath, praying his ordeal was over. "Please, help the pain," he said, eyes open and pleading with his captor.

"As you wish." Chuikov nodded then pivoted on one foot and reached for a long narrow object hanging on the wall behind Pyotr's head. He loved the feel of the smooth rosewood handle and the shine of the Damascus steel blade. He wheeled around, raised the Chinese sword high over his head, and made a swift, powerful move. Straightening, he pulled a cloth from his rear pocket, carefully wiped the blade and returned the sword to its place on the wall. Then he stalked from the room without looking back, a satisfied smirk on his face.

Pyotr's open mouth was frozen in a silent scream, his eyes like marbles staring with confusion and fear. Gravity slowly gained the advantage when his head slowly began to tilt to one side. Then it rolled once, fell of the table, and landed on the floor with a sickening thud. It was a sound nobody heard.

CHAPTER 7

Sinclair Island, San Juan Islands, Washington, USA

Fifty seven year old Colin Farthington settled back in his office chair and gazed out the huge picture window. Across the shimmering sea the rocky cliffs of neighboring Cypress Island were shrouded in darkness. Farther to the west storm clouds hung low over Vancouver Island. The simply decorated office was on the second floor of Colin's rustic home. He owned nearly eighty percent of Sinclair Island, a thousand acre spit of land located some twelve miles southeast of Bellingham, Washington. A handful of seasonal residents, many of whom flew their own airplanes to the island's small airstrip, inhabited the remainder of the island. Most residents, while friendly, kept to themselves. Except for two or three annual get-togethers, social life on the island was non-existent.

Colin gazed at a passing car ferry and smiled. He was glad they didn't stop at Sinclair Island. Colin had never married and treasured his privacy as much as he enjoyed the fabulous views of the other islands that dotted the ocean to the southeast of Vancouver Island. He'd certainly entertained many beautiful women over the years, but bachelorhood suited him just fine. His thoughts were interrupted by a gentle beeping sound coming from his computer. He turned his attention to the screen and studied the face of a one of his assistants.

"OK, Phil, so you recommend we take a position in Uranium? I read your report and agree. I know it's risky, but how much do you recommend?" Colin said.

"I'm confident that in six to eight years you'll triple your initial investment. I suggest forty to fifty," the young man on the screen spoke animatedly.

Colin's private telephone began to chirp.

He lifted his brow and said, "I agree, Phil. Up to fifty million dollars. I gotta go. I've got another call coming in. Do what you do best."

He hesitated for a moment as he eyed the rapidly blinking yellow light. He snatched up the phone and said, "Yes, Jane."

"Gabrielle is on the secure line from Belarus. She sounds frantic," Jane replied.

Colin frowned and punched a button on the phone.

"Yes Gabbi?"

"Colin I need help! Pyotr has been kidnapped! The men who grabbed him almost got me, too. I am afraid to try to call him on his cell phone. They might be looking for me too. What should I do?"

Colin's mouth tightened.

"This is bad Gabrielle. Make no mistake. Tell me exactly what happened."

"It was at the train station. Two men appeared from nowhere. I kept watch before Pyotr arrived but didn't see them until it was too late. They shot him in the neck with some sort of a dart. I'm sorry. It's my fault. I should have been more careful. But I am frightened that the men will find me too! Please help me! And please find Pyotr."

"OK Gabbi, hold on. You did all you could. Stay in your apartment. Do not answer the telephone. Don't go near the windows. You will be safe. I'll send Tom Smithers over to your place as soon as I can. Trust him, completely, you'll be OK," Colin replied.

Better get Kristen out of Moscow too. His sister would strangle him if anything happened to her daughter.

He hung up the telephone and scowled out the window. The rain began to fall in heavy sheets. The seas outside Bellingham Bay had become steely gray and ominous. He had to make sure the men who had kidnapped Pyotr couldn't get the girls too. They were valuable assets. Even more, they were like family. Time was no longer on his side. He had to assume Pyotr told his captors everything. Soon others would be closing in on the nuclear weapons.

He drummed his fingers on the table for a moment then picked up the phone again and rang for Jane.

CHAPTER 8

The Kremlin, Moscow, Russia

Just after midnight on a moonless night three men crept along the southwest corner of the Kremlin, avoiding the bright lights shining from the top of the high red brick wall surrounding the huge complex. Each man was dressed in black and wore a small backpack and a harness, similar to those used by rock climbers. They crouched in the shadows watching the sparse traffic on the Bolshoy Kamenny Bridge that spanned the Moscow River. Silently they attached short climbing spikes to each boot, and when the road was empty of cars each took his turn to run to the base of a large tree and scurry up until he was well hidden by foliage. As they reached the top of the tree they removed their spikes and stowed them in their backpacks. A warm breeze blew across the river carrying with it a hint of diesel fumes and rustled the leaves around the three men. The five meter high brick wall of the Kremlin loomed eight meters away. The walls brought to mind images of a castle with one and a half meter wide notches cut into the top of the wall at regular intervals.

"OK, Goguniv, our position is perfect, do your thing now," Pavel Dubkov, the leader of the team, whispered into the microphone of his headset radio. He continued his scan of the open area between the Moscow River and the Kremlin wall. The traffic on the four lane road that skirted the river moved along at a steady pace. A lone bicyclist cruised past on the sidewalk concentrating on the crosswalk ahead. They had at least four hours to break into the Kremlin, find the map showing the location of the nuclear weapons, and make their escape. But Dubkov was nervous. Nikolai Chuikov had entrusted him with the mission and would never accept failure. Pavel was well aware of Chuikov's short temper and ruthlessness. He was certain that failure would result in a painful and slow death for his entire team.

Fadey Goguniv, a lanky twenty-five year old with extensive tattoos covering his arms and neck, opened his pack and removed a small crossbow, aimed for the top of the Kremlin wall and squeezed the trigger. A three-pronged hook hurtled forward, a thin wire trailing behind. A quiet *thunk* told him he had hit his mark. Quickly he yanked the wire tight and attached the end to the tree.

"Go Kerensky, hide yourself when you get across and signal when we can cross over without being detected. Keep an eye on the road," said Dubkov.

Jasha Kerensky, the youngest of the three at only nineteen years of age, attached a wheeled trolley to the wire, lifted his wiry legs and silently slid toward the top of the wall, less than one-half meter below their position in the tree. As he approached, he used his feet to halt his slide, then unlatched the trolley and scooted through one of the notches in the wall. Finally he stepped down one meter to the narrow battle platform that ran along the inside of the wall. Peering through one of the notches he scanned the bridge and the river. A few cars sped past, but he was well hidden in the shadows. His comrades squatted in silence and waited. At the next lull in traffic Jasha flashed his light.

Minutes later the three intruders lowered themselves to the ground inside the Kremlin, an old fortress surrounded by more than 2200 meters of brick wall. They tugged on the rope until it dropped at their feet, then they hid it behind a shrub. Twenty defensive towers were irregularly spaced along the walls. One of these, 300 meters east of their point of entrance, was their target. The men waited without moving for five minutes to make sure security guards hadn't detected them. They crept silently, keeping to the trees that littered the dark southern portion of the Kremlin.

After a seven minute trek, they halted outside Tainitskaya Tower, more commonly known as The Secret Tower. Built over five hundred years ago, the red brick tower's primary purpose was to protect the river side of the Kremlin. The Secret Tower was unique in its design. As a key component of Kremlin defense, the Tower had a cache-well and underground tunnel that led to the Moscow River. This tunnel led from the well to the river and, if there was a siege against the Kremlin, defenders could either use it to escape or get water from the river. The Soviets filled in the tunnel in the early 1930's. During the following decades homeless people and drug peddlers scoured out small passageways deep into the tunnel. Recently the government had sealed the entrance so that access from the river side became impossible. The only access was from the inside of the Kremlin.

Pavel Dubkov, a small, thin man in his late 30's with a clipped military-style haircut, removed his backpack and dug out a small canvas case. He unrolled it and selected two narrow metal tools. In less than a minute he picked the heavy lock on the front door and slipped into the Tower. Fadey and Jasha eyed each other, shook their heads, and smiled. More than once they had been amazed at the strength and dexterity of their leader. Both of the men were at least fifteen centimeters taller and fifteen kilos heavier than Dubkov; but they could match neither his power nor his agility. Fadey followed Pavel into the tower; Jasha hid a small wireless microphone under a nearby shrub and followed moments later—they would be alerted by any sound—and secured the door from the inside.

Pavel Dubkov led his team from the front door of the tower to a circular well filled with cobblestones. It was at the bottom of this old cache-well where they expected to find the tunnel leading to the river. Working with a sense of urgency, they began to remove the fist-sized rocks from the well. Forty-five minutes later they reached the bottom. Dubkov donned a headlamp, climbed two meters to the bottom of the well, and wriggled his way into the narrow tunnel.

"Do you see the map?" Fadey asked. "Chuikov thought we'd have to dig about one meter."

"Nothing yet," Dubkov said with a grunt as he squirmed farther into the narrowing space. He searched every inch of the exposed wall of the tunnel but couldn't find the drawing. Fine dust coated the inside of his nose. He rested for a minute while the dust settled to the ground. He reached into a rear pocket, removed a bandana and tied it around his face. More comfortable, he renewed his search for the map. He cleared away several rocks to clear a larger path. He rolled to his side to move one of the larger rocks out of his way. He started to roll back to his stomach when he caught a glimpse of something out of the corner of his eye. He squinted at the ceiling and discovered small dark etchings scoured deep into the stone.

"I think I found the map!" he shouted with satisfaction and relief.

"Pavel be quiet, someone is coming!" Jasha whispered as loud as he dared. "Turn off your lamp!"

The three Russians froze in place, holding their breaths, as the microphone Jasha had hidden picked up the sounds of someone approaching the Secret Tower's front door. Fadey's hand drifted to the pistol strapped to his right hip.

"Da, Svetlana, she is a beauty, Uri, but I do not think she will go out with you," one guard said and laughed.

"Well, I can hope. You know she has not turned me down yet," the other replied.

"Ah, two more hours until our shift is over and then you can visit her and I will go home to my lovely fat wife and cheap vodka. I think she is cooking shashlik for me tonight," the first said and laughed loudly.

"All clear," whispered Jasha as the sounds of the guards faded.

Pavel relaxed, rolled over on his back and tugged a small digital camera from his pocket. He adjusted his headlamp as the dust settled and went to work.

When he finished photographing the map that was etched into the roof of the tunnel, Pavel climbed out of the tunnel and helped Jasha and Fadey refill the well. Gathering their gear they crept out of the Tower, closing the unlocked door behind them.

The night was still dark and quiet when the three intruders approached the interior Kremlin wall where their rope was hidden behind a low hedge. They scaled the brick wall and worked their way back to the tree. Minutes later they raced down the Moscow River in a small motorboat, similar to many that would cruise the river when the sun rose.

Pavel reached into a compartment under one of the seats for a 2-way radio and flipped a toggle switch.

"We found the map. It will probably be days before they discover the Tower's unlocked door. By then, it won't matter," he said with a broad smile on his narrow face.

CHAPTER 9

National Hurricane Center, Miami, Florida

Charlie Holly leaned back in his ergonomic chair with his eyes closed. He'd been on duty for nearly fifteen hours after agreeing to fill in for Maggie Booth, who had taken time off work to assist her ailing mother. Soon his head fell to his chest and his breathing became slow and quiet.

The National Hurricane Center's main operation center occupied a medium sized room with soft brown paint on the walls and muted lighting. A large map of North America, the Atlantic Ocean, Western Europe, and Africa took up most of one wall. Eighteen computer stations were situated around the rest of the room. A large desk in the center of the room housed advanced communications equipment and was used as the main control station for the Center. The computer screen on Charlie's desk displayed nothing more than a small, but intense, weather system off the African coast.

Gentle snoring filled the room with a soothing regularity as Charlie dreamed of marlin fishing and girls in skimpy bikinis. When his screen automatically refreshed itself the small orange dot surrounded by yellow where the thunderstorm had been turned a deep red and became much larger.

The door banged as senior hurricane specialist Sally Riggs hurried into the room.

"Wake up deadhead!" she said as Charlie's body jerked and his eyes opened.

"Uh, sorry, Boss. I've done a double shift and the weather has been real quiet."

"Well, what the heck is that red blob on your screen?" Sally asked, her forehead knitted into a frown.

"I have no idea. I only closed my eyes a minute ago," he said. "Let's check the barometric pressure."

Sally eased into her chair, clicked her wireless mouse several times, then sat back and waited. Two seconds later she leaned forward and studied the data that had appeared on her computer screen.

"No worries yet," she said. "Pressure's 1012 mb, just a bit below normal. I'll watch for a while. The storm might blow itself out near the Cape Verde Islands. I'll take over here."

Sally settled back in her chair and frowned. Something didn't look right to her. She wasn't concerned about a tropical storm because the barometric pressure was normal and most big storms formed farther west than this one. But it had grown much larger in the few minutes she'd been in the center. Maybe it was only a local storm.

She checked the pressure reading again.

1002 and dropping. No worries, yet.

CHAPTER 10

Fort Belvoir, Virginia

L t. Colonel Brad Wilkerson sat alone in his office on the second floor of a non-descript brick building at Fort Belvoir, Virginia, fifteen miles south of Washington DC. His second floor office was plain, with only a desk, comfortable office chair, and several filing cabinets. Photos of Wilkerson posing with small groups of soldiers covered the walls. An American Flag on a tall metal pole stood in one corner. His assistant occupied a small adjoining office. They shared a men's room with others on the same floor. Only Wilkerson's name was on a plaque attached to the outside door of their suite. There was no indication that he was assigned to the US Army Intelligence Support Activity (ISA), a relatively unknown foreign intelligence-gathering unit of the Army.

After reading the single paragraph report for a second time he stood up, walked over to the window, and looked out, unsure whether he should contact the man at the White House immediately or wait for more information. Majestic maple trees waved gently in the breeze. Beyond the trees dense woods separated the fort from upscale suburban neighborhoods. He stared at the vacant grounds for two minutes, and then returned to his chair, picked up his secure cellular phone, and pressed a speed dial button.

It was answered immediately.

"What is it, Colonel?"

"Well, sir, our listening post intercepted a transmission between someone in Moscow and an American businessman located on an island near Seattle. The key words of the communication were 'Davy Crockett.' We're confident the communication concerns the nuclear weapons stolen from our Army troops in West Germany back in 1959 when the Cold War was hot, but before the Wall went up in Berlin. We haven't picked up a reference to Davy Crockett in years. The rest of the communication was a jumble of phrases we don't yet understand, but my analyst is working on it."

Vice President Gordon leaned back in his chair and stared at the ceiling. A moment later he blinked his eyes several times and nodded.

"Well, Brad, keep me in the loop, but keep a tight lid on this. You know there are only a few of us who know the Russians stole our nuclear weapons. We've got to get them back. We're lucky neither the media nor my opponents have stumbled on the truth of what really happened. This new development is promising, though. I can't stress enough how important this is and that you've got to keep the situation under wraps. Inside your office. We can't share our intel with any of the other intelligence agencies. Especially those bastards over at NSA. OK? Anyway, who's this contact on the island near Seattle? Any chance we can bring him in to our side?" said Gordon.

"He's Colin Farthington, sir. We've had our eye on that rich sucker for a long time. U.S. Customs suspects that many of the weapons he reportedly has are illegal, but none of the agents has been able to catch him in the act of bringing them into the country. He's a sneaky son-of-a-bitch. I don't think he would ever help President Anderson's administration. I'm sure you are aware they're about as far apart politically as any two people can be. When we learn where the nukes are kept, I'll send a team to retrieve them."

Gordon rolled his eyes, his mouth tight.

"Colin Farthington? Shit. I haven't had contact with that scoundrel for years. We attended the same college and joined the same fraternity. I couldn't get a dime out of him for the campaign. Do whatever is required to get those weapons back. Don't bore me with the details, but you have clearance to take extreme measures if necessary. I'll get you whatever funding or equipment you need. You'll be responsible for securing your own weapons, though. Remember, the honor of the United States is at stake here," the Vice President replied.

Lt. Colonel Wilkerson hung up and smiled. He'd worked with Vice President Gordon enough times to see behind his phony remark about honor. Politicians were stupid, he thought.

Wilkerson had seen the Vice President whore himself for personal political gain. Sydney Gordon rose to his position by using his law enforcement experience. After serving four years in the US Army 18th Military Police Brigade, he attended law school at Harvard. At age thirty two he was elected Attorney General of Maryland, followed by eight years as Governor. Then President Anderson chose him as the Vice Presidential nominee.

Wilkerson's thoughts shifted to the problem at hand. He felt certain that the Davy Crocketts were within his grasp, but getting them back could be tricky. Weighing only 76 pounds, these missile launched warheads were the smallest nuclear weapons ever built, measuring only 30 inches long and less than a foot wide. They have a kill radius of 500 feet and expel a lethal dose of radiation up to a quarter mile. A detonation would render an area uninhabitable for as little as two days, depending on the wind and terrain. Perfect for a terrorist group planning to attack the President or the Senate Office building. Or a compound like Camp David, the President's private retreat.

Wilkerson shuddered at the thought and checked his watch, hoping his assistant would report soon. The secret of the theft of the weapons had been kept within a tight circle. Previous Directors of the ISA had kept the information close to the vest; the troops who had been on duty when the Russians stole the nukes from under their noses had been systematically silenced. The few low level staffers and analysts that worked on the project were aware their families would be in grave danger if they leaked the information. Wilkerson was confident the secret would be kept in a tight circle. Damage contained for now. But not forever. The internet wasn't called the information superhighway for nothing. As well, he had no control over what the Russians might do; security breaches were very common in Russia and bribes ruled the day. Still, he had to learn the location of the weapons.

His phone rang.

"OK, sergeant. You'd better have something for me."

"I do, sir," Staff Sergeant Jack Smith said. "At first the analyst thought 'fortune' and 'island' referred to Fortuna Island near Croatia, but that didn't pan out. The geology's all wrong. I—"

"I don't care where they aren't, sergeant. Get on with it," Wilkerson interrupted.

"Yes, sir. We found this small island east of Cuba named El Fortunato. It's only about 15 miles long, but we discovered a reference to a geological tourist attraction called Bonny's Abyss. It's a good bet that's where the Russians hid the Davy Crockett nuclear weapons."

"Who controls the island, sergeant?" Wilkerson asked.

"Well sir, the British run it as one of their Overseas Territories. We can't invade it. And we'd never get permission to explore the abyss," Smith replied.

"Of course not. Make sure you shred everything. That will be all," Wilkerson snapped as he hung up the phone. He smiled to himself and nodded his head. They would be in and out before anybody knew they were even there, he mused.

Brad Wilkerson turned to his computer and printed a file listing his select teams from Seaspray, a covert Army unit formed during the Iran hostage crisis in 1980. Good thing his units were no longer working with the CIA. He could not risk other agencies learning about this situation.

Wilkerson studied the list and shook his head. His worst fears were confirmed. The best teams were stationed in South Korea or Pakistan. Several in

Venezuela and Libya. He told himself this job would be easy and he wouldn't need a crack team. But he hated to take unnecessary risks. He moved his finger down the list until he came to the last name.

Wilkerson closed his eyes and settled back in his chair. He sat without moving for five minutes. Then he lifted his spit-shined shoes with their one inch lifts onto his desk and crossed his ankles. He rubbed his chin and pulled at his nose. With a jerk he got to his feet, reached for the phone, and called Lieutenant Troy Baker.

He said a silent prayer while the phone rang.

CHAPTER 11

Washington DC

Vice President Sydney Gordon settled into his chair and stared at the telephone. He was a good looking man, six foot two inches tall, with a square jaw and dark brown hair combed straight back. A bit of gray at the temples gave him a distinguished look. Yet his cold eyes only softened when it was politically expedient. After plotting for years to become President he had just fallen short of gaining his party's nomination five years earlier. He'd accepted second place on the ticket, understanding the Presidential nominee, Senator Marge Anderson of Oregon, chose him only because of the electoral votes he could deliver. It had worked; they'd won a very close election. Their reelection last year had been much easier.

Most of the political insiders understood she had preferred Senator Grayson Wythe of Virginia over Gordon. Wythe came from a family long entrenched in Virginian politics, even claiming lineage to George Wythe, one of the signers of the Declaration of Independence. But Gordon had ruthlessly out-maneuvered him in order to gain the Vice Presidential nomination.

Gordon had discovered that Wythe's father had been careless while posted in Germany. He'd been sent to Berlin as a military attaché responsible for the Davy Crockett weapons and had become involved with a young German woman who'd been an agent for the Soviets. When the Davy Crockett nuclear warheads had disappeared, so had she. The elder Wythe had quietly been demoted and sent to an outpost in Alaska.

Gordon also had information that Senator Wythe, as Chairman of an important foreign affairs subcommittee, had secretly buried this information. When Gordon had presented the proof to Wythe, the Senator had no choice to drop out of the race, citing "family considerations."

Sydney Gordon had never been able get his arms around the high approval rate the President enjoyed. Her dovish foreign policy agenda did not match the serious dangers all free nations faced from terrorism. But when he ultimately became President he'd lead the United States to its rightful place in the world, no matter who got hurt in the process. He was confident he would succeed her if he played his cards right and if Wilkerson did his job. In three short years he'd be the most powerful man in the world.

He picked up the secure phone, studied his address book, and punched in the numbers, not trusting an assistant to place a call.

"Colin Farthington's office, how can I help you?" a young woman's voice said pleasantly.

"I'd like to speak with Mr. Farthington. Please tell him William Teller is calling," the Vice President replied in a steady tone.

After a brief silence, "Hey, Sydney, er—Mr. Vice President, it's been a long time. Why the cloak and dagger? You haven't used that ridiculous alias since our fraternity days at Tufts. What can I do for you?" Colin said in a friendly voice that did not match his mood.

"I'll get right to the point. We've obtained information you might be interested in some extremely rare military weapons from the fifties. Cold War items. What can you tell me?" the Vice President said.

"What is this, Mr. Vice President? You guys spying on me? I did have a lead on several unique Russian bazookas, supposed to be in the basement of an old bombed out building in Minsk. Unfortunately, nothing came of it," Colin said.

"Oh, you understand how it is, Colin. Some bureaucrat from West Point contacted my office. They'd like to fill out their museum collection of World War II weaponry and wanted my help. I know you're an old weapons collector and thought you might be able to help. I'm sure you're aware that some up here on the Hill, not to mention the FBI and a bunch of other Federal agencies, think you are crossing a legal line by obtaining some of your weapons. I've got no concerns about the methods you use," the Vice President said.

"Well, sorry to disappoint, Syd. But as I said, I reached a dead end. And remember what I said. I'm a law-abiding loyal citizen. Tell me, how did you learn of my interest in these particular weapons?"

Gordon reclined in his chair without speaking for nearly fifteen seconds. He enjoyed this kind of bullshit.

"Sorry Colin, you don't have clearance for sensitive information. Security has tightened up since 9–11, even with the policies of the current President. Contact me if you hear anything."

"Sure thing Mr. Vice President. You can count on me," Colin said in a flat voice.

After he hung up the phone, Sydney Gordon rose to his feet and withdrew to the window. He paid little attention to the beautiful white flowering shrubs outside and the neatly trimmed lawn. His eyes hardened into narrow slits.

"Fucking liar," he muttered.

CHAPTER 12

Sinclair Island, Washington State

Colin Farthington paced on his elevated outdoor deck. A foggy mist filled the air, hindering his view of the strait thirty five feet below his perch, but he didn't care. Passing whales and soaring eagles, had he been able to see them, would have held no interest for him today. Impatiently he glanced again through the window at the clock hanging on the wall of his office. There was much he needed to learn. He felt certain Pyotr was dead and prayed Gabrielle and Kristen had reached safety. Why hadn't Smithers reported in yet? Was he in danger too?

Colin questioned whether his passion for rare weapons was worth the loss of people he cared for. But he refused to give up. Especially now that the stakes had risen. Russian thugs might not be the only group hunting for the weapons. Sydney Gordon's call had complicated things further. The situation was getting a little dicey, but he had not become incredibly wealthy by panicking at the first sign of trouble. Experience told him that adversity often creates its own opportunities.

Colin's thoughts were interrupted by the sound of footsteps on the wooden deck. He turned as his administrative assistant hurried toward him. Wearing only a light sweater and knee length skirt, she shivered in the chilly air. Born in tropical Cairns, Australia, Jane Evers was used to rain but was still adjusting to the cool temperatures of the Pacific Northwest. Though only 5'2" she was a tough Aussie with medium length brown hair and blue-gray eyes. At the age of twenty two she'd come to visit the Canadian Gulf Islands, located a few miles north of Sinclair Island, after finishing her University studies in Brisbane.

She'd been sea kayaking with a group of friends when a sudden freak storm raged in from the Pacific and separated the kayakers. Huge waves and strong winds prevented the group from staying together. Jane found herself alone and battling rough waves and frigid water. Reaching a small uninhabited island she stayed alive using the survival skills she'd learned while trekking in the harsh Australian outback. She rode out the storm by building a crude shelter under a rock overhang and dining on the beach oysters that littered the beach. She even managed to trap a Dungeness crab in an old bucket found lying in the underbrush. Two days later, after the storm had subsided and the sun had come out, she spotted a yacht passing close to the island and used a small signal mirror to attract attention of the people on the boat. She learned from the sailor, Colin Farthington, that her friends had survived the ordeal and had organized a rescue effort.

Jane was still with Colin, and even though he was her employer, they had a close personal relationship. He respected her intellect, determination, and loyalty. She admired his brilliance and level-headed approach to every situation.

Colin raised his eyebrows and asked, "Any news?"

"Yes, and it's mostly good," Jane replied. "Gabrielle and Kristen are safe. Tom Smithers called and reported a successful mission. He's got them both hidden in a secure apartment and is waiting for a transport plane to send them here. A shipment of precious gems is scheduled to leave Belarus tomorrow and the girls will be on board. He'll get them here safely."

"Thank God for that. But what about Pyotr?"

"Nothing yet," Jane said. "He's vanished. Smithers thinks he's been murdered, but has no proof. We don't know what, if anything, he told the thugs who kidnapped him."

Colin stared into the darkening sky. A sudden breeze riffled his hair out of place. He brushed his fingers through his hair and frowned.

"We'll assume they learned everything. We have to move fast. Most likely they're in possession of the same information we have and are mobilizing their forces to recover the nukes as we speak. How are we doing with what Pyotr told us?"

"Our team should have an answer soon, I'm told. They're not sure there's really a map in the Secret Tower of the Kremlin but are convinced the weapons were hidden in a cave on an island near Cuba. We're still trying to identify the island," Jane said.

"Yes, it's too risky for us to search the Tower. There's plenty of data and information from Kennedy's blockade and the Russian retreat. Our guys will figure out what happened."

Colin's intercom buzzed, interrupting their conversation. He raced into his office and punched the transmit button.

"Colin here," he barked. "What have you got?"

"Edwards here, sir. We've identified the island as El Fortunato, not far to the east of Cuba, sort of in the Bahamas chain. That's the 'fortune' Alexei mentioned. And bonnie, well it doesn't really refer to a woman's first name like you might think. We're sure the reference is to the famous female pirate Anne Bonny who prowled the waters around El Fortunato during the early 1700's. She was one of the fiercest and most feared pirates of her time. She was an incredible woman because during that era few pirates even allowed females onboard their ships. Women had few rights back in those days and rarely made important decisions. But as one of the pirate leaders, she was bloodthirsty and ruthless."

"You've got to be kidding. I know the island very well. Get to the point. What's all this have to do with the nukes?"

"I'm getting to that. There's a big sinkhole on the island. Supposedly Anne Bonny captured a Spanish galleon and murdered the entire crew by throwing them down into the hole. That's how it got its name. You're familiar with it, Colin. Bonny's Abyss near Magic Bay on El Fortunato Island. We're certain the weapons were hidden in a cave at the bottom of the sinkhole. They might still be there."

Colin dropped into his chair and stared at the antique clock on his desk. Bonny's Abyss at Magic Bay used to be a limestone cavern connected to the ocean by underground streams. Long ago the roof of the cavern collapsed, creating a hole some 80 feet deep and 40 feet across. The bottom still filled with water at high tide.

He stood up, leaned on his desk and turned his head toward Jane.

"This is good news, Jane. KC Jameson is living on El Fortunato. Get him on the secure phone. Hurry."

CHAPTER 13

El Fortunato Island, Bonny's Abyss

KC Jameson edged toward the rim of Bonny's Abyss and stared into its eighty foot depth. The rough limestone walls dropped nearly straight down and disappeared into murky water. His knees weakened and vision blurred. He stumbled backward and slumped on the rocky outcrop. KC realized his fear of heights and of tight spaces was irrational. Flying in airplanes was no problem. Heck, he'd even logged nearly twenty hours piloting a small Robinson 22 helicopter back in Seattle, but standing at the edge of this deep hole was a different story altogether.

The edge of the Abyss was sheltered from the ocean breeze, and the late afternoon sun had turned the air hot and humid. The air was heavy, a sure sign of an impending storm. Sweat trickled down his nose and fell on his shorts. Shortly his heartbeat returned to near-normal. He rose to his feet and stumbled the short distance to his dust-covered truck. He leaned against his truck, a gray 2005 Toyota Tundra with four-wheel drive and an extended cab, relieved to be away from the deep Abyss. KC breathed deeply and stared blankly at the few homes that were nestled on the breezy hilltops. Sudden movement caught his attention, and he turned as a pelican glided past just a few yards offshore searching for its breakfast. "Well, that was interesting," he muttered to himself as he jumped into his truck.

KC drove towards a marina at the south end of the island, needing the calming security a flat and expansive ocean offered. Earlier that morning he had received an urgent call from his boss, Colin Farthington. Colin was adamant that KC find a way to climb down into Bonny's Abyss, find the cave, and search for some nuclear weapons.

"There's nobody else, KC. I can try to get you some help, but there's a good possibility Russian thugs are following the scent, and the US Government might be getting involved as well. I had a man in Moscow who learned the weapons might be in Bonny's Abyss, but he's gone missing. He was kidnapped and is probably dead. Then I got a rather strange call from Vice President Gordon asking me about my weapons collection. I suspect he's aware we're after the nukes. We must be careful—Gordon is as immoral as they come. Time is running short. Find the weapons and hide them in the secret room in your lab. Then we'll get them to Sinclair Island," Colin had said over the secure satellite phone.

KC had argued he didn't have the ability to climb into Bonny's Abyss, but Colin refused to accept that. He reminded KC of where he might be today had Colin not plucked him from the streets of Seattle, given him a good job, and paid for his college education.

KC replayed the conversation in his mind.

"I want those weapons, KC," Colin had said. "I don't want some foreigner to get them first. God only knows what they might do with them. I don't even trust our own federal government. This current administration is a complete mess. Anderson and Gordon despise each other. I don't know Gordon's end game, but it can't be good. That arrogant son of a bitch will stop at nothing to achieve his goals. I'm going out on a limb here, KC, and taking a huge risk. But I'm willing to do it. The weapons will be safer in my collection than under Gordon's control or in a terrorist camp. Nobody will steal them from me, I can tell you that!"

KC's shoulders had sagged and he'd replied, "OK Colin, I'll try. But please try to send someone down here to help me. You have to remember I'm no good with heights. I freeze up and my brain doesn't work. You know I get claustrophobia, too."

Watching the calm seas, KC went through a list of people who might be able to help him. Most of his friends were ex-patriots with good jobs who would face certain deportation, if not a long prison term, if they were caught with nuclear weapons. He'd learned from Colin that the warheads themselves were not large, less than three feet long and weighing about 75 pounds, so he wouldn't need a lot of help. Intelligence reports indicated some sort of launcher was with the warheads. Probably one additional person would be enough to do the job, but he had to get someone to help him get into Bonny's Abyss. He considered several friends who might help if they could take time off from their jobs, but he couldn't afford to wait until the weekend. He grabbed his cell phone and made a call.

"Oh, hello KC, how's it goin'?" said the man who answered his phone.

"Hi Doug, I'm good. Say, I've got a little situation and need help finding some old artifacts here on the island. An assignment from my boss that I can't do very easily by myself. I could really use your help. Any chance you're free tomorrow? You'll have to do some rock climbing. And probably crawl into a cave. Should be a lot of fun," KC said.

"Sorry man, but my girlfriend's parents are visiting and I promised I'd take her old man deep sea fishing. He's a real nut for it, so I'll be tied up for the next three, four days. Unless the storm heading our way turns into a hurricane. Then I'm gonna sit tight," Doug replied.

KC hung up the phone. Who else he pondered. He'd need someone trustworthy. He didn't need the local police breathing down his neck, and the thought of spending time in the squalid local jail turned his stomach. What about the Russians? Were they even coming? Maybe they'd already landed on the island!

His gaze fell upon a colorful sailboat heading for Sunday Cove, a sheltered bay on the south west corner of the island. The boat, overloaded with people, floated dangerously low in the water. Haitians most likely. The invasion of illegals had become a huge problem for El Fortunato. Not only did they work without the proper permits, but they were also blamed for much of the crime on the island. Everybody would be better off if the Coast Guard intercepted them before they reached land, but the island had limited resources and the bureaucracy trudged along at a snail's pace. Island life was wonderful, he thought, as long as you're not in a hurry.

The sailboat disappeared behind Cooper's Hill. Then it hit him.

"That's it!" he shouted.

The snotty woman on the beach, Nikki. A climber and a caver! He smiled, feeling good for the first time since he got the call from Colin.

Then he frowned. What if she just laughs again? He'd just have to swallow his pride and persuade her to help him.

CHAPTER 14

Gibara, Northeast Coast of Cuba

D ust hung low in the early morning sun. Time had left this seaside port city of seventy thousand residents behind, even by Cuban standards, and had transformed the once important sugar trading port into a city of ruins and run-down huts. Colorful graffiti was present on many buildings, and while Spanish architecture was still in evidence, most were without a complete roof or had no glass in their windows. Tourists came to visit the museums, but few stayed more than one day. Several long piers jutted out into the sheltered harbor, home for both small fishing boats and a handful of modern cruising yachts.

Few people paid attention as three young men, dressed in baggy swimsuits, lugged three heavy bags and two large plastic coolers to a silver Maiora luxury yacht. The 55' low profile boat was built for speed as well as comfort; the enclosed cockpit sat toward the aft end of the sleek arrow shaped boat. Two elderly gentlemen sat at the water's edge hunched over on their low wooden stools. They gripped long bamboo fishing poles in their withered hands, stared at the young men, and scowled.

"Rich Canadians," one muttered to his companion. "They ruin our waters and our fish with their fast oily boats."

However, his scowl became a leer when a taxi screeched to a halt near the boat and two young women wearing skimpy bikinis poured out. Giggling, they carried colorful bags aboard a moment before one of the young men untied the mooring lines and shoved off. The twin diesel inboard engines roared to life and slowly propelled the boat through the calm waters of the harbor. Jasha Kerensky reached into a cooler and pulled out a can of beer while Vilma Revnikova rose to her feet, arched her back, and looked up at the cloudless blue sky, taking in the full force of the hot sun. She turned toward the dock, smiled at the old fishermen and wiggled a forefinger. They returned her gaze, sighed and returned to their fishing and their unfulfilled dreams.

The man at the helm gently pressed the dual throttles to full power. He gave little thought to how the yacht had been acquired. He only assumed the previous owner and crew rested somewhere deep below the shimmering aquamarine waves of the Caribbean Sea. He cast a glance to the inner cabin of the yacht and was pleased his crew was no longer acting like carefree tourists. The women, now fully dressed in casual clothes, carefully checked the weapons and ammunition they'd hidden in the coolers.

Alena Lukova held one of the Makarov semi-automatic pistols in her right hand. The short weapon fit her hand perfectly and, with the 8 round clip inserted, was perfectly balanced. She'd spent many hours at the pistol range outside Moscow and had fired hundreds of rounds. Alena was, by all accounts, an expert marksman. After returning the weapon to a box with four other Makarovs she grabbed one of the two AR-15 assault rifles they'd brought along. She was quite proficient with the AR's, but preferred the Makarov. The final item in the cooler was a box containing four RGD-5 hand grenades. Alena hoped they wouldn't have to use them.

Ten minutes later, the man at the helm studied the GPS unit mounted on the console. "Less than four hundred kilometers. We'll be within pissing distance of El Fortunato Island before dark," said Pavel Dubkov with a huge grin on his face.

§ § §

Cairns Army Airfield, Fort Rucker, Alabama

A gentle rain fell as Lieutenant Troy Baker drove his army issued blue Ford sedan along Wallace Street. In spite of the drizzle Baker wore reflective wrap-around Oakley sunglasses. He increased his speed to thirty five miles per hour as he drove past several large hangars. Among the hangars he spied rows of helicopters and beyond a runway for fixed wing aircraft. He checked his rear view mirror and saw an MP jeep gaining on him as he turned on Herron Street. Moments later he pulled into a parking lot adjacent to the red and white control tower building.

The MP's vehicle drew up close behind him as he parked in front of the tower. The driver remained behind the wheel while his passenger sprang from the jeep and approached as Baker peeled his six foot four inch frame out of the small sedan.

"Excuse me sir, we had you at ten over the limit. I'm sure you are aware that twenty five means twenty five here at Cairns Field," said the MP in a clipped voice.

Baker rose to his full height and adjusted his sunglasses.

"Sorry, Sergeant, but I'm here on direct orders from Lieutenant Colonel Brad Wilkerson of U.S. Army Intelligence. Here's my authorization. You can return it to me inside. I don't have time to chat with you boys," Baker said as he removed an envelope from his briefcase. Without giving the Sergeant time to respond, Baker spun on his heels and strutted into the building. The two soldiers stared open-mouthed at his retreating frame, but said nothing.

Inside, Baker approached the reception desk where a Corporal spoke on the telephone. Baker abruptly snatched the telephone from the man's grip and slammed it on the receiver. The shocked soldier scrambled to his feet and saluted the superior officer.

Ignoring the salute, Baker said in a firm voice, "I need your commander. Go get him now."

The Corporal picked up the telephone again. A frown flushed across Baker's face and he snatched the phone from the soldier's hand.

"I said go and get him."

The Corporal sprang up, almost knocking over his chair, and scurried down the hallway. Baker turned as the MP approached him with papers in hand.

"Sorry for the bother, sir, everything's in order. Enjoy your stay at Fort Rucker," he said and turned to walk away.

"Sergeant, for your information, I was never here. You never laid an eye on me," Baker said in an even tone.

"Yes sir!"

Moments later, the reception Corporal hurried up to Baker and said, "The Major is on his way sir. He asked if you would wait a minute."

"I ordered you to get him!" Baker replied.

"Er, sorry, sir, I'm doing the best I can."

"Not good enough, soldier. Lucky you aren't a member of my squad."

Moments later, Major Doug Coulter hurried down the hallway with a frown on his face and approached Lieutenant Baker. Baker slowly removed his sunglasses.

"Now, what's all this about, Lieutenant?" Coulter said.

"Please read these orders, Major. They will explain everything. My men will be here in fifteen minutes. Here's a list of what we need. And Major, we are in a hurry. This is Priority One—straight from the top," Baker said pulling another sheet of paper from his briefcase. He offered a quick salute to his superior officer. Coulter read the document, and then stared at Baker for a few seconds.

"No problem, Lieutenant. Let me know if I can get you anything else."

"Thank you, sir."

One hour and thirty minutes later Troy Baker and four soldiers climbed aboard the blue and white Beechcraft King Air 100. There were no military markings on the twin engine prop airplane. The interior had been reconfigured from its usual 13 seat capacity to accommodate Baker, his men, and their gear. Baker stared at the men under his command and shook his head. Only Sergeant "Bud" Walker, his helicopter pilot, was a seasoned soldier. The rest were raw rookies, only weeks out of advanced infantry training. The only one who had shown any leadership potential was a 20 year old Corporal named Peter Garcia. Even though each of the rookies had graduated in the top ten percent of his class, they'd never been tested in battle. Baker had no idea how they would react to live fire, if they met any.

But this should be an easy assignment, he reflected. Fly to Gitmo, helicopter to the island, pick up the nukes, and leave before anybody became aware of their presence. He had been informed that one of Colin Farthington's people was on El Fortunato looking for them as well, but Baker did not waste his energy worrying about a single civilian.

Should be a piece of cake, a good training mission for the new men, Baker mused. He welcomed his new assignment. His last one had been a complete screw-up. Ruined because he neglected to check the air pressure in the spare tire. Well, that was history; now he was getting another chance to prove he should be promoted to Captain.

He gazed out the window at the shimmering waters of the Gulf of Mexico below, and then closed his eyes, losing himself in the dull drone of the twin turboprop engines.

The pilot's voice came over the intercom, interrupting his thoughts.

"ETA Guantanamo Base, Cuba, three hours forty minutes, sir. I've received confirmation that a civilian model Eurocopter helicopter will be waiting for you when we land."

CHAPTER 15

El Fortunato

For the first time in weeks KC's morning swim was a quick in-and-out affair. He was motivated by the urgency in Colin Farthington's voice and was anxious to find someone to help him retrieve the nuclear weapons before anyone else.

He'd set the timer on his coffee maker for 6:30 a.m. the night before and woke to the noise of the brew percolating. After his quick swim he poured himself a cup and trekked back to the bathroom where he shaved. He dressed in cargo shorts, pulled on a green golf shirt and was out the door at 7:15.

"Looks like a storm coming" he said to nobody as he got in his Toyota pickup truck. The eastern sky was dark with clouds, but the wind was relatively calm. Humidity hung heavy in the air.

After he had returned from the Abyss the day before, he'd made a few more phone calls trying to find someone to help him retrieve the weapons but wasn't surprised when no one offered to help. That left only one final possibility. He hoped the woman he had met on the beach, Nikki, was still at the Blue Wave Bed and Breakfast. KC had not seen her since the towel incident on the beach and had tried to put that embarrassment out of his mind. It wasn't easy, especially when he recalled the way she laughed at him and the derisive comment about his manhood. He wondered how he would be received when he asked her to help him climb down into Bonny's Abyss and find the cave.

He angled his vehicle into the lower highway and had to slow for a dump truck that was backing into the construction site of the newest condominium development. He edged toward the center line of the highway and peered around the truck. As soon an oncoming motorbike passed he swerved around the truck, sped up, and headed towards the Blue Wave, only a few minutes down the road.

The Blue Wave Bed and Breakfast was run by an elderly Canadian lady named Emma Cameroon who had taken a liking to KC when they first met. He'd stayed with her for a few weeks while he arranged permanent accommodations. She had four rental units housed in two brightly painted two story buildings. Emma lived alone in a separate single story stone cottage where she prepared a daily breakfast for her guests. The bed and breakfast had a small swimming pool and hugged the beach at Secret Bay.

"Hey Emma, how's it going?" KC asked as he pulled up to Emma's house.

"Oh, hi KC, long time no see. Actually, business is a little slow. You never know what's going to happen during hurricane season. Looks like a big storm coming in the next couple of days. What brings you around so early?" she said, peering up at the cloudy sky.

"Well, I met one of your guests the other morning on the beach. I've got a little project and I hoped she might be able to help. Her name is Nikki. Is she still around?" said KC.

"I'd be careful with her, KC. She's a real firecracker, that one. Can't wait to get off this island. I never understand you young folks these days. Here we are in paradise, and all she wants to do is climb a mountain or crawl into a cramped little cave. She's a looker, though. I'll give her that. She's over in Magnolia Two, Unit 1 on the lower level. Bring her over for breakfast. I'll buy," Emma chuckled.

The sliding patio door of the bright blue building was wide open. KC approached slowly, rapped his knuckles on the glass and, seeing nobody in the room, said "Hello, anybody home?"

Moments later Nikki Colt strolled to the doorway and eyed KC. She was wearing a long sleeved shirt, baggy shorts, and hiking boots. She pursed her lips and frowned at KC. After a few seconds, a twinkle crept into her eyes.

"Come over to show off again have you?" she said.

"Er, um, no I…um," was all KC could muster. He felt himself flushing and stepped away from the door, unsure of his next move.

Nikki grabbed her car keys and strode out the door. Pausing, she turned and stared at KC. The edge of her mouth twitched once.

"When the cat gives you back your tongue, I'd like to know why you're here. In the meantime, I've got a busy day ahead. My fiancé gets here tomorrow, and I have a lot to do before then," Nikki said.

KC shifted his weight. "Well, er, sorry. I was wondering if you might be able to help me on a little project I gotta do for my boss," KC stammered.

"Oh sure, I can only imagine what the 'project' of yours might be. Didn't you hear me tell you my fiancé is on his way here? Look, I know lots of people like islands like this. But not me. It sucks. It's dry, it's dusty, and it's scrubby. Sure the water is beautiful, but swimming isn't really my thing. I want to get my work done and get to someplace more exciting. I can't take the time for some ridiculous project of yours," Nikki said.

KC pointed a finger at her and said, "You don't understand. I shouldn't be telling you this, but the situation might be dangerous. You told me you're an experienced rock climber and caver. I'm no good at either, but the project my boss assigned me requires both. I'd like you to help me. We'll be happy to pay you for your time. Please."

"Oh, get real. Who is this boss of yours? Why doesn't he help you? I cannot believe something could be dangerous on this island," Nikki said, glancing at her watch.

"My boss is a wealthy man who lives near Seattle. He wants me to recover some rare artifacts for one of his collections. He thinks Russian terrorists might be searching for them too. My job is to get them first," said KC.

"Oh, sure. This is insane. A rich boss? Russian terrorists? What would they be hunting for here, in the middle of nowhere? Madness. You've got to be kidding. Hey, I gotta go. I'll be with my fiancé for a few days. Try me next week, but I'll probably be busy," Nikki said as she got in her small Suzuki SUV and slammed the door.

"But—wait, it's complicated. Nikki, please."

Nikki rolled her blue eyes and drove away.

KC remained in the open patio door staring at the dust kicked up by her vehicle. "Shit. Back to the drawing board," KC muttered, pulling at his ear.

CHAPTER 16

National Hurricane Center

Sally Riggs frowned. She couldn't believe the image on her computer screen. The storm that had sprung up near the African coast had not hit Cape Verde, but had shifted and tracked northwest instead. During the first six hours of her shift, the storm grew larger and traveled three hundred miles. Incredibly fast. It was definitely a tropical depression with internal sustained winds at 35 mph and its pressure continuing to drop. The reading was 990 mb and falling. A tropical storm was surely brewing.

While too early to know for sure, experience told her a hurricane was imminent. Sally entered the information on the Center's tracking website. She hoped she wasn't too late. Small boats in the way of this storm would be in trouble.

Two hours fifteen minutes and three cups of strong black coffee later, a door banged and Charlie Holly hurried into the Center.

"Sorry I'm late, Sally. I had a hard time getting up; the double shift last night completely wore me out," Charlie said.

"Sure, Charlie, and your date with Amy had nothing to do with it?" Sally laughed as she grabbed her jacket and headed for the exit.

"Be sure to monitor the storm. It's moving like a race horse. Moved 85 miles in the past two hours and the pressure is still dropping. I can't say for sure, but I think Haiti can expect high winds and torrential rain in 40 to 48 hours," Sally said.

"See ya, Boss. I'll keep a sharp eye." Charlie said as he poured himself a cup of coffee and folded the newspaper to the crossword puzzle.

He didn't notice that the storm's pressure had dropped to 985 mb, only 5 mb above a Category 1 hurricane, and the winds had increased to 60 mph, closing in on the 74 mph needed for a true hurricane.

CHAPTER 17

Sinclair Island, Washington

Colin Farthington stared out his large picture window at the gray sky. The majestic cedar and fir trees shivered in the slight breeze, and small rivulets of water trickled down the glass. The drizzle had started at daybreak.

"Well, Jane, I think we're in trouble," Colin said to his assistant. "KC can't find anyone to help him, and he's afraid of heights so he doesn't think he can climb down into Bonny's Abyss and retrieve the weapons. I need those weapons, not only for selfish reasons, but also to keep them out of the hands of terrorists. The longer KC delays, the higher the risks become. I don't know what the US Government might be doing about them. I don't trust Sydney Gordon. I'm too familiar with his tactics. He was President of our fraternity at Tufts the year I pledged. Even then he was a shady character. Rumors spread around the University that he had devised a system to obtain copies of exams in advance. He had a high grade point average and always had money to spend on beer and girls. His phone call tells me that he's involved up to his eyeballs in this weapons fiasco. This situation is going to get real messy. And dangerous."

"Don't we have someone we can send to help KC?" Jane asked.

"Time is of the essence, Jane. We need those weapons now, before anybody else gets them. El Fortunato isn't the easiest place in the world to get to. Our Cessna Citation can't fly that far without a refueling stop. The trip will take at least a day, probably two, from Seattle, assuming favorable weather," Colin replied.

"Well, let's see where our own agents are located," she said, studying several sheets of paper on her clipboard.

"Allenby is in Western Australia working on the uranium project, Franks is in South Africa on the titanium pollution situation, and Carlson's in a remote province of Chile negotiating the copper deal. Rogers is finishing up his fishing vacation in British Columbia and is flying to Seattle tomorrow," Jane replied.

"He'll do. Contact him. And check the weather. I picked up something on the news about a big storm out in the Atlantic. It's moving fast and might be headed towards El Fortunato," Colin said.

"I'll get right on it, Colin."

"Do you have more news from our people in Belarus? Any sign of Pyotr?" Colin asked.

Jane gazed out the window then said "Sorry boss, not a word."

Thirty five miles to the south, about half way to Seattle, fog banks began forming close to the surface of Puget Sound. The breeze died and the drizzle eased to a heavy mist.

Fog became thick as whipped cream, slowly oozing south toward downtown Seattle. Traffic began to slow as visibility dropped to less than 100 yards. Local television stations interrupted programming to issue warnings. Ship captains stared at their GPS units, peered blindly ahead, and limped back to their ports. Sea-Tac airport began diverting planes. There would be no flights, in or out, for at least the next 24 hours. Maybe longer.

At about the same time, seven hundred miles to the north, Howie Rogers lounged on the dock at Muncho Lake in Northern British Columbia as he waited for his seaplane. The sun was bright and the air fresh and crisp. The plane was three hours overdue and he couldn't have been happier. He loved the solitude of this country and had nothing pressing back at work. Hopefully the plane wouldn't get here and he'd have another day of trout fishing. He turned his attention inland and watched as the old man who managed the lodge hobbled down the hill toward him.

"You can unpack your bags, Howie. You ain't going nowhere. Bad weather down south. Nothing in or out for a few days. Good thing for you the fish are still biting."

"Thanks Eddie. I'd better get back to the lodge and call my boss. I hope he didn't plan anything important for me," Howie said, grinning from ear to ear.

CHAPTER 18

El Fortunato

KC lounged on his front porch holding a bottle of Presidente lager and gazed past the succulent shrubs to the ocean just a few yards beyond. A northeast breeze freshened in advance of the impending storm, and a lone power boat cruised the choppy waters. Humidity still hung heavy in the air, unaffected by the breeze. Hopefully the storm would change course and miss the island, but he'd learned that some tourists were fleeing the island amid rumors that the airport would be shut down.

He had few worries, however, because both his house and office were well stocked with food, water, flashlights, and kerosene lamps. He spent a few minutes securing his outdoor furniture and checking the hardware on his wood hurricane shutters. It would take a few minutes to shut them if a hurricane actually hit the island.

KC had come no closer to finding someone to help with the recovery of the nuclear weapons and seriously considered contacting Colin again to ask for someone else to find the weapons, but didn't make the phone call. He owed Colin too much. Facing challenges was not a problem, but fear of heights and claustrophobia had always proved to be difficult obstacles to overcome. Perhaps he could hold off until the storm passed. Climbing alone into Bonny's Abyss would be difficult enough in good weather, but nearly impossible in rain and wind. Stepping back into his house he kicked off his Chacos sandals and grabbed another beer. He popped the bottle cap and was reaching for the television remote control when a car door slammed.

Nikki Colt stormed into his house without knocking, her face red with rage.

"Your goddamn Russians! They're here," she shouted to KC.

"What are you talking about?" KC said. "Calm down. Take a breath and start from the beginning. What's going on?"

"I don't know what they were doing on such a remote part of the island, anyway. I hate Russians. You shoulda seen what some of them did to my team two years ago when we were working in Poland. Acted like they owned the whole God forsaken country. Treated us like dirt. Trust me. The Russians I just ran into are bad. I can see it in their eyes—and I've seen plenty of shit-bag Russians," Nikki said, her blue eyes on fire.

"Whoa, hold on, Nikki. You have to tell me what's going on," KC said calmly. "Here, sit down. You want some lemonade or something?"

"Shit no. And what can you do? Got any guns around here? Because they do."

"Guns? What kind?"

"Rifles, most likely AR-15's. You know, the so-called assault weapons. Come on, let's go. You wanted my help, well now you're stuck with me."

KC gazed out to the ocean for a moment. "Calm down Nikki. Where did you find the Russians and what were they doing?" KC said.

Nikki wiped her mouth with her sleeve.

"Ok," Nikki said more calmly. "I was down near the southwest point where the road gets real rough and you need four-wheel drive. I went to scout a site for a radar relay station and came across a pick-up truck carrying five people, three men and two women, stuck in the sand right up to both axles. They wore casual clothes, like tourists, but I'll bet my bottom dollar they're up to no good," she said.

"Why?"

"I'm getting to that. I got out and asked if they needed my help and noticed that they had some stuff hidden in the back of the truck under big pieces of burlap. They spoke English well enough, but I know Russians when I see and hear them. The men had short military style haircuts. But probably not soldiers. More likely free-lance mercenaries. I also know a lot about guns. My name is Colt, remember. They had at least two rifles under a piece of burlap, but the butt end of one was sticking out. Just like the newer rifles with adjustable stocks. They acted kind of friendly and asked for help, but I couldn't do anything for them without a chain. Anyway, my car is too small to pull them out," she said.

KC took a sip of his beer. "I wonder where they got a truck."

"Shit, I don't care! But they got one."

"What color?"

"Light blue. An old Ford, I think. I'm not much into cars, but the truck was sort of boxy looking and in pretty good shape. Not curvy like the new trucks."

"Good. I wonder why they weren't over near Magic Bay, closer to Bonny's Abyss."

"Abyss? They asked about that. What is it?"

"It's a deep hole in the ground." KC smiled briefly. "And the place where I need your help."

"Well, they don't have a clue where it's located," Nikki said. "They asked how to get to it. I told them I'm new to the island and never heard of it. Which is actually the truth," Nikki said.

64

"Let's go," urged KC.

"We have some time, I guess. I told them I'd send someone to help them. What a joke. I wonder when they'll realize nobody's coming," Nikki said with a satisfied smirk. "Oh yeah, when I drove away, up a little hill, I glanced back at the ocean. I think their boat is stuck on one of the sand bars in the bay. I doubt they'll get off very easily, even at high tide. What a bunch of losers. Anyway, what's this project of yours?"

"Oh, not much. We just have to find some old nuclear weapons the Russians left here," KC said with a twinkle in his eye.

Nikki's jaw dropped. "You gotta be shitting me. Is it safe?"

"I think so. The weapons should still work, but they won't just explode for no reason. I gotta get them before the Russians do. And maybe some Americans."

"Shit, KC. This gets crazier by the minute."

"You got that right. Come on. We gotta do this before the hurricane hits."

Nikki paused and turned to KC, looking directly into his green eyes. "Hurricane? I've never been in one."

KC smiled. "Yea, one's bearing down on the island now. We've got a day or two before it hits us."

CHAPTER 19

The Cave

O K," Nikki said. "I'll need some information about the Abyss. How deep is it and what type of rock is it made of?"

"Oh, boy. I tried not to look down into it—makes me lightheaded. But I guess it's about seventy five feet deep and half that across. The rock, I know, is limestone. It's rough and there are plants growing right out of the stone. And the walls go straight down," said KC.

Nikki rolled her eyes and said, "Good. We'll need some climbing gear. I've got a good rope and two harnesses at the B&B. You'll need a pair of thick gloves and a headlamp. Got any water bottles?"

"No problem," KC muttered and turned toward his back hallway. A minute later he emerged with an armful of gear.

"Let's go. Are you sure you'll need me down there?"

"Nice try," Nikki said with a smirk.

When they reached Bonny's Abyss, Nikki quickly went to work. She secured one end of the long rope to a rock outcropping, attached her harness, and paused.

"Pay attention, KC. You'll only get one chance to do this."

Stepping into the void she repelled down the near vertical walls until reaching a narrow, flat protrusion in the cliff face and searched for the cave. The air in the Abyss was heavy with humidity and before long she was dripping with sweat. Finding nothing she continued down until she reached a narrow ledge about 8" wide. The water was only 25 feet below her.

She released the rope, removed her gloves, and eased her way nearly twelve feet around along the ledge, clinging to the rock face, finding handholds in the tiniest of cracks in the stone. Her goal was to reach a small circular indentation in the rock face four or five feet above a clump of bushes growing out of the rock. Just below the indentation was a ledge four feet long and 15 inches wide. Grabbing a thick branch she hoisted herself up to the ledge and studied the indentation. Here the vertical walls of the Abyss had become less steep and smaller stones and gravel had collected in the area.

After resting just long enough to catch her breath, Nikki removed a trowel from her belt and began digging into the loose gravel. Moments later the trowel broke through the outer layer of stones. She dug furiously for several minutes, eventually opening a hole large enough for her shoulders to fit into. Donning her headlamp she propelled herself headfirst into the void. The first few feet angled downward. Nikki wriggled her way in, flat on her stomach until she reached a large rock that prevented her from going any farther. She dug around the edges for a minute then gave the rock a shove. To her surprise it slid easily and disappeared into the darkness.

Aiming her headlamp forward, Nikki continued onward, finally sliding into a large cavern, perhaps fifteen feet around and at least as high. The rough floor of the cavern was only three feet below the entrance. A single stalactite hung from the ceiling, nearly reaching the floor. "Aha," she said after spotting two tunnels branching off the cavern and into pitch black. This is what we're looking for, she thought, then climbed back out of the cavern.

"Get your ass down here Jameson! Now! I found the cave." Nikki shouted up to KC as he peeked over the edge of the deep pit.

High above, KC stepped back from the edge. Even then his knees wobbled and he became light-headed. His heart hammered and his breath came in short gasps. In an attempt to pull himself together he crawled up to higher ground and took several deep breaths. He edged closer to the pit but stopped when he heard a faint, unusual sound. Curious, he wheeled around toward the noise, searching the houses and road near Bonny's Abyss, but found nothing. The wind suddenly dropped and the noise became more distinct. KC scanned the ocean, beginning at the nearby marina and swept his eyes to the west. Shading his eyes, he detected movement close to shore. He watched carefully until he recognized a medium sized civilian helicopter flying only a few feet above the rising ocean swell. It was heading directly for him.

That's gotta be trouble, he thought as he pulled on his gloves and edged toward Bonny's Abyss. Refusing the urge to look down, he grabbed the rope, holding on like Nikki had shown him when she began her decent, and slowly edged backward down the limestone wall. Out of the wind, a sudden calmness overtook him, his heartbeat slowed, and his breathing became regular. Still, he refused to look down.

"Come on Jameson. Move it!"

"Piece of cake," he muttered, hoping his bravado would cover up his real fear of heights. Several minutes later, as a light rain began to fall, he reached the small ledge.

"I made it, Nikki!" he yelled with relief.

"Not so fast Jameson. You've got some more climbing to do. Look down to your left and you'll see a smaller ledge. Slide down and work your way over here to the cave. You only have to go about 10 feet."

"Yea, right," KC muttered as he backed over the ledge and felt his way to a foothold. He found one easily, but found it difficult to shuffle his way over to the cave without falling.

"How the hell do I hold on?"

"Use your fingers. Find little handholds. Feel for small cracks in the wall. Come on, hurry."

"I know. I spotted a strange helicopter flying only fifty feet above the waves coming this way. Something tells me it's not a tourist flight," KC shouted as he inched his way across the rocks.

Moments later he reached the cave and peered into the opening. Nikki grabbed his shoulders and dragged him through the narrow entrance. KC fell on her in the darkened space, tearing skin off his elbow.

"Get your headlamp on," Nikki ordered. "We've got some searching to do."

KC reached into his small backpack, found his flashlight and turned it on. He froze.

Eerie shadows danced on the rough walls of the cave and the ceiling appeared to be melting slowly toward his head.

"Come on Jameson. Snap out of it. You're doing just fine." Nikki said, shaking her head.

"I...I cannot move, this place is closing in on me," KC stuttered.

"Look KC, pretend it's night and we're out for a stroll. You'll be alright. Take a couple of deep breaths. Follow me. "

Nikki grabbed his hand and gave it a tug.

"I'll try," KC said slowly and took a small step forward.

They scrutinized the cavern and studied the two tunnels Nikki had seen earlier. One was seven or eight feet high, the other wasn't more than five feet high and narrower than the first. Reasoning that the Russians had been in a hurry to hide the weapons, Nikki and KC started down the largest tunnel. As she went in, Nikki removed a large piece of white chalk from her pack and drew a large "X" on the wall.

"Wouldn't want to get lost down here," she said with a smirk. Every twenty feet she made another chalk mark on the wall. It would be easy to retrace their steps.

The tunnel sloped downward making travel easy. The air in the cave was cool and dry, a welcome relief from the warm humid air outside. KC couldn't place the smell, but found it not at all unpleasant; a bit stale perhaps, but not offensive. The floor was smooth rock, long ago worn by tidal flows and runoff from rain. However, the walls were a rougher limestone so KC and Nikki had to be careful not to scrape their arms on the jagged stone. With measured steps, they moved slowly through the blackness.

After covering about sixty feet into the tunnel, they found a small opening in the right side of the wall. Nikki stuck her head inside, headlamp scanning the interior. A few seconds later, she drew back, shook her head, and continued on. Occasionally they encountered a small pile of rocks that had broken off the ceiling of the cave. KC peered upward at each rock pile, certain the massive hill above them would come crashing down at any minute. In spite of the cool air, sweat trickled into his eyes and down his nose. The walls of the tunnel soon became narrower and the floor rougher. They had to slow down and bend over at times to maneuver past low hanging rocks. KC closed his eyes and tried not to think of the tons of rock above his head.

Suddenly, the tunnel opened into another cavern, slightly smaller in diameter than the first one. It was circular in shape, perhaps 12 feet across, but the ceiling rose much higher than the first cavern. KC breathed a little easier. The larger space lifted his spirits and calmed his fears. The walls were a shade lighter than those in the tunnel, giving the room a dim glow from their headlamps. KC realized he was in an ancient underwater cave. His professional instincts kicked in after a few seconds. He neared one of the sidewalls and studied the etchings and fossil remnants left in the rock face by long ago sea life. The walls were rough, pockmarked with several shades of gray coloring.

Here they found two more tunnels branching off at forty five degree angles. One angled upward and the other down. Nikki studied both for a minute and came to a decision.

"The left one. It slopes downward and it's bigger. Come on let's go. You can come back another time and explore the right one," she said and scampered into the darkness.

KC followed close behind her, a tight smile on his face. "That'll be the day." He muttered to himself.

§ § §

The Eurocopter EC-145 came in fast and low. The chop of the ocean below increased as frothy white waves sent a spray up toward the chopper. Lieutenant Troy Baker scanned the scrubby uneven terrain and searched for Bonny's Abyss.

His map indicated a unique geological formation located two hundred meters inland from the salt flats. Corporal Garcia spotted it first.

"Sir! Look. The Abyss. Two o'clock."

"Good eye, Garcia! Okay, Sergeant, set her down on the beach. We'll be out of the wind and out of sight. I doubt anyone will bother the helo in this weather."

Sergeant Walker eased the helicopter down to the flats, its spinning rotors only feet from the low rock cliffs.

"Listen up people," Lieutenant Baker shouted as Walker shut down the twin engines. "Hand guns only for this one, and we all go. The chopper will be secure here. We're in and out in one hour, two, tops. When we get to Bonny's Abyss, four of us will go down. Corporal Garcia will be on watch above and will handle the ropes. We'll get the package, haul it up and be out of here before this storm gets worse. Grab your climbing gear and let's go. Any questions?"

Sergeant Walker turned to Baker and said in a hushed voice, "Uh, sir, shouldn't we leave someone here to guard the helo and act as a scout—just in case some baddies show up?"

Baker glared at Walker, ducked his head, sprang from the helicopter and trotted away.

Walker closed his eyes, shook his head, and followed the squad.

CHAPTER 20

Arlington, Virginia

Lt. Colonel Brad Wilkerson sat behind his mahogany desk and stared out the window. A small dog trotted across the street, paused at a road sign, and sniffed. Then he lifted his leg. Wilkerson didn't know what the next few days might bring and hoped the dog's action wasn't a bad omen. He wasn't afraid of Vice President Gordon, but the man was ruthless and dangerous so he'd have to watch his back. His eyes shifted to a small photo on the wall next to his desk. He smiled, remembering his first days in uniform.

Thirty years ago he'd signed up for the Army Reserve Officers' Training Corps at Lehigh University in Pennsylvania. He'd excelled in the program and at his chosen major, Engineering Physics. Upon graduation he began his four year obligation at Fort Ord in California training new recruits. The end of the military draft in the early 1970's had led to an important change in the armed forces as recruits willingly volunteered for service to their country. For the most part, these new soldiers tackled the challenges of basic training with eager enthusiasm. In spite of the Vietnam debacle, morale throughout the various branches of the military had reached highs not seen since the late 1950's.

Wilkerson had loved Army life and had always loved his country, but he was frustrated with the civilians who controlled the military. He loved reading about Russian history and was appalled when he learned that Russia had beaten the United States into space, first with Sputnik and then when Yuri Gagarin became the first human to be launched into space. But his hatred of the USSR was solidified when he saw photos and read stories of the Berlin Wall.

Wilkerson had been lucky. His military career allowed him to actively fight against the spread of Communism. He considered himself to be a true patriot with a mission to battle tyrants and terrorists. His idols included Lieutenant Colonel Oliver North, the controversial Marine officer involved in the Iran-Contra Affair back in the 1980's, and the fiery World War II hero General George Patton, a devout opponent of Communism.

After sixteen years of service around the globe Wilkerson had been promoted to Lt. Colonel and been installed high in the command structure of the

Intelligence Support Activity, or ISA, an army unit charged with collecting actionable intelligence in advance of counter-terrorism missions. He'd met many like-minded soldiers who detested Russia, the Soviets, Communism, Liberal politicians, and everything they represented. He'd recruited many of these soldiers to serve under his command in covert units, first fighting the Communist menace and later radical Islamic terrorism.

However, he was worried about his team on its way to El Fortunato. Lieutenant Baker, a loyal soldier, had shown a lapse in judgment during his last mission, resulting in embarrassment for the ISA and the wrath of several US Senators. Senator Rothberg of Wisconsin had personally warned Wilkerson to keep his activities above board and to focus on collecting intelligence.

Now he was stuck outside of Washington, far from the action and unable to directly assist his men. Securing audio transmissions from the Caribbean area was difficult with the numerous intelligence agencies listening in on every communication to and from Cuba. As the hours passed, he became more anxious. He rose from his chair and began pacing in a precise circle around his large office.

Five minutes later he made a decision.

He leaned over his desk and pressed the intercom button. "Sergeant Smith. Now."

Moments later Smith hurried into the office and stood at attention. "Yes sir."

Wilkerson stood with his hands clasped behind his back and looked up at the Sergeant.

"I'm going to Guantanamo Base, Sergeant. I've got to get closer to the action and can better control communications with Lieutenant Baker from there. You're coming, too. Get working on the paperwork, I want to leave in two hours, tops."

"Yes sir," said Smith with a smirk on his face. "I'm assuming we'll be going to Cuba on a humanitarian mission?"

"Of course, we'll need a good cover story," Wilkerson said grabbing his duffel bag from a closet. "Figure something out before we leave."

CHAPTER 21

National Hurricane Center

The storm intensified as the internal pressure continued to drop. Earlier that day it had officially become a Category 1 hurricane named Ida when its winds reached 74 mph. The barometric pressure had dropped further to 955 mb and the wind increased to 115 mph. Forecasters didn't expect the storm to intensify further because current water temperatures would not support a more powerful storm. The storm had raced across the Atlantic Ocean, often reaching speeds in excess of 60 mph, but would likely slow down as it approached Haiti.

Charlie Holly and Sally Riggs watched the storm's progress on their computer screen.

"Looks like the eye will skirt the north side of Puerto Rico and Haiti and then veer northward. The storm will pummel the south Bahamas and El Fortunato in the next 30 to 36 hours and the projections indicate a direct hit somewhere in South Carolina. We should update the hurricane warnings for all these areas." Sally said as she began tapping on her computer keyboard.

"What about the storm speed?" Charlie asked.

"Once it starts bumping the island land masses it will slow down to about 20 miles an hour. The winds should ease a bit, maybe to about 100 mph. Still a Cat 2 hurricane," Sally said. "I think the eye will pass directly over El Fortunato Island."

"Any chance we'll get hit here in Miami?" Charlie said, hoping for some excitement to break up the long boring days.

"Slim, very slim. But possible."

"Awww," Charlie said.

Sally rolled her eyes and started tapping on her keyboard.

CHAPTER 22

Bonny's Abyss, El Fortunato

In the depths of the cave, Nikki turned toward a small alcove, partially hidden by several limestone pillars. She was in her element and hummed quietly to herself. The cool small spaces evoked pleasant memories of other caves she'd explored. Here the tunnels were wider and the floor smoother than many of the caves she'd explored. But she loved it just the same. Even KC appeared more at ease deep in the cave. An inner peace descended upon him. He didn't appear to be sweating as much as when they first came in. More important he was breathing normally.

Distracted by her comfort, Nikki nearly missed it. Relaxing a little too much, she tripped over an irregular rock lying on the uneven floor and stumbled forward. Recovering her balance, her head swung sharply to the left wall of the cave. Her headlamp reflected off a shape that didn't fit in with the cave's natural rock strata.

Something smooth. Geometric.

"Whoa."

Nikki bent over and squeezed into the small alcove where she discovered another recessed area only a few feet high. Dropping to all fours, she adjusted her headlamp and peered into the recess. Lying before her lay three long wooden boxes, each with its top closed and secured by a single latch. They were painted olive green and had a leather handle on each end. Nikki gave a little shudder. They reminded her of caskets.

"They're here! Look, this looks like Russian lettering stenciled on the side. Come help me. They must be heavy," she said, grabbing at the handle of the closest box.

"Careful, we don't want to set off the bombs."

Nikki rolled her eyes and pulled hard on the handle of the container. KC shifted his stance to help her just as she came crashing backward into him. They both fell roughly against the pillars, then on the floor, the box landing on top of them.

"What the hell?" KC said as he shoved the box off of him.

Nikki rubbed her elbow and discovered a smear of blood on her hand. She rested for a moment and stared at the box.

"They're empty, Nikki," KC said softly.

"Oh shit! Where are the damn things?" Nikki said.

"Damned if I know. Stash the box where you found it. Let's get out of here."

She rolled over to get her hands under her and began to stand up when she spotted something shiny in a pile of tiny rocks at the edge of the tunnel wall. She aimed her headlamp toward the object and leaned forward.

"Hello what's this?" she said as she reached over and gently pawed through the pile of rubble until her fingers settled on something smooth. She picked it up and inspected it for several seconds.

KC stopped, turned, and raised his eyebrows.

"Look, a ring. With an inscription," she said.

She grabbed a corner of her shirt and brushed dust and dirt off the ring. By the size it certainly appeared to be a man's ring. The band was platinum, with a dark oval stone on top. Inscribed into the stone were the letters "J. C. 1965"

"Couldn't have been left here when the nukes were hidden here; that happened in 1962. But maybe when someone moved them? All we gotta do is find someone with the initials JC and we'll find the weapons," KC said.

"Yea, sure, that should be easy. Piece of cake. What if the inscription means something else? Jesus Christ or some high school or college?" Nikki said.

KC shook his head, dropped the ring in his pocket and turned to retrace their steps.

"Let's get the hell out of here. My head is clear now, but I don't want to press my luck. Don't forget about the helicopter I saw approaching the coast."

They hurried back up the tunnel, following the chalk marks. Within minutes they broke into the smaller of the two caverns they'd passed through earlier and slowed their pace.

"Wait a minute," she said. "I'm going to take a quick look up this other tunnel. Maybe the nukes are in another part of the cave."

"OK, but hurry."

KC waited as she scurried up the *right hand* tunnel, making chalk marks on the walls as she trotted. Three long minutes later she rejoined KC.

"Bare as a bone, as far as I went." Nikki said.

KC and Nikki trotted along the tunnel toward the cave's entrance. KC kept his head down, focusing on each step. The closer they got to the entrance the more KC longed for fresh air and daylight. Even rain would be welcomed. They emerged from the tunnel and rushed into the first large cavern. KC smiled. A speck of light from the small opening to Bonny's Abyss beckoned. They raced toward the exit.

They didn't get far.

"Halt! Don't move or you will be shot."

KC and Nikki stopped and spun toward the voice. Four lamps flicked on, one after the other blinding the pair with their brilliance.

"Point your lights to the ground. Now," the voice ordered.

"Who the hell are you to order me around?" Nikki shouted, turning her eyes from the intruders' bright lights.

"I'm First Lieutenant Troy Baker of the US Army. I've got a pistol pointed at your head, so don't get any cute ideas. I'm here to retrieve government property. I think you know where it is. We are on direct orders from Washington. Tell me where they are!" Baker ordered.

"What are you talking about?" Nikki said. "We're a couple of cavers exploring this neat place."

Baker stepped toward Nikki.

"That's enough, Miss," Baker said. "Private Evans, search these prisoners for weapons."

"Nobody's touching me, asshole!" Nikki shouted as she backed to the side of the cavern with fists clenched and eyes like coal.

"Hold everything," KC growled. "We are US citizens and you have no authority here. I know the local government wouldn't take kindly to an invasion by the US Army. Now what are you looking for?"

"You know, Buster. We know all about your boss, Colin Farthington. We know what he collects and what you are after. The weapons are official property of the United States Government and we are here to get them back. Tell me where they are and we'll let you go. We have no interest in harming US citizens," Baker sneered.

KC wiped the bottom of his nose with a forefinger.

"Okay, I'll tell you. All you have to do is follow the chalk marks through that tunnel. There's another cavern with two tunnels. Make sure you take the one on the right. The one that slopes up. When you reach the end of the marks, you'll have to go another hundred feet or so because we ran out of our marking chalk. There is a small room on the right side of the tunnel. Kind of hard to find. You'll find three green boxes in there. Can we go now?" KC said.

"Get lost. Just remember, you never saw us. I've got a man at the rim with a rope waiting to haul the cargo. Name's Garcia. Tell him I said you could go," Baker said as he pivoted and spoke to his men.

"Private Turner, you've got point. Move out."

"Sir—" Sergeant Walker began.

"I said move out. Everyone." ordered Baker.

When the last of the American soldiers disappeared into the dark tunnel, KC and Nikki leaped for the exit.

"Quick. Before they realize we sent them on a wild goose chase," Nikki said. "You go first."

KC didn't argue and stuck his head out into Bonny's Abyss. The rain had stopped and KC turned an eye toward the sun peeking out from behind a cloud. He grinned and gulped the fresh air while his eyes adjusted to the bright light, then crawled out on the small ledge next to the opening. But as he got his footing and began to edge his way along the wall of Bonny's Abyss a large object hurtled past him and splashed into the water below.

"What the hell?" he said in a shocked voice. KC's mouth sagged when his eyes fell on the object below.

Floating face down was a human body, a red pool seeping from its head.

Suddenly the stone next to him exploded in a cloud of dust and several small fragments hit KC's bare legs. KC snapped his head up toward the rim of Bonny's Abyss and his stomach turned to jelly. Four people, dressed in combat gear, were rappelling down the sheer walls directly toward his position on the narrow ledge. One other remained on top, gun in hand, giving covering fire to the descending invaders.

KC scanned the rock walls hoping to find an escape route but found none. Nikki started to poke her head out of the cave. KC dove into the opening, shoved her back inside. He wriggled through and landed on top of her.

"What the hell are you doing Jameson? Get off me!" Nikki shouted.

"Hold on, Nikki. The Russians are here. They're right above us. They killed Garcia up top and are climbing down here."

"Oh shit, let's go. Over there," she said, ducking into the second low tunnel they'd not yet explored. This tunnel was narrower with rougher walls than the tunnel they'd first explored. They stumbled on, going up a steep passageway, hoping to find some place to hide or another exit. The tunnel made several turns, but gave no evidence of a way out. They moved at a rapid, but careful pace. Still, their knees and elbows became raw from scraping the rough walls of the cave.

Three minutes later KC grabbed the back of Nikki's shirt.

"Wait. Listen." KC whispered. From far behind them someone yelled. Followed by more screaming. Mostly in English.

They ducked instinctively and covered their ears when a sudden burst of gunfire drowned out the shouting. When the gunfire stopped, the shouting continued for a moment longer. The smell of gunpowder rose up into the tunnel. The pungent odor grabbed at their throats.

Then, a piercing scream was followed by a single shot.

After that there was nothing but silence. KC's ears still rang from the gunshots. Then they heard a woman laugh.

"Come on, let's go. My guess is the Russians won the battle. We gotta stay ahead of them. They saw me and have to figure we're still in here somewhere," KC said.

Sixty seconds later the sound of footsteps scraped on the rocky floor behind them. They stopped to listen. Someone was coming.

KC scrambled farther up the sloped path. He rounded a sharp bend in the tunnel when Nikki grabbed him by his belt.

"What the hell!" he hissed. "What are you doing?"

"There!" she whispered, pointing above her head. Wisps of gun smoke and limestone dust disappeared into the ceiling of the tunnel.

"An opening. Stand back," she said, drawing a rope from her backpack. With nimble fingers she tied a metal hook to the end and hurled it up into the two foot circular dark hole above their heads. She jerked the rope until the hook caught on a rock or crevice. Like a spider she climbed up and disappeared. Seconds later she poked her head out and said,

"KC, get the hell up here! What are you waiting for? There's plenty of room for us to hide."

Muffled voices echoed up the tunnel toward them. KC sighed, grabbed the rope and hauled himself through the small opening. He found himself in a small narrow cavern about six feet long and four feet high. He squeezed next to Nikki and willed his heart to slow its rapid beating. Then they caught the sound of voices coming from below. Nikki reeled in the last bit of rope a second before two Russians rounded the sharp bend of the tunnel.

"Ah, Lukova. The American soldiers were weak. The job was almost too easy. Now we find the others and have some fun with them."

"No Jasha, we must retrieve the weapons first. We can kill them slowly after. Good. The smoke has cleared. Are there signs they came this way?" Alena Lukova said.

"Not here, but let's keep going. They have to be somewhere," said Jasha, studying the floor of the tunnel.

KC held his breath, afraid the slightest noise would give away their position. He felt the curve of Nikki's body next to him and realized they had never been this close. He closed his eyes and slowed his breathing. Her scent was good, feminine without being overpowering, in spite of the sweat and dust that covered them both. An unusual comfort engulfed him and he felt safe and secure in the closeness of Nikki.

Nikki quickly brought him back to reality.

"They're gone. We can't go back—let's keep climbing," Nikki whispered.

Nikki switched on her headlamp. KC stared up the narrow shaft angling upward from the small cavern. His stomach tightened as the space began to close in on him again. He closed his eyes for a moment and didn't move. His heart throbbed and sweat drenched his face. He heard Nikki continue her crawl up the steep shaft. She pivoted and aimed her light into his face.

"Move it, KC. Come on, hurry. There must be an opening somewhere. The smoke has almost disappeared," she whispered.

KC shook his head. The first step is the hardest, he told himself. Once I start, I can do this. And slowly he began to move up through the narrow slit in the rocks. Sweat trickled down his back. The air in the shaft became hotter, with a musty smell. Dust caked the inside of his nostrils.

Jagged limestone rocks tore at his shirt and soon blood oozed down his knees and shins. He moved on, always looking up, hoping to see the smallest spot of light. The shaft narrowed further. Nikki removed her backpack and dragged it behind her.

The floor gradually became less steep and the tunnel opened up a little. KC and Nikki continued their climb unobstructed. No pinhole of light broke through the darkness ahead. KC convinced himself the tunnel was a dead end. He was about to suggest they turn back and wait for the Russians to leave when they heard an explosion and felt a shudder come from far below them. The shaft trembled, dirt and small rocks pelting them from above. Their headlamps reflected off thick dust. KC and Nikki closed their eyes and stuck their noses into their shirts.

Four long minutes later, the dust cleared enough for them to breathe without inhaling the fine particles.

"What the hell was that?" Nikki said.

"Shit, Nikki, I think they blew up one of the tunnels, or the exit hole. Probably sealed the American soldiers inside the cave. We won't get out that way. If we don't find a way out up here soon we'll be stuck here forever. I don't want to die like this."

"No use crying over something we can't control," she said and resumed her climb. Two minutes later she stopped abruptly.

"What is it?" KC asked.

"I think we're at the dead end you worried about."

KC's shoulders sagged. "Let's go back and find another exit. The gun smoke had to go somewhere."

"Sorry KC. I didn't want to say anything, but there's a small opening below us about twenty five feet where most of the smoke and dust went out. Not even big enough for your head. There's no way out behind us."

"But you said we're at a dead end. We're screwed."

CHAPTER 23

Bonny's Abyss, EL Fortunato

Hold on a minute," Nikki said as she grabbed her pack and rummaged inside. She removed a thin metal object, unscrewed it, and extended it to a length of about eighteen inches.

"Might as well probe above us. Maybe we'll get lucky," she said and began poking the rod into the soil and rock above her head.

"Hey, be careful," he said as fine debris rained down on him, clogging his nostrils even more.

"Oh, cut it out. You got a better idea?" Nikki grunted. "Cover your head."

Before he had time to react, small rocks crashed inches from KC's head, followed by buckets of dirt, pebbles, and sharp stones. KC peered at the shaft above him. A dull ray of light fell through the opening. In an instant KC's stomach relaxed, his breathing returned to normal, and a huge grin spread on his face.

Nikki clawed at the dirt and pebbles clearing an opening barely big enough for them to scramble out. They emerged on relatively flat ground in the middle of a thicket of shrubs. They rolled onto their backs and filled their lungs with the fresh air.

A minute later they crawled to the edge of the thicket. Bonny's Abyss lay twenty five yards in front and perhaps fifteen feet below them. A lone woman was standing at the rim of the Abyss peering over the edge and talking on a two-way radio. She straightened up and pivoted directly toward KC and Nikki's position. They flattened further into the dirt and held their breaths. Turning slowly, the Russian scanned her immediate area but didn't spot them. Only then did she pull a pistol from her belt and begin a search on foot. Luckily for KC and Nikki she headed in a direction opposite from where they were hidden.

"Where's she going?" Nikki whispered.

"Toward the road I think. Lucky for us I parked the truck the other way. We can get to it without her seeing us as long as she keeps going toward the road."

"OK, let's get out of here before the rest of the Russians climb to the top"

"No kidding. There's a shallow ravine behind us. It'll get us close to the truck. Come on."

KC led Nikki through the thicket, stopping often to watch for the Russian. When they reached the edge, KC grabbed her hand and trotted down a short slope to a shallow rocky ravine where a scattering of shrubs gave them enough cover that the sentry couldn't spot them. They worked their way up the ravine toward the road, taking care not to stumble on the loose rocks. The wind had increased and the rain had returned as a fine mist. They crouched lower and made their way along the edge of the dense vegetation. At last KC let go of Nikki's hand. He went to his hands and knees and crawled to a point where he spotted the Russians' truck parked at the side of the narrow road. He stared at the truck for only a minute, expecting the Russian woman to appear at any moment.

"Let's go. Now," said KC, as he sprung up and sprinted across the road.

Nikki followed close on his heels until they reached the safety of a tall stone wall surrounding a large vacation home. They raced around one end of the wall and hurried down a narrow path through dense vegetation. Ten yards later they broke out into the small clearing where KC had parked his truck.

Before Nikki fully closed the passenger side door, KC started the engine and pressed the accelerator to the floor. Nikki's door slammed shut as she was thrown to the back of the seat. When they reached the road, KC spun away from the Russian truck and sped as fast as he could down the rough unpaved road. Just before reaching a sharp curve he glanced in the rear view mirror. The Russian stepped out from the tall shrubs that hid Bonny's Abyss from the road, spotted them, and raised her pistol. KC slid the truck around the corner and increased his speed.

"Shit that was too close," KC said, smiled at Nikki, and laughed.

"What's so funny?"

"I hope I don't look as silly as you do, with all that dust caked to your face."

"You look worse," Nikki said after she studied her face in the mirror on the back of the truck's visor.

"Thanks. Let's go and clean up."

"And then what? All we've got is a ring. And no weapons," Nikki said.

"I don't know, Nikki. I'll call Colin. He knows a lot about the islanders here. Hopefully he'll have an idea."

CHAPTER 24

National Hurricane Center, Miami

W hat the hell?" Charlie Holly muttered.
Hurricane Ida had stalled near the north coast of Haiti. The large storm had raced across the Atlantic at an astounding pace, the eye passing Haiti by a mere thirty miles. An hour ago its winds had dropped to 60 mph, below hurricane strength and was retracing its path, moving slowly southeast, threatening Haiti with torrential rain and strong winds.

"I've seen something like this before," replied Sally. "Six years ago a small tropical storm moved northward over Bermuda and then went south about fifty kilometers. Did this for the better part of a week. But that one wasn't as strong as this one. It might strengthen again and move back north. We'll monitor the situation. The islanders on El Fortunato must be confused. We warned them of a direct hit, but the rain stopped half an hour ago and the cloud cover is breaking up."

"Never a boring day in the Caribbean," Charlie chuckled.

Sally didn't catch his sarcasm.

CHAPTER 25

El Fortunato

KC and Nikki arrived at his office and parked the truck behind a large dumpster. His office was housed in a drab concrete structure situated on a gravel road in dire need of repair. The only other tenant, a fitness center, occupied the entire second floor. The pair rushed inside KC's first floor office as the sun emerged from behind massive dark clouds. Their mood brightened with the sunshine and the reality they'd survived an attack from a vicious and dangerous squad of commandos.

"Not bad, Jameson," Nikki said, a twinkle in her eye. "Even for a science geek."

"Yea, yea. But don't ask me to climb another mountain or crawl into another gopher hole. Give me the open sea."

They cleaned up their scrapes and bruises and washed off most of the dust that was caked on their faces. KC called Colin Farthington on his encrypted satellite phone. After informing Colin about the empty trunks and the strange ring, KC told him about the massacre.

"Oh my, KC," Colin said. "What a tragedy our soldiers were killed. We're doing all we can to identify the Russian commandos. We'll do what we can to nail the bastards. There were three men and two women? I'm confident my contacts in Russia will be able to give us a solid lead. Not that it will do those American soldiers any good. But it might help if we know who we are up against. In the meantime, stay alert."

Colin went on to explain that he'd spent several winters on El Fortunato when he was in his early twenties and had become good friends with an American ex-patriot by the name of Jimmy Calhoun. The island was very primitive in those days, with little development, only two or three pay telephones, no television, and rough gravel roads. Many people relied on generators for their power, but the island was a fun and adventurous place.

"Calhoun came with some of the first developers on the island. Quite a character and ladies' man in his day. Awed them with his straw hat, guitar, and risqué lyrics. Pretty good singer, too. He must be close to eighty by now. Last I heard he works at the El Fortunato Golf Club, regaling folks with outlandish tales of island adventures and escapades with exotic women. Go visit him at the Club, but don't let him bullshit you. It's possible the ring is his. Tell him I'll come down there and fill his Rum Punch with salt water if he doesn't help you. Let me know what you find out. Remember, be careful."

KC was exhausted from the ordeal in the cave and their narrow escape. He dropped Nikki off at the Blue Waves Bed and Breakfast, agreed to pick her up later that afternoon and visit the golf course, and then drove directly to his house. Once inside he grabbed a bottle of Fortunato Lager and collapsed in a comfortable chair on his front porch. He sipped his beer slowly and watched tourists enjoy paragliding and windsurfing. He emptied the bottle, got up, and caught sight of a group riding horses along the beach past his house. He ambled into his bathroom, undressed and turned on the shower, letting the hot liquid pour over his body, soothing his aches and pains. Ten minutes later, an eternity in the shower for someone who relied on rainfall for all his water needs, he returned to the porch, removed the ring from his pocket, and studied it closely.

It was a typical man's ring, similar in style to the type usually acquired after graduation from college, except it had personal initials rather than the insignia of a college or university. KC pondered the meaning of "JC." What if it didn't belong to Jimmy Calhoun? What else could JC stand for? Could it be a religious ring referring to Jesus Christ?

Curious to learn more, he moved to his computer chair, logged online, and brought up a search engine. After typing in "JC" and "ring" he scanned several pages of listings associated with the letters. The only items of minor interest referred to a college in the Midwest and a music disc jockey somewhere in the Northeast part of the U.S. He doubted anyone connected to either would have had reason to visit El Fortunato and explore the cave, but he filed the information in the back of his mind in case something came up.

At ten minutes to three he locked his house, mindful that five dangerous killers remained on the loose, and climbed into his truck. He drove slowly to the end of his driveway and waited several minutes. Satisfied that he wasn't in any danger, he continued on, taking care to avoid the many potholes on the gravel road.

Five minutes later, he drove into the compound and parked near Nikki's room. Emma Cameroon hurried to his truck with a nasty scowl on her face. She stared at KC with narrowed eyes and folded her arms across her chest.

"She came back all dirty and bruised and bloody. What'd you do to her KC? That's no way to treat a lady," she said sourly.

"Hey, Emma, she went into the cave first. Not my fault!" KC said defensively.

"Well, okay. Anyway, looks like the hurricane might miss us. Might get some wind and rain again, but nothing serious," Emma said.

"Excellent. Say we're kind of in a hurry. I gotta grab Nikki and scoot. Good to see ya Emma."

Nikki stepped out of her room and slid into KC's truck.

"You know KC, I was thinking. Why didn't you call the police? I mean, my God, men got killed today. And the killers are still on the island. Shouldn't we tell somebody?" she said.

"I considered it. But if we did, we'd spend at least a full day, probably more, answering questions from the police, and if the US government became involved we'd have an embarrassing international incident. If the authorities find out about this, we'll never find the nukes. They'd probably hold us for questioning, maybe even arrest us. Believe me, you don't want to spend even one minute in one of the jail cells here. At some point Colin will inform his contacts in the US Government. But he's got to be careful because he's no friend of the current administration. Until then we'll have to watch our backs. We don't know where the Russians are holed up. They probably realize we escaped from the cave. You can bet they are looking for us. Come on, let's go find Jimmy Calhoun."

CHAPTER 26

Santiago de Cuba, Southeast Coast, Cuba

The thin man was dressed in tan silk slacks and a white long sleeved shirt open at the collar. A straw hat covered his shaved head, nearly touching the dark glasses perched on his long pointed nose. A brown leather bag hung from his shoulder on a narrow strap. He strolled down the street, paying little attention to the small groups of women traipsing down the sidewalk, shopping bags in hand. The few shoppers who did look at him lowered their eyes immediately and quickened their pace when they took in his gray skin and vulture-like nose. They understood instinctively this was a man to avoid.

He approached an old stone building on the corner of two narrow streets overlooking a long bay sweeping in five miles from the Caribbean Sea. He glanced up and down the street searching dark doorways. Classic American cars from the 1950's lined the streets. At the corner a horse-drawn carriage waited for a fare. He didn't spot anyone following him, but he couldn't take any chances. Finally, he opened a massive wooden door and stepped inside the building.

He climbed a wood staircase to the second floor and stopped in front of the third door on the right side of the corridor. He knocked once and waited. A moment later, he detected footsteps and listened to the clicking sounds of dead bolts being unlocked. The door opened and he stepped in.

Without a word a small man, five feet six inches tall with a bald head and skin the color of coffee ice cream, locked the door behind him and hurried down a hallway into a large room. White wicker furniture dominated the room. None of the pieces matched but all had worn cushions with faded floral designs. The thin man followed at a leisurely pace.

"What have you learned, Juan?" he asked.

"Good news, bad news, Mr. Chuikov," he said with a huge grin.

Nikolai Chuikov's head snapped up. He gave his host a withering stare, but remained silent.

"Yes, I know who you are. Not to worry. There will be no trouble. Now, please, the money first. Then we will get to the details."

Nikolai reached into his leather bag, withdrew a wad of bills, and handed them to the small man. Juan smiled broadly and began counting the American currency.

"It's all there, Juan. Three thousand American dollars. I'm not here to cheat you. I just want information and assistance."

Juan Diaz shrugged his shoulders and offered a weak smile. "Yes, yes, my friend. Old habit I suppose. We don't trust anyone here in Cuba. Can I offer you a cool drink? Please sit down."

Without waiting for an answer, he stepped to a small kitchenette at the far side of the room, poured two glasses of lemonade and passed one to Chuikov. He approached his desk, pulled open a drawer, and grabbed a notebook. After a long minute Juan looked at Chuikov and cleared his throat.

"Your people got to the island, but their boat became disabled. Somehow they got to shore and stole a truck. But, alas, they got stuck in soft sand on a back road. An American woman happened by but offered no assistance. That is the last word from them. It appears they have lost their satellite phone."

"What?"

"I have not been contacted by your people. But I have an informant on the island. He found your people."

"What?" Chuikov crossed his legs and removed his hat. Diaz gaped at his vulture-like features.

"Er, yes, I always prepare contingency plans. My man learned of an explosion of some sort. Your team was spotted later, so they must be safe. A helicopter was abandoned on the salt flats, and presumably belongs to the Americans. They seem to have vanished. But a pickup truck with a man and a woman was seen leaving the area."

"Did they bring anything out of the Abyss?"

"That is unknown."

Chuikov closed his eyes and rubbed his bald head. "How can I contact my people?"

"We must wait until they contact us."

"There is no other way?" Chuikov asked.

Diaz stood with his arms outstretched, palms facing up. "You are in Cuba, señor. What a foolish question. Efficiency is unknown here."

Nikolai's eyes flared for a split second. He knew Juan Diaz was lying. How could the man learn what was happening on the island and not know where his team was holed up? Chuikov would not tolerate deceit.

"So they are on their own."

"Yes. So now you can spend time on the beach with beautiful women, no? Or maybe you go down the highway a short distance and harass the Americans at Guantanamo?" Juan said with a chuckle.

Nikolai Chuikov said nothing but rose to his feet and finished his lemonade, edged to the window, and stared at the shimmering blue-green water. He placed his empty glass on the windowsill and slid the bag off his shoulder, unhooked the latch, and reached inside. In a single smooth movement, he pivoted and shot Juan Diaz twice—once in the throat and then in the middle of his forehead. The small man slumped to the floor as his heart pumped the last of his blood, soaking his bright flowered shirt and oozing onto brightly patterned tiles.

Nikolai returned the silenced Beretta Tomcat to his bag, glared at the dead Cuban, and stepped over the growing pool. He bent down and picked up Juan's notebook, the wad of money, and his shell casings, then strode from the room. He didn't notice the hint of a smile on Juan Diaz's frozen face.

Angry about the incompetence of his team and that his identity had been compromised so easily, Chuikov clenched his fists and hurried to his rental car. He regretted having to kill the Cuban, but the man knew too much and might have alerted the authorities to Chuikov's presence on the island. He gunned the engine of the small Skoda station wagon and drove south toward the Caribbean Sea.

He drove aimlessly trying to come up with a workable plan. He had to find a way to get to El Fortunato and search for the nuclear weapons. He'd overesti-mated the expertise of Pavel Dubkov. Now he had no choice except to locate the weapons on his own. Dubkov and his team could no longer be counted on. No one in Cuba owed him anything. He'd spent all his financial capital when he'd secured the boat for his team and used Juan as an information conduit. A small gang of local thugs who loved American dollars had helped him. Now they were even. Chuikov had no doubt that the gang would double cross him if the price was right. As well, Castro's Policia would have his neck if they discovered he was in their country. They were very protective of their authority and power and resented anyone from Moscow carrying out covert operations on their island. His fake German passport had garnered little scrutiny when he cleared customs, but he had to be careful.

His stomach growled uncharacteristically and he decided to find a restau-rant. *Killing does increase the appetite*, he mused. He was aware that most of the restaurants in the city of Santiago de Cuba served incredibly bad food, so he continued his journey south toward the sea.

Minutes later he left the city behind and drove toward the airport. The road rose and fell over the rolling terrain, open fields mixed with dense woodlots. As he neared the airport, industrial and storage buildings dotted the hillsides. He approached a large round-about where he turned to the coast, away from the airport. He slowed and edged over to the gravel shoulder and studied the map the rental agency had given him. A list of tourist attractions included an old stone fortress named El Morro and a restaurant. His map indicated they were located around the next bend in the road. He folded the map and tossed it on the seat next to him. As he pulled the car back onto the road he felt a sudden stabbing pain in his stomach. A moment later it disappeared.

Chuikov shrugged then drove on until he reached the El Morro. The fortress loomed in the distance. The parking area at the restaurant was more than half full, giving him hope that the food was at least passable. Fifteen minutes after leaving Diaz' building he parked the vehicle, opened the door, and began to get out when a sharp stab of pain shot from his rib cage to his lower bowels. He grabbed his abdomen and farted. That should do it, he thought. Must have been the travel that upset my stomach. He took three deep breaths and relaxed his shoulders.

Nikolai Chuikov stepped up the restaurant's wide staircase when the sharp pain returned with a vengeance. He doubled over and belched, both smelling and tasting lemonade. His throat began to tighten and his vision blurred. He stumbled on the next step and nearly fell down. If he could get a glass of water, he'd be fine. A small cry escaped his lips, but his tongue was frozen in his mouth. He fell back down the steps and rolled over. He struggled to sit up but pain spread into his chest so intensely that his breath came in small gulps. His belly was on fire, and his tongue had swollen and had become so big his mouth didn't have room for the large fleshy muscle. Clarity hit him in an instant.

Diaz—the son of a bitch.

Nikolai Chuikov's body twitched twice, and then lay still.

Unseeing eyes stared at the young woman rushing down the steps toward him.

§ § §

Three hours later and six thousand miles away, an elderly man settled into the chair at his desk, opened a small envelope, and withdrew a single sheet of paper. One sentence was written in small script.

"An unidentified male died today of an apparent burst appendix at the El Morro restaurant outside the city of Santiago de Cuba, on the southeast shore of Cuba."

The man smiled, swung his chair around, and fed the letter into his shredder.

Everything was coming together nicely. When this mission was completed, all Russians would hold his family in high esteem. Especially the President himself.

He and his daughter would be set for life.

CHAPTER 27

About Forty Miles East of Santiago de Cuba

Goddammit Sergeant! What's happened to Baker and his team? When was the last time we heard from them?" Brad Wilkerson screamed at his assistant. "Ah, sir, like I told you. The last transmission came as they landed the chopper at the edge of shallow salt flats on El Fortunato. They found Bonny's Abyss only a few hundred meters from where they landed. They planned to be in and out in less than two hours," Sergeant Jack Smith said.

"And how long ago was that?"

"Uh, eight hours, sir."

"I'm going out. Stay with the radio," Wilkerson ordered as he rose and marched out the door.

Wilkerson and Smith had hitched a ride on a military aircraft from Andrews Air Force base outside Washington D.C. arriving in Guantanamo earlier the same day. To hide the true reason for their visit, they'd told base authorities they had come at the request of a local politician to visit with a soldier whose mother had recently died. Apparently, the soldier wanted to resign from the Army, but his family had contacted Wilkerson and told him his mother's dying wish was that her son remain in the Army. As a proud mother, she had high hopes that he would climb easily in the military ranks if he worked a little harder. While there was a hint of truth to the story, the soldier was actually a distant relative of Sergeant Smith. An extra week's leave was an excellent incentive for his cooperation.

Sergeant Smith waited until he was certain Wilkerson was well on his way to the Officer's Club. He reached in his duffel bag and grabbed his satellite telephone. He punched in a number and waited.

"Yes? Activate your scrambler," a voice said on the other end.

"Yes, sir. Looks like it has gone bad sir. No contact for eight hours. Their helicopter is sitting on an isolated salt flat. Good thing it's a civilian model. Can't be traced to us."

"Give them until tomorrow morning. If we don't make contact, we'll know they failed. You know what to do. I will not allow any loose ends. Understand?"

"Yes, sir. You can count on me." Smith replied without hesitation and hung up.

Sergeant Smith rose early the next day. Dawn was breaking when he poured himself a cup of black coffee while sitting at the window of his small room, looking toward the ocean. Colors changed with every passing minute, but Smith was too absorbed in his thoughts to absorb the beauty of the early morning sea. There had been no report from Lieutenant Baker or his team.

Finishing his coffee with a quick gulp, he went into the bathroom where he showered, shaved both his face and his head, and then dressed in a clean starched uniform. With cold eyes he checked himself in the mirror. Gig line straight up, boots polished, creases sharp. He strode to the door and marched down the hall, through a set of doors and knocked on another door.

"Enter!" came a quick reply.

"What's the news, Sergeant?"

"We've had no communication at all from Lieutenant Baker. There's no signal from his GPS unit either. Seems they vanished into thin air."

"We'll assume they're still in the cave. And likely very dead. We've got to take over the mission ourselves, Sergeant. The two of us. It's a good thing we came down here, closer to the action. Find us a fast boat and we'll go to El Fortunato and secure the nuclear weapons ourselves. But we have to be very careful. The mission should have been easy, even for Baker. How or why he's apparently failed is of no concern."

"Sir, may I speak freely?" Smith said.

Wilkerson looked up at the Sergeant. "Go ahead, Sergeant, but don't waste words."

"Sir, you've not been in the field for at least five years. El Fortunato is hot and humid, the weather people have issued a hurricane watch for the island, and our Russian enemies are good. Are you sure this is wise?"

Wilkerson's eyes narrowed.

"I appreciate your concern, Sergeant, but I'm in excellent shape. I work out for at least an hour every day. Do not think for a minute I have forgotten what it's like in the field. I've been in Kuwait, Iraq, and places I cannot even tell you about. Now go and find us a boat. We can't leave from here. Find us a local marina or something. Tell them we want to rent a boat to go fishing. Or whatever, I can't be bothered with the details."

"Yes sir!"

Two hours later the two military men, now dressed in civilian clothing, drove along the south coast of Cuba, heading west from Guantanamo Bay. The highway toward Santiago de Cuba rose and fell, weaving through the countryside. Pretty farms dotted the hillsides, showing little evidence that Castro's Communist party controlled the island nation. They met with little traffic for most of the trip, but the going was slow as large potholes kept their speed below thirty miles per hour. Sergeant Smith drove with agility and enjoyed the challenge. They passed dense woods, occasional glimpses of the Caribbean Sea, and scattered shabby houses but few people or cars. Two hours later they began to hear sounds of aircraft taking off and landing.

"We've got to be getting close to the Bay," Wilkerson said. "It's not far past the airport."

"Sir, I've brought some provisions for the trip but think we should get a good meal before we leave."

"Right. Looks like there's a place ahead, up on that small hill."

They pulled into a parking stall near the entrance of the El Morro restaurant as an ambulance screeched to a halt behind them. EMTs sprang out and raced toward a body lying on the pavement. A young woman stood wringing her hands and sobbing. Wilkerson and Smith hurried past on their way to the front of the restaurant. Wilkerson glanced at the figure lying on the ground. The man's eyes remained closed and his skin white and chalky. Evidently the EMTs had arrived too late to save the poor fellow.

Sergeant Smith glanced at the dead man. His face paled and he stumbled on the bottom step leading up to the restaurant.

"What was that all about, Sergeant? I've never seen you trip on anything before. You're pretty nimble for such a big guy," Wilkerson joked.

"Well, sir, the dead man looked familiar, but I can't put a name to his face. Just a vague memory with some bad vibes. I'll place him, eventually. Oh well, let's eat. I'm hungry."

The restaurant provided a splendid view of the Sea and the food was much better than either man had expected. A humid breeze blew onshore, and the Caribbean sparkled in the bright sunlight. Fresh broiled fish and a garden salad swallowed with imported beer set them in a good mood. In spite of the challenges ahead, Wilkerson was eager to get back into the field. He wouldn't want to do this all the time, but some action once in a while was good for the spirit. *Keeps me young*, he mused.

After leaving the restaurant, the two men drove north along the coast. They passed a beautiful deserted beach and then the road began to climb, following a treacherous cliff that dropped at least fifty feet to the sea. The road finally turned inland passing through dense forests before once again dropping back to sea level. Wilkerson spotted a sign announcing the location of Ciudamar Yacht Club as Sergeant Smith slowed the car and made a left turn on a narrow lane. They cruised into a parking area behind a large blue and white building, got out of their car, and grabbed their gear bags. They had not seen a single person or moving vehicle since turning off the main road. They hiked around the large building and found a small marina that appeared abandoned. A sleek white boat with a broad blue stripe along the side was secured to the long dock. The rest of the slips were vacant.

They approached the boat and Wilkerson grinned.

"A Sea Ray 410 Sundancer with an enclosed hardtop cockpit. I know this boat fairly well. My cousin has a smaller version up in the Chesapeake and has taken me out fishing a few times. It's an impressive boat. I really like the Cummins diesels. Look, it's even got a wood grained steering wheel. How long is the trip, Sergeant?"

"Well sir, it's powered by twin 375 horsepower inboards and we've got plenty of fuel. It's less than 300 miles to El Fortunato and the sea is relatively calm. If the weather cooperates, we'll arrive in six or seven hours. Probably be near dusk."

"We're cutting it kind of close, Sergeant. I hope we can reach El Fortunato before dark. I think our lunch break was a bad idea. Well let's get going."

"You bet, sir, not to worry. This boat is well equipped with excellent electronics. We'll take the shortest and fastest route to the island. But if we have to we can sleep on board. There are a couple of nice cabins. I've packed fresh water, sandwiches, and a few snacks. A six pack of beer, too. Why don't you take the wheel first? I'll spell you later. If it's OK with you, I think I'll take a nap. Follow the coastline east, but we should stay as far offshore as possible. We're near the end of the Cayman Trench. Twenty thousand feet deep in places. We don't have to worry about bumping into anything."

"What about Cuban police boats?"

"Shouldn't be a problem. We're close enough to Gitmo. They'll give us some protection, even if they don't know it," Smith replied as he squeezed his large bulk down the steps to the forward cabin.

As soon as the boat motored out to sea, a man emerged from the shadows of the marina headquarters building. He checked his watch and smiled.

CHAPTER 28

The Caribbean Sea

Ninety minutes into the journey, Sergeant Smith, who had not slept at all, emerged from the cabin and squinted in the bright sunlight. A few scattered clouds floated lazily above. Smith spotted a few sails far in the distance. He settled behind Brad Wilkerson as his superior officer piloted the boat. Smith scanned the horizon, finding the sea empty. They had passed Guantanamo and were rapidly approaching the eastern end of Cuba. The sea was calm and Wilkerson was able to keep the throttle wide open.

Smith turned to Wilkerson, his feet at shoulder width, giving him a steady stance. He reached into his waistband and withdrew a long narrow object encased in leather. Slowly, he removed an eight-inch dagger and took a long slow breath. Then, in a swift and precise move, he thrust the razor sharp point into the back of Brad Wilkerson's neck.

Wilkerson lurched forward and made a feeble attempt to grab his neck with his left hand. Smith twisted the instrument once and thrust harder. The razor point opened the front of Wilkerson's throat and blood spewed all over the cockpit. His body slumped over the steering wheel, blood splattering all over the controls. Sergeant Smith withdrew the knife and let the dead man fall to the deck.

Smith pulled a handkerchief from his pocket, shifted the engines into neutral, and wiped the blood off the throttle controls. He climbed down to the front cabin and returned with three heavy weight belts which he secured to Wilkerson's body, then hauled the corpse back to the swim platform and rolled it into the sea. He felt confident that the weights would counteract the natural buoyancy of salt water and hold the body at the bottom of the ocean for a long time. It may never surface, at least not in one piece.

"Twenty thousand feet should be a suitable grave for you, sir." Smith sneered as Wilkerson's corpse disappeared under the gentle waves. "The Vice President does not tolerate failure."

Taking the controls, he spun the boat around and headed back to the Ciudamar Yacht Club.

As he approached the dock, a man emerged again from the shadows, grabbed a mooring line and secured the boat. The two men worked in silence for twenty minutes until all visible traces of blood had been removed. They wiped down all surfaces, removed fingerprint evidence, and packed their gear.

"Leave the key. Someone will steal it," the man said.

Smith grinned. "Excellent idea. How far to your airplane?" Smith said.

"Ten minutes. You'll be sipping margaritas in Key West in a few hours, but we have to fly low across Cuba until we are close to the Bahamas. Then we'll head northwest to Florida. Our flight plan has us arriving from Mobile Alabama," the man chuckled.

As the pilot finished prepping the Beechcraft Model 18 twin engine airplane, Smith stepped thirty yards away and fetched his satellite phone from his satchel. He punched in a number and waited.

"Yes?"

"Mission accomplished. But you should know Nikolai Chuikov is dead too."

"How do you know?"

Smith explained their trip to the restaurant and the encounter with the emergency medical team. He'd crossed paths with Chuikov several times over the years. Once Chuikov had even winked at Smith when both had the same man under surveillance. The last time was in Berlin five years earlier. He'd been following a suspected East German spy when another man trotted out of a small garage and bumped into Smith. Chuikov had glared at him and hurried away. Two days later, Smith read a newspaper report of four individuals, including two small children, who had been brutally murdered in the same garage. He instinctively knew Chuikov was guilty of the murders.

When he was finished with his explanation, Smith listened for the click, stuffed the phone back in his bag, and strolled back to the aircraft. He had a satisfied smile on his face.

The pilot had the airplane warmed up by the time Smith strapped himself into the co-pilot's seat. He adjusted his sunglasses as the pilot eased the throttle forward. The small airplane rose and, once airborne, the pilot angled to the northeast barely clearing the trees below. They flew east of the large city of Santiago de Cuba, and reached the north coast in less than twenty minutes. Still flying low, they kept on the same northeast heading for another half an hour before turning north toward Florida.

"We're home free," said the pilot. "I've got a cooler in the seat behind you. Grab a beer if you want."

"Sounds good to me," Sergeant Smith replied.

They flew in silence as the coast of Cuba disappeared behind them with Florida still over the horizon. The shimmering sea was mesmerizing and Sergeant Smith began to nod off, relaxed by his beer and the thoughts of the reward Vice President Gordon owed him. The droning of the engines lulled him into a contented and well needed sleep

§ § §

Not far below, Frederick Lockhart pointed his small fishing boat toward his homeport on Ragged Island, about twenty miles northeast of his current position. The fishing had been excellent and he looked forward to sharing stories with the men at the Bone Fish Bar. As he increased the power on his two hundred horsepower Yamaha outboard engine a small speck in the distant sky drew his attention. He eased off the throttle and soon picked up the hum of engines. He wondered why the airplane was flying so low.

"Fools," he muttered.

The airplane flew by a few hundred yards off his port side. He shrugged and turned his attention to his compass.

A loud explosion jolted Lockhart. He spun around and watched in horror as the airplane fell from the sky and crashed into the ocean. The tail section was missing, and one wing snapped off when it hit the water. Lockhart gripped the gunwale as the concussion from the explosion rocked his boat. When the sea calmed, he shaded his eyes and searched the water. The airplane had disappeared below the waves. Small bits of the aircraft and its contents bobbed harmlessly, but Lockhart did not detect any other movement. The fisherman shook his head and sank into the seat. Probably drug smugglers, he supposed. They got what they deserved

Just as he began to engage the throttle, he detected a faint noise over the hum of the boat motor. Lockhart shut the engine off and searched the water for the source of the noise. He scanned the horizon and saw something move. A few hundred yards away, an arm waved above the flat ocean.

Hours later Lockhart was a hero at the Bone Fish Bar and Grill. He entertained the crowd with his story of the pilot who had leaped from his airplane seconds before it exploded in midair. Apparently, he'd detected gas fumes and feared the plane would explode.

Luckily, the pilot reported, he was the only person on board the airplane. Also lucky that his only injury was a broken ankle. He'd been wearing a life jacket and was able to inflate it just before he hit the water.

§ § §

Later, 1100 miles north of Frederick Lockhart's position

Vice President Gordon's aide knocked on the door and waited without moving, hands clenched behind his back. Sixty seconds later a voice from the other side of the door boomed.

"Enter!"

He twisted the knob, tiptoed in, and eased the door shut. He was in awe of the expensive decor with its plush burgundy colored carpeting, hunter green velvet drapes, and original oil paintings on the walls. A large antique desk sat at the far end of the room and a well-stocked bar occupied one corner. The place even smelled rich.

The aide approached the desk and waited, hands clasped behind his back.

Sydney Gordon leaned forward and said, "Well?"

The aide shuffled his feet and said, "The GPS tracking device stopped sending a signal sixty-five minutes ago, sir. The plane was over open water in the southern Bahamas near Ragged Island. As of ten minutes ago, there have been no reports of a crash."

"That's all. You can go. Say, son, how's the wife and new baby? I hope you're keeping them safe. We live in dangerous times, you know."

"Oh, fine, thank you for asking, sir," the aide stuttered, his face becoming ashen. He retreated from the room, closed the door quietly, and slumped on a nearby bench. His heart hammered and his breath came in short gasps. *My God,* he thought, *the man's a monster. I've got to watch my back.*

Behind the closed doors, Vice President Gordon sipped his Woodford Reserve Bourbon. In spite of their dedication, Colonel Wilkerson had proven to be unreliable and Smith knew too much. It was a pity they had to be eliminated, but there could be no loose ends.

Gordon sat in silence and stared at nothing for a full minute. He drummed his fingers on the desktop then stood up.

"I'm not finished yet. I've still got one more option left," he said. "Probably should have used this one first."

CHAPTER 29

El Fortunato

KC and Nikki drove along the back roads of El Fortunato with one eye on the rear view mirror. They passed native houses painted in colorful blues and oranges and caught glimpses of the beach and the beautiful waters beyond. The island was enjoying a tourism boom, yet the expansive beaches were not overcrowded. El Fortunato was still relatively unknown. Commercial development had been slow, especially when compared with the more well-known destinations like the Cayman Islands and Bahamas. Traffic was light.

Fifteen minutes after leaving Nikki's bed and breakfast, they turned into the parking lot of the El Fortunato Golf Club. The first, and only, eighteen hole golf course on the island, El Fortunato Golf Club was well regarded, having won a design award from a major golf magazine. It was a beautiful course with views of both the ocean and inland lagoons. The challenging design proved to be a good test for golfers of all abilities. Fairways snaked through groves of Palm trees while expansive sand bunkers threatened to gobble up errant golf shots. On several holes, water came into play, and the steady wind pushed many players to the limits of their ability.

KC parked the truck and they proceeded around the clubhouse on foot. They approached the first tee where a foursome prepared to tee off.

"Ho there, pardner!" a voice boomed nearby. "You two can't play without sticks. Well look what we have here, what's your handicap, darlin'?" the man said, smiling at Nikki.

KC and Nikki turned together as a man carrying a clipboard hurried toward them. His gray hair stuck out at all angles from beneath the well-worn straw hat perched on his head. Dark sunglasses hid his eyes. His weathered and deeply tanned face was engraved with a permanent smile. He appeared to be in his seventies at least, but was trim with well-toned arms and a flat belly.

"I remember your face sonny, but not your name," he said to KC. "Seems I remember you play to about a 14 handicap, right? Now who is this delicious creature you've brought with you?"

"Well, I've played here a few times. Nice try, but my handicap is much higher than 14. I'm KC Jameson, and this is my friend Nikki Colt. We're here to see Jimmy Calhoun."

"At your service, sonny boy. Say, my shift is about over; how about we sit down and have an iced tea, or something stronger if you like. I never like to pass up the opportunity to spend time with a beautiful young lady. What do you say? I'll buy."

KC raised his eyebrows and looked at Nikki. She stared at Jimmy with her mouth open.

"Uh, Nikki?"

"Oh. Okay. Sure," Nikki said quietly

KC chuckled and followed Jimmy up the stairs to a raised patio set with umbrella tables. Sitting at a table out of direct sunlight, they ordered iced teas and a side order of cracked conch.

"Well, to what do I owe the honor of this visit?" Jimmy said as he gazed around the lush patio. "You like this place? You should have been here in the early days when the only real watering hole was the Pink Grouper. There were plenty of young ladies to entertain with my guitar and Caribbean songs. I was quite a catch back then. So, what can I do for you two?"

KC explained how he and Nikki had met on the beach and how they decided to explore Bonny's Abyss. He skipped any mention of nuclear weapons, Russians, and the dead American troops.

"Haven't been to the Abyss in years," Jimmy said in a low voice. "But why are you telling me all this? I'm too old to climb down into that hole. Better for the young people. I like these open spaces here at the golf course."

KC glanced at Nikki and she nodded back at him. He reached in his pocket, withdrew the ring they'd found in the cave, and placed it on a napkin in front of Jimmy. Nobody said a word.

Jimmy didn't move. His permanent smile sagged into a slight frown. He stared at the ring, drumming his fingers on the table, and then shifted his gaze to Nikki. His fingers went silent. He closed his eyes and sat without moving.

Then, with a sigh, he removed his straw hat and leaned back in his chair. After taking a sip of his iced tea he said, "Shoulda ordered something a little stronger I guess."

KC leaned back then, waited a moment, and asked, "Your ring?"

Jimmy sat for almost a full minute. He stared out to the golf course where a man was lining up his putt on the eighteenth green.

"Tough putt, that one."

"The ring?"

Jimmy shrugged his shoulders and said, "Yup, it belonged to me a long time ago. I must have dropped it when I was down in the Abyss, crawling in the same cave you and 'simply gorgeous' here explored. I always wondered where I lost it."

"I'm sure by now you've realized we're not only here to return your ring. We have to find what was in those trunks. You know they're empty now, but maybe you don't know what was in them. Small nuclear weapons. And we're not the only ones who are looking for them," Nikki said.

Jimmy sighed and spoke in a low monotone. KC and Nikki settled back in their chairs and listened.

Jimmy explained that as one of the first white settlers, he'd explored every inch of the island and surrounding waters. He'd found remnants of old British cotton plantations, shipwrecks in shallow waters, and evidence of ancient fishing villages. He'd befriended much of the local populace and had become accepted almost as one of their own. The natives taught him how to find the best places to dive and fish. They caught conch and lobsters in shallow coral reefs and steamed the lobsters right on the beach. He also learned their lore, the stories of pirates and astronauts—John Glenn splashed down nearby at the conclusion of his historic space flight—and of men in uniforms hiding something in Bonny's Abyss.

"But when I crawled deep in the cave, the trunks you found were empty. I figured they had to be big trouble when I saw the Russian letters stenciled on the sides. But I didn't actually know what was in 'em. That's when I lost the ring, I guess, and the last time I entered the cave. Must have been at least 20 years ago. It's surprising, but only a few native islanders know about the cave, and they think it's possessed by evil spirits. I think they're afraid to pass on the knowledge, afraid something bad will happen to them if they enter the cave."

KC told Jimmy about the Russian commandos and the battle with the American troops. He left out no detail, trusting that Jimmy would keep the information to himself.

"So except for your girlfriend here, you'd be a quivering sack of jelly buried in the cave, huh?" Jimmy laughed. "I'll tell you what. Lewis Michaelson, an old hermit, is a friend of mine. He used to live out near the Abyss when there weren't many roads in the area. He lived from the sea, fishing and shelling, and only went to the island market once a month for supplies. A good guy, but didn't take to living around people. He knew that part of the island better than anybody, even me. Probably even better than many of the natives. If there is anybody who knows what happened at the Abyss in the early 60's or where those weapons are located, it's him. But he moved to another island a good fifteen years ago when the first house went up a half mile from the Abyss. He's got a little place on

Big Cave Cay. But development is starting up there too, so I don't know where he'll move to next. You can get there by boat or a small plane and rent a car. Take a map of the island with you and follow the main road to the northeast point. His shack is about a quarter mile walk from the dead end. Ya can't miss it. You should go see him. Use my name and he'll talk to you, I hope." Jimmy said with a chuckle.

KC rose to his feet. "Thanks Jimmy, we'll take my boat and visit him today. We appreciate your help," he said.

"No worries, KC. Be sure to bring your spunky partner back again for a cup of tea. Or something stronger. I might even buy her one," Jimmy replied with a grin.

Without a word Nikki spun on her heels and strode to their truck. A small smile was painted on her face.

As they pulled on to the main highway KC turned to Nikki. "Think he was telling the truth?"

Nikki shivered, in spite of the warm weather. "Of course not. He knows more about this than he's letting on."

CHAPTER 30

El Fortunato

Nikki was quiet as they drove away from the golf club. KC chose to take the lower main road but kept an eye out for the Russians. Nikki appeared deep in thought, unaware of the beautiful blue waters beyond the broad white sand beach.

KC glanced at her and frowned. "What's up?" he asked.

"I don't think I can do this anymore, KC. I did what you asked when I led you into the cave. I never imagined I'd feel lucky to get out alive. I've been in tight spots before, but not at the other end of an assault rifle. I'm through with this scavenger hunt. Take me home. I have work to do. I can't afford to lose my job."

"Come on Nikki. I know we had a close call, but I need your help. I want your help."

Nikki looked at KC and shook her head. "Take me home."

"Okay," KC said after a brief hesitation.

They drove another four minutes before KC slowed his truck to negotiate a small roundabout. "Well how about you humor me one last time? Then I'll take you home. Promise."

"What!"

"I want to check out the helicopter the Americans came in."

"Why?"

"I'm a helicopter nut. I'd like to take a peek at it. It's a Eurocopter, made in Germany, I think. Look, it's only a short detour. Someone will get suspicious and call the police. We should notify someone. Probably Colin."

"Okay Jameson. One more time, then take me home. But step on it."

KC turned left opposite the Club Med entrance and drove up the hill to the main upper highway. Traffic was heavy; the break in the weather had brought both tourists and residents from the security of their rooms. At the large round-about KC angled right and drove slowly looking for the road he expected would take them near the helicopter. Passing the miniature golf course, he recognized a familiar small lane fifty yards ahead. As he made the left turn, he had to slow down to maneuver around a flooded pothole. The truck crept through a one foot deep pool of water.

"Shit!" Nikki yelled.

"What now?" KC said.

"Get out of here! Fast. It's the Russians. They must have entered the round-about right behind us and recognized me. Hurry, they just turned onto this road! They're gaining on us."

KC didn't hesitate but pressed the accelerator to the floor. Mud splattered on the windshield as the truck bounced down the road. Nikki peered out the back window as the Russian vehicle continued down the lane after them.

As KC and Nikki came over a small rise, KC spotted the Eurocopter sitting on the salt flats a quarter mile ahead. They plunged down a steep hill across a shallow ravine. Ahead, the road rose steeply before disappearing around a sharp bend. At the bottom of the ravine another large pool of water had collected, with no place to drain. It was deeper than the first one they had negotiated. He had to slow the truck to avoid stalling the engine.

"What are you doing? They're catching up!" Nikki shouted.

"No worries. Watch this." KC said as he drove the truck along the edge of the road, scraping his door along the thick undergrowth of brush and trees. The truck tipped dangerously as Nikki's side sank deep into the pool of water, but the road bed was firm. Moments later, they reached dry land and increased their speed. The Russians sped after them, closing the gap.

Nikki turned, held on to the back of her seat, and watched the road behind them.

"They've stopped!" she shouted.

The Russian truck was stalled deep in the middle of the pool of water at the bottom of the ravine. Steam poured out from under the hood as the Russian driver tried to restart the engine.

"That should give us some time. Let's get to the helicopter," KC said.

Nikki gave KC a strange look, eyebrows furrowed but a hint of a smile on her lips. Then she snapped her head around toward the helicopter.

"The hell with the helicopter! Let's drive out of here!"

"Can't do it. There's only one road out and it's behind us. We'd never make it overland and that leaves only one way out, and I don't mean by swimming. I figure we've got maybe a five minute head start."

Speeding up, KC drove over the last hill before the beach and turned toward the helicopter. The tide was coming in, but was still a good fifty feet from the chopper. Moments later he slammed on the brakes, skidded to a stop, and flew out of the truck.

"Have you flown one of these before?" Nikki asked as they ran to the helicopter.

"Uh, not this model. I've flown a smaller one. A two-passenger Robinson 22.

When I was in Seattle, I was a passenger in one of these a few times. I think I can remember how to find the ignition switch. Once we're in the air, we'll be fine."

"Great, Jameson, just great."

"Shut up and get in. This is our only option."

They climbed into the Eurocopter and fastened their seat belts. KC studied the control panel, trying to remember how the pilot had started the engines. The display was totally different than a Robinson 22, much more complicated, with more dials and switches. Sweat poured from his forehead, stinging his eyes and blurring his vision.

"Jameson, now," Nikki urged glancing behind her.

"I know. Please, give me a minute," he said, wiping his eyes.

"We don't have a minute! Hurry. They're coming on foot! Get us out of here."

KC found what he was looking for and flipped a toggle switch to activate the starter generator. The rotors started turning when KC reached down for the collective stick next to his seat. He slowly twisted the end of the stick, and the sound of the engines increased. He should have let the engine warm up for several minutes, but with the Russians so close he didn't have time. He placed his feet on the anti-torque pedals with more pressure on the right one. He twisted the throttle on the collective until the helicopter began to shake and rise. They lurched twenty feet above the salt flats and KC inched the cyclic forward.

"Jameson, they're coming down the hill. Move it!" Nikki shouted as the Russians appeared seventy five yards behind the rising helicopter.

KC gave the throttle a full turn and rammed the cyclic forward. To his dismay, the helicopter flew at a sharp downward angle with its nose facing the ground. KC and Nikki were thrown forward toward the windshield. Luckily, their seat belts held them in their seats, but the chopper shot down toward the light blue water. Just as the front skids kissed the water, KC tugged back on the cyclic but overcompensated again and caused the chopper to lurch backwards toward the advancing Russians.

"KC, what the hell are you doing?"

"No worries," KC said under his breath. "I can do this."

He relaxed his fingers, gently manipulating the cyclic control. At the same time he steadily increased the throttle. The helicopter rose steadily and edged over rising tide.

Nikki held their pursuers in view. Her eyes grew wide. One of the Russians was down on one knee aiming his rifle at the retreating helicopter.

"They're going to kill us. Do something!"

"Got it."

Now in complete control, KC moved the cyclic from side to side flying in a zigzag pattern away from the attacking soldiers. They heard one loud thunk as a bullet smacked harmlessly into the chopper's tail boom.

"We've been hit!" shouted Nikki.

KC flew on for a minute without saying a word. He studied the gauges in front of him.

"We'll be Okay. I'm pretty sure their shot missed the fuel tank and the controls haven't been damaged. We'll be Okay."

They flew on steadily, the Russians becoming like small ants far behind. KC angled the helicopter to a northeast heading and grinned.

"Shouldn't take more than a half hour. We've got plenty of fuel. Sit back and enjoy the ride."

The El Fortunato chain consisted of over twenty separate islands and cays. Most were small and uninhabited, but four had been fairly well developed. Tourism was the primary source of revenue for most islanders, although the construction industry provided many jobs. Fancy condo-hotels and all-inclusive resorts lined the expansive white beaches of Secret Bay. Where the beach was narrower a blend of expensive mansions, some owned by Hollywood movie stars, and older, more modest homes dotted the landscape.

KC and Nikki scanned the ocean below where boats churned through the water. Just beyond the salt flats sport fishing boats inched along in search of the elusive bonefish. They passed over coral reefs, still beautiful in spite of the detrimental effects of over development and warm ocean waters. Recent years had seen some significant recovery of coral as effects of climate change had eased.

They flew one thousand feet above the shimmering turquoise of the open ocean. Twenty minutes later they spotted Big Cave Cay. KC had visited the island a few times and was familiar with the layout of the airport. It had a single runway near the island's north central coast. In contrast to their narrow escape from the Russians, the flight over to Big Cave Cay was smooth.

As they approached the small airport, KC's stomach tightened and his grip on the cyclic strengthened. His flying experience consisted of about twenty five hours as a student. He was actually not qualified to carry passengers and had only flown solo three times. That was several years ago. As the airport structures became larger, he rehearsed the procedures for landing. He adjusted the throttle and slowed the chopper. He managed a deep breath and steered the helicopter away from the lone hangar at the end of the runway. He eased into something of a hover twenty feet above ground. Below, a man opened a side door of the building and stepped out. He shaded his eyes and watched the descending helicopter.

KC clutched the cyclic with tightened fingers and reduced altitude. With his strong grip, he lost some of the feel of the craft. The helicopter smacked into the runway with a thud, bounced back up about six feet, and spun nearly thirty degrees. The man below fled into the safety of the hangar. KC struggled with the controls, but managed to set down squarely on the ground. He shut down the power and the chopper settled on the tarmac, rotors still spinning.

"Well, that was interesting," Nikki said. "Can we do it again?"

"Hey," KC said as if his landing had been perfect.

KC shut down the helicopter, stepped out, and strolled to the hangar. The man remained in the doorway and frowned.

"Hello! My friend and I are out for a day of sightseeing. Can I get a rental car here?" KC said.

"Sir, may I see your papers? I am Kirkwood Lundy, the immigration agent for the island, and I can handle the car for you as well. Where did your helicopter come from? I've never seen one like this before on the islands. I must say, that was quite a landing."

KC handed him his identification and explained he lived and worked on El Fortunato conducting ocean research for a company located in the State of Washington. The chopper had recently been delivered to help him with his research. He was still learning how to fly this model.

"And this is my girlfriend," he said. "She works on El Fortunato too. We're both from the States."

"I—I—uh. That's right," Nikki stammered after KC gave her a quick wink.

Lundy scrutinized their papers for several minutes. He stared at their photo ID's comparing their faces to the photos again. He looked at KC a little longer tapping his lower lip with a forefinger. Finally satisfied, he stepped over to his steel desk. The desktop was bare except for a small rattling electric fan that did little to cool the heavy, humid air in the office. He opened a drawer on the left side of the desk and selected a set of car keys. He tossed them to KC.

"You meeting friends here?" Lundy asked.

"Uh, no. Why do you ask?"

"Oh, nothing. Fifty dollars for the car. Pay me now. Return by four p.m. Your helicopter will be safe with me. Don't be late."

KC drew two twenties and a ten from his wallet and handed them to the man. Then he found another twenty, folded it twice and slipped it to the immigration agent.

KC grinned. Lundy slipped his hand into his pocket and looked away.

CHAPTER 31

Big Cave Cay

For all its size Big Cave Cay was one of the least populated islands of the El Fortunato chain. A few resorts, each powered by huge generators, were nestled along pristine beaches. The interior of the island was thick with vegetation that somehow survived the hot, dry climate. In spite of the recent rains, most of the plant life appeared dry and barely alive. The island had few roads and none were paved.

KC and Nikki turned their rental car inland and passed a small cluster of stone buildings which housed a few offices, a grocery store, and gas station. Checking his map, KC found the road leading to the northeast point. After a few miles he turned left off the main road and slowed to a crawl, weaving his way around deep pot holes, basketball-sized boulders, and tree branches littering the road. They bumped along for fifteen minutes kicking up mounds of dust. The only living creatures they passed were two skinny dogs. Finally they came to a dead end.

KC parked the car and they stepped out. A narrow path disappeared into the thick brush. Without a word, KC pointed toward the sandy path and stepped toward it. KC and Nikki plunged ahead, ducking under low hanging branches. Soon they caught the sound of the surf lapping on the shore. The heat was stifling, humidity soaking their shirts, sweat trickling from their noses. They followed the narrow path through lush tropical vegetation that blocked out most of the sunlight. After slogging through the bush for three or four minutes they came upon a small sand dune at the edge of a narrow white sand beach. They stopped at a fork in the path and stood for a moment letting the gentle on-shore breeze cool their sweaty bodies. KC pointed to their left.

"That way."

A hundred yards ahead they spotted a grove of large mahogany trees with a shabby wooden hut tucked at the base of one of them. A low grassy dune separated it from the narrow beach. They neared the hut and stopped at the edge of a small clearing. The place was deserted. Two windows hung open, the door stood ajar.

"Hello?" Nikki squeaked.

Silence.

KC stepped toward the partially opened door and peeked inside the darkened building. He took several steps back and stood with his hands on his hips, unsure of his next move.

Nikki shouted and KC sensed something falling. The next thing KC knew he was lying on the ground with a terrible headache. He touched the side of his head with two fingers. They came away bloody.

A second later a man dropped from nowhere and landed on the ground next to KC. Nikki jumped back a step.

"What's going on here?" she shouted, taking a step toward the man.

"Sorry about that, young man," the old man said to KC.

KC groaned and said, "I think I'll be all right."

"I sit way up in that tree and study the ocean. Very peaceful. When you two came along, I just kept watch. Wanted to know what you're up to. Then the coconut sort of slipped from my fingers. You'll be fine, I figure. So why are you here?"" Lewis said with a straight face.

In spite of his sore head, KC got to his feet and stared at the old man. His features didn't give a clue of his age, but KC sensed he was well past seventy, more likely in his eighties. His weathered face reminded KC of old leather, and his white hair was long and stringy. He wore a dirty T-shirt, cutoff jeans, and a pair of worn sandals. KC wondered how he was able to shave his wrinkled face and if he ever took a hot bath.

KC took a moment to explain that Jimmy Calhoun had sent them because of his knowledge of the area around Bonny's Abyss.

"Yup, that Jimmy's a good man. If he sent you, it must be okay. Come on in for a cup of tea. It's the least I can do," Lewis continued. "I use island heather that grows near here. A few sips of this and your headache will disappear. Guaranteed."

They stepped inside the small wooden building that KC judged to be no more than fourteen feet on a side. In spite of the ocean breeze, the single room was warm and stuffy. An unmade bed occupied one corner, an old overstuffed chair in another, and a small kitchenette lined the wall opposite the front door. A small table with one chair filled most of the center of the room. Several kerosene lamps hung on the otherwise bare walls. A pile of books littered another corner.

Lewis started to heat water on an old Coleman two-burner propane stove as KC sank into the large chair.

"Wait, sonny. This ain't no resort. I got two wood boxes outside for you. Girlie, why don't you go get them."

For the second time in half a day, Nikki was tongue-tied. Few men had ever dared to treat her in such a rude and brusque way. She didn't know what to make of the old man and was irritated by his gruff manner, but she thought he might be the key to finding the nuclear weapons so she kept her mouth shut.

They sat in silence while the water heated. KC pressed a dirty cloth to his wound. Shortly, Lewis poured the brew into faded ceramic cups and lowered himself into his comfortable chair.

"You'll have to share. I got only two cups. I don't get no visitors." Lewis muttered. "OK, tell me why you are here. Come on hurry up. I got things to do."

KC could not imagine what the old hermit did every day. He certainly didn't spend his time cleaning either his dwelling or himself. He checked his watch and was glad they still had plenty of time before they had to return the rental car. He told Lewis about their search for the nuclear weapons. He mentioned neither the American soldiers nor the Russian squad. He summed up by saying, "Jimmy Calhoun thought you might know where the old weapons are hidden. You see, my boss up in Seattle collects old military artifacts and wants them for his museum. Can you help us?"

"Why should I? Them things might be dangerous, you know. Best to leave them buried where they can't hurt nobody," Lewis said.

Nikki raised her eyebrows and gave KC an inquisitive look. He nodded in understanding.

"Well, Lewis, there's something KC didn't tell you."

"What?"

"One important fact that should change your mind."

"Well don't just sit there girlie, spit it out. Huh!" Lewis said, shaking his head.

Nikki straddled the wooden box, leaned forward and smiled at Lewis. She took a breath and continued. She told Lewis about the shoot-out in the cave and the attack on their helicopter. When she finished, Lewis lay back in his chair and closed his eyes. He did not move a muscle; only the slow rise and fall of his chest was proof he was still alive. KC and Nikki waited patiently, wondering if the old man had fallen asleep. KC checked his watch again, and tapped its face.

Nikki nodded and said softly, "Lewis. Will you please help us?"

One eye opened, and then the other, as Lewis stirred to life. He rose slowly and sighed. He appeared older and paler than he had only moments before. His red eyes became watery and dull.

"You'll have to do some figuring on your own," he said.

"What do you mean?"

"Don't interrupt me again, boy. Or our visit will be over. Understand?"

Lewis rose to his feet, ambled to a corner of the cabin, bent over, and lifted the lid of an old wooden trunk. In stark contrast to the rest of the shack, the trunk was a beautiful piece of furniture with brass hardware and leather handles. It would be a prime piece in any antique shop. He rummaged around for several seconds, and then removed a folded piece of paper. He returned to the table, opened the paper and used his hands to spread it out. The three of them stared the paper for a few seconds.

"A map?" Nikki asked.

"Yup. I was with Jimmy Calhoun down in the Abyss, in the cave, some time after the trunks were emptied. The natives spoke about something dangerous. No specific details, just rumors. We found a rolled up scroll in the bottom of one of them trunks. Nothing else. I took it with me."

"What was in the scroll? Where is it?" Nikki blurted.

"I'll get to that. I studied the writing on it many times, but ain't got no clue what it means. I didn't like having it near me so I took it away from here. I don't know why, but I couldn't bring myself to destroy it. Maybe it's cursed."

"What did you do?"

"Shut up and listen. I'll tell you if you'll let me. This line here," Lewis said pointing to the map. "You'll find a path. Follow it back toward your car, but stay to your left when you get to the fork. You'll run into a bunch of caves a little ways down. No more than a half-mile from here. Use this map to find where I hid the scroll in the cave. When you get to the right place, crawl in about fifteen feet. I'm done with you two. Here, take this flashlight. Leave it near the path where you parked your vehicle."

Lewis sat in his chair, folded his hands across his belly, and closed his eyes.

KC rose hastily to his feet. "Come on Nikki, time's running out. We better hurry. Thanks Lewis. You won't regret this."

KC grabbed Nikki's hand and hurried out of the cabin. They followed the path along the sand dune, thankful for the fresh breeze blowing in from the ocean. When the path forked, they veered left instead of heading toward their car. The path turned inland into the hot and muggy forest. Soon sweat stained both their shirts. KC estimated they covered a hundred yards before emerging again from the dense vegetation. They found themselves near the beach, but what caught their attention was a huge rock structure rising straight out of the sea.

"The caves. Come on," urged Nikki.

KC's stomach tightened as he stared at a large opening in the rock wall. "Here we go again."

"Jameson, you did just fine before. This time will be easier."

They ducked down low and entered the cave. KC was confused by the brightness of the interior. Nikki led the way. After only a few yards, they stepped into a large cavern that was open on the ocean side. Ahead of them stalactites and stalagmites had joined to create a series of columns which reflected brightly from the outside light. The spaces behind the columns were inky black. Smiling tightly, KC grabbed the map and traced his finger along one of the lines. Beyond the columns four tunnels led off the main cavern leading away from the beach. KC pointed to the nearest tunnel.

"This one."

"Hurry, tide's coming in and we don't know if the water will rise in here."

Without either a safety line or chalk the pair passed into the large tunnel. After walking just a few yards the floor began to slope downward and narrowed. Their pace slowed as the rough floor became slippery and the low ceiling was pockmarked with holes. Several times Nikki tripped on the back of KC's heels. They continued their downward trek in silence. The tunnel widened but KC had to bend over to avoid hitting the roof.

KC came to an abrupt halt. "Whoa."

Nikki squeezed past him and looked where KC was pointing. A dark pit in the floor of the cave spanned the width of the tunnel. KC shined the flashlight across the hole.

"Too far to jump," he said. "It's got to be at least twenty feet."

"Careful, some of these can be really deep. Bottomless, in fact. Give me the flashlight."

Nikki aimed the light into the pit and standing water.

"Oh, crap," KC muttered.

"No, it will be OK. The pit's about six feet deep, but the water is only about 18 inches. I can see the bottom. And the sides of the pit are wet. I think when the tide comes in this fills part way with water, and then seeps out cracks or crevices at the bottom. We'll be fine if you don't mind wet feet."

Less than two minutes later they resumed their trek. The tunnel was V-shaped and they found themselves on the upward leg. At the top of the rise the floor leveled out and the tunnel became several feet wider. KC breathed more easily as he sensed a dim light entering the cave from somewhere ahead. He checked the map again and counted the smaller side tunnels as they passed them and stopped at the fifth one.

"Here. This is it," KC said, looking up from the map. He pointed to a small opening about five feet above the tunnel floor. "Lewis said we should crawl in fifteen or twenty feet. You'll find the scroll up on a ledge."

"Wait," Nikki said.

"What now?"

"Sometimes bats live in caves like this. I didn't say anything before, but I think I heard some when we first entered the cave."

KC snapped his head around and down. "That would make my day."

Nikki took the flashlight and shined it into the opening. A few seconds later they heard squealing noises and the first bat burst out and flew over their heads. Suddenly they came by the dozen. Fluttering sounds filled the tunnel. Nikki stood still, but KC dove for the floor.

Nikki laughed.

"OK, should be all clear now. They won't come back as long as I keep the flashlight on."

KC gave her a boost as she scampered up the rock wall into the narrow opening and disappeared. With nothing to do, KC wandered farther down the tunnel keeping an eye out for more bats. The dim light brightened a little, and KC detected something moving in the shadows. The hairs on the back of his neck tingled and he froze in place. He stepped back the way he had come keeping an eye for whatever might be stalking him.

"Got it!" came a voice behind him. He flinched and spun around.

"Shit, Nikki, you scared the hell out of me!"

"Oh don't be a sissy. Wow. Look at them!" she said, pointing the flashlight ahead. "First time I've seen iguanas on the islands. Just like little dinosaurs," she giggled.

"They give me the creeps. They stare at us with those big eyes like we're their next dinner. Come on, let's go."

Nikki pivoted and trudged down the tunnel, KC following several paces behind. A minute later she came to an abrupt halt.

"Uh oh."

"What the hell now?" KC said.

"Look." she said, pointing the flashlight ahead. Where only a few minutes before they had negotiated the pit in the floor of the cave, they saw nothing but water. Seawater reached the ceiling of the cave.

"The tide's up. Flooded our only way out. We'll have to swim."

"Not me. Nikki. I've got to keep the scroll dry. Let's wait until the water recedes."

"That will take too long. Remember, we have to get the car back. Don't worry. The scroll's wrapped in some kind of plastic. Come on. You're not afraid, are you?"

"Oh, no, of course not. Piece of cake. Swimming into a flooded tunnel. Not knowing how far we have to swim. In the dark."

"Oh, come on."

"This might be a piece of cake for you, but I'm scared. Terrified in fact."

"Suck it up, Jameson. I'll go first. We don't have far to go. Wait thirty seconds before you go. You can even keep the flashlight. Just keep your hand in front of your face so you don't swim into the wall we climbed down," she said and dove into the water.

KC waited a full minute expecting Nikki to return and tell him they were trapped. That they'd have to wait for the tide to go out.

The surface of the water shimmered, inching toward him with the rising tide. He took several deep breaths and relaxed his shoulders. Offering a silent prayer he slid into the dark water. The salt stung his eyes, but he wouldn't close them for fear of losing his way. His hands scraped the floor until he felt it turn upward. The water above his head had become a little lighter. Moments later he burst to the surface and scrambled out. Nikki was standing in three inches of water smiling at him.

"Nice job, Jameson. I'll make a caver out of you yet."

"Come on. We gotta get the car back. I'll feel better when we're up in the air," KC said. Without another word he trotted down the tunnel, splashing through ankle deep water, until he reached the large main cavern. Sunlight raised his spirits and calmed his hammering heart.

Back in the car they bumped along the gravel road for fifteen minutes, their clothes still damp.

"Read the scroll, Nikki."

Nikki unrolled the plastic protector and carefully removed the scroll. She frowned as she studied the document. "Hey, it's some sort of poem."

> *"Oh, how they flew from wave to wave*
> *When the devil came to our blessed shore*
> *And with smoke and fire defiled the cave.*
> *The Abyss now bare, spears no more*
> *They lie below her most sweet soul*
> *That, stabbed with seven sorrows."*

They sat in silence for several minutes. "What does it mean?" asked Nikki.

"I have no idea. Looks like we have some homework to do."

Just before 4 pm they pulled up to the airport hangar and parked the car. Their clothes were still damp but they looked reasonably presentable; only their shoes remained soaking wet. Nobody was in sight when KC carried the car keys into the office. The fan on the desk was still purring. KC dropped the keys next to the fan, found a piece of paper and wrote a short note thanking Kirkwood Lundy.

He hurried out to the tarmac, going through the helicopter start-up procedure. He opened the helicopter door and saw Nikki standing on the other side with another person. *Kirkwood's here,* he thought. *Guess I didn't have to write the note after all.*

"Come on Nikki, let's go so we can get home before dark" he shouted.

Nikki didn't move.

"Come on kid, let's go!"

"I don't think so, Mr. Jameson," Kirkwood Lundy said as he scurried around the front of the helicopter.

He had a pistol in his hand, pointing directly at KC.

"What's this?"

"Well, Mr. Jameson. I came to admire your fine Eurocopter here. I'm a fan of all flying machines, especially helicopters. We don't get many of them around here."

"Okay."

"Yes. But I'm wondering how it got damaged. Look right here," Lundy said as he pointed to the rear of the helicopter. "I wonder how a nice new helicopter with a fine pilot and beautiful crew could have been punctured by what appears to be a bullet. I'm sure you can explain."

"Gee, how did that happen? We'll have to call the manufacturer and file a complaint," KC stammered.

Lundy smirked and said, "Good try, Mr. Jameson. Perhaps both of you should come with me and be my guest for the night. Something is fishy about all this. I need to check you out."

"But you verified our identification. We're here legally."

Kirkwood Lundy nodded. "Maybe so. But I'm not sure if your activities are legal. As immigration officer I must contact the police. You come back here with damp clothes and wet shoes. Where did you go? I checked around and no one observed you in the village or at the tourist caves. You guys into dealing drugs or running guns?"

Nikki stepped forward with clenched fists.

"Of course not! We got wet from the surf at the beach," KC said and took hold of Nikki's arm.

With raised eyebrows Lundy said, "I don't think so. Now, both of you. Turn around. Hands up. Start walking."

CHAPTER 32

The Airport on Big Cave Cay

KC and Nikki trudged back to the hangar where Kirkwood Lundy directed them through a small game room and kitchen and pointed to a storage room at the far end of the building.

"You can't hold us in here," KC said.

"I can and I will. I'll leave you alone for a few minutes and get you some food and water. You might get a little warm in here," Lundy said, waving his pistol at them.

"But what about a bathroom?" Nikki said gritting her teeth.

"Ah, yes. A problem perhaps, but with luck the police from El Fortunato will be here early in the morning. This is a storage room. I suspect you might find a bucket in the corner. I might be able to arrange a proper bathroom break in several hours. Get in there. Do not think of escaping. This building is built of heavy gauge steel strong enough to withstand any hurricane."

Lundy locked the door behind Nikki and KC, secured a heavy beam across the door then made a quick stop in the rest room. On his way out he looked at himself in the mirror, ran a hand over his hair and smiled. Satisfied that his prisoners could not escape, he sauntered out of the hangar to his truck.

Shifting into third gear, he chuckled to himself. The police would not be arriving the next day. Anyone with such a fine and expensive helicopter had plenty of money. Somebody would be slipping him more than twenty dollars for Jameson and the woman's freedom. A lot more.

§ § §

KC surveyed their makeshift jail cell. The room wasn't more than six feet wide, but at least fifteen feet long and had one small window about two thirds of the way along the long wall and five feet above the floor. An assortment of mops and brooms lay in one corner; cleaning solutions and kitchen items occupied several narrow shelves. Six almond colored folding tables, their metal legs folded underneath, leaned against the back wall. The window was closed and the air was stale, humid, and smelled of lemon cleanser.

Nikki stepped to the door, placed her shoulder against the heavy steel panels and shoved hard. Nothing happened. She hurried to the single window, pulled the latch and yanked it open. It swung upward with a creaking noise. Heavy mesh was bolted across the opening. She gave the mesh a quick push, hoping it was either old or rusted enough to break away. It held tightly, even when she grabbed a broom handle and thrust violently at the tough screen.

"Shit, shit, shit."

KC ignored her outburst. Instead he began searching the shelves for something to help them escape. He pawed through an assortment of bottles and jars of kitchen cleansers, carefully reading the product label on each one.

Nikki breathed hard, her shirt dark with sweat. She turned to KC and said, "What the hell are you doing Jameson? Get your ass over here and help me with this window, It's our only way out."

KC ignored her and continued rummaging through the shelves. "Ah ha!" he said, grabbing one of the bottles of cleaning solution. "Nikki, pull one of those tables over here and find three or four of the longest mop handles. Use another table or two and make a shelter for us as far from the window as possible. I have a plan."

Nikki eyed him curiously, but didn't question his orders.

KC grabbed two two-liter bottles of soda, unscrewed the caps, and emptied the contents on the floor. Then he picked up a small roll of aluminum foil and a plastic bottle of liquid cleaning solution. He carefully tore the foil into long thin strips. He pawed through the bottom shelves and found a five-pound box of galvanized roofing nails. He removed several handfuls and slid them inside the bottles. Finally, he added the strips.

"Here's what we're going to do. I'm gonna fill these bottles with the cleaning solution and tighten the caps. Then, and I gotta be quick, I'll push them against the mesh, then shut the window to hold them in place."

"What for?"

"We're making a bomb."

Nikki's jaw dropped and her blue eyes grew bigger. "Oh, shit."

"Right. We have to move fast. After I close the window we'll put one of these tables up against it, then wedge the mop handles between the wall and the table. We'll only have a minute, maybe a little longer. Make sure you cover your ears and keep your eyes closed. Ready?"

"Are you sure this will work?"

"It has to."

Nikki nodded and gripped the table she had brought over from the end of the room.

KC checked the time and began to work. He filled the plastic bottles about half way with the cleaning solution and tightened the caps.

Twelve seconds had passed

He slammed the window shut and helped Nikki brace the table against the window as per their plan. They wedged the mop handles against the wall to hold the table securely in place.

Twenty seconds.

Nikki raced to their little shelter with KC behind her. They ducked low and covered their ears. Sweat dripped off Nikki's nose. The only sound she heard was the hammering of her heart. She tried to cross her fingers.

Fifty-five seconds.

Sweat streamed down KC's cheeks, but he kept his eyes on the second hand.

Seventy seconds. Too long. He found himself holding his breath.

Nikki turned toward him, a questioning look in her eyes. KC sensed fear, too. He shrugged and held his breath.

BOOM!

The soda bottles exploded violently, sending roofing nails through the wire mesh and shearing off the bolts that held it in place. A pungent odor filled the room. The strong smell of cleaning solution stung their eyes. KC paid little attention and raced to the window. He tore the table away. One of the mop handles had fallen to the floor, but the others had done their job. The main force of the explosion had thrust outward instead of back into the storage room.

"Holy shit!"

"Of course," said KC with a grin, his green eyes sparkling with satisfaction.

KC snatched a large rag from a nearby shelf and brushed away shards of broken glass and bent the wire to make a larger opening.

"You won't fit." Nikki said. "Help me up. I'll squeeze through, run around, and open the door. Hurry."

Minutes later the pair raced down the tarmac to their helicopter. Kirkwood Lundy apparently thought his makeshift jail cell would hold his prisoners and had done nothing to disable the chopper.

After reaching an altitude of two hundred feet they spied a small pick-up truck racing along the road toward the airport, a long dust cloud trailing behind.

KC smiled and nodded toward their former captor. He eased the stick forward and the helicopter raced toward safety.

CHAPTER 33

El Fortunato

KC lazed in his bed and listened to the coffee machine do its thing. The back of his neck hurt and his shoulders ached. A nice swim would cure his ills, he thought, as he swung his feet over the side of the bed. A stabbing pain shot into his right knee. He sat at the edge of the bed for several minutes. He looked at the jumble of sheets and shook his head.

Good thing my housekeeper is coming in a couple of days, he thought.

KC's thoughts shifted to Nikki and the mixed feelings he had about her. She certainly was a beautiful woman, but he wasn't sure about her brusque personality. He'd been content in his solitude after dropping her off at her bed and breakfast last night, but this morning he couldn't get her out of his thoughts. What is it about her? He wasn't even sure how she felt about him but wondered why she didn't talk about her fiancé. Wasn't he supposed to arrive soon? Well, he'd see her today. It wasn't safe for her to move freely around the island. The Russians wouldn't hesitate to kill them both if they thought murder would serve their purpose.

The flight back from Big Cave Cay had been uneventful. KC made a perfect landing near the salt flats with plenty of daylight remaining. The Russian commandos were nowhere to be seen. His truck sat where he'd left it earlier in the day. Surprisingly, the Russians had left the scene without disabling the vehicle.

He'd dropped Nikki off at Emma's and told her he'd come by early the next day. She'd said nothing, but nodded her head in silent assent.

After his morning swim and a cup of coffee, KC drove to her unit at the Blue Waves Bed and Breakfast only to find the door to Nikki's unit locked and her car gone.

Emma Cameroon stepped out of her house and marched over to KC. She stood with her harms folded across her chest and glared at him.

"What's going on here KC? She got up early, skipped breakfast, and raced out of here in a cloud of dust. Didn't even say a word to me."

"We gotta find her, Emma. There's trouble here, but I can't tell you about it quite yet. You know her cell phone number?"

Emma hurried back to her office with KC close at her heels. She opened her guest ledger book and spun it around to KC. He opened his phone and punched in her number.

"What!" Nikki answered.

"Nikki, the island's not safe. We need to finish what we started. I'm going to call Colin and get some protection. Now come on back. I'm here with Emma."

He heard a "click," then silence. He pressed the redial button and listened to her voice mail message.

"Emma, what's going on with Nikki?"

"She left me a note saying that I shouldn't set another place for breakfast tomorrow. I guess her fiancé isn't coming."

KC raised his eyebrows and turned toward his truck.

"I gotta go. Call me when she comes back. And watch out for strangers. Don't trust anyone," KC said.

CHAPTER 34

KC's house, El Fortunato

Thirty minutes later, KC reclined in his comfortable chair and unrolled the scroll. Still concerned about Nikki, he was determined to focus on the task at hand. He'd called Colin and begged for someone to come and help. He explained their narrow escape from the Russians, the strange meeting with Lewis Michaelson, their difficulties with the immigration officer on Big Cave Cay, and their complete confusion regarding the poem. While sympathetic, Colin couldn't promise to send additional help anytime soon because of bad weather in the Seattle area and the possibility that the tropical storm in the Caribbean might turn back toward El Fortunato and become a full-fledged hurricane. The presence of the Russian commandos worried him, but he laughed heartily at the story about Kirkwood Lundy. He expected to uncover clues about the poem and would call back when he had some hard information.

KC read the document over and over in an attempt to unlock its meaning.

"Oh, how they flew from wave to wave
When the devil came to our blessed shore
And with smoke and fire defiled the cave.
The abyss now bare, spears no more
They lie below her most sweet soul
That, stabbed with seven sorrows."

The first part appeared clear enough: evil people arrived on the island. The last lines remained a complete mystery. Checking his watch, KC rose and drifted outside to the beachside porch. He paced back and forth, paying no attention to the beautiful turquoise water a hundred feet away. He needed help and could not afford to wait for Colin.

Nikki was his only option.

He had to find her, find out what had made her so angry, and convince her help one more time.

"Gotta get moving," he said to himself. "I'm not doing much good staying here."

He locked the house, got into his truck, and tore off down the driveway, hoping for inspiration to help him find Nikki.

§ § §

Cooper's Beach, El Fortunato

Nikki parked her car along the side of the road and followed the rocky trail through scrubby vegetation toward the beach. Beer bottles and plastic bags littered the path. She reached the edge of the rocks and gazed out to sea at the retreating tide. She jumped down onto a rock ledge then stepped to the beach. Several times she waded knee deep into the ocean to get around rock outcroppings that extended beyond the end of the beach. The cool water gave her some relief from the heat and humidity.

After a quarter mile she ran out of beach as a tall rocky cliff rose from the water. She trudged inland into a small sandy box canyon she'd discovered only a week ago. Rock walls rose straight up ten or twelve feet on three sides. A narrow opening on the fourth side led to the beach. Tourists rarely ventured this far from the parking area which made it the perfect place to be alone with her thoughts.

Nikki lowered herself to the sand and stared at the water gently lapping against the shore only fifteen feet away. She leaned back into the shade of an overhanging rock and thought about the events of the past few days. She'd actually enjoyed her time with KC, but she sensed a certain unhappiness within him. She realized that KC had been sneaking peeks at her. He hadn't given any other indication of interest in her, other than the help she could give him in his quest. Maybe it's because she was engaged.

"I should say *no longer engaged*," she muttered. Frank Milburn, her fiancé, had phoned her last night after KC dropped her off. She had expected he was confirming his arrival, but was astonished when he informed her he cancelled his airline ticket. She was unprepared for what came next. He told her he still cared for her, but he had met another woman at a business conference in San Francisco the previous month. They fell for each other immediately. A short whirlwind courtship followed, and five days later he asked her to marry him. They planned an intimate wedding later in the year.

Nikki closed her eyes and rubbed her forehead. *Was I nuts to fall for him in the first place?* He'd been the perfect gentlemen and appeared genuinely pleased that she had a promising career. He was athletic but was not a rugged outdoors type. Even so, he'd gamely gone hiking and kayaking with her. In turn, she attended Broadway plays and the Symphony with him. They both enjoyed these new experiences. In spite of these differences, they had a lot in common. Similar upbringing, excellent educations, a love of good food and wine, and travel.

Curiously, she wasn't hopping mad. She had a short temper and had blown off steam the night before, stopping before throwing a wine glass against the wall. She regretted treating Emma so rudely this morning, and would make it up to her later. The sweet old lady had treated her almost like family. Now she didn't know how she felt. She should feel empty, but curiously, she felt excited, in spite of a bruised ego. Almost free.

A droning sound broke her from her reverie. She squinted above the ocean toward the source of the noise. A red and white Coast Guard helicopter flew past her on one of their routine patrols.

She tapped her lower lip with a forefinger, sighed, and then leapt to her feet and started running back down the beach. The tide was on its way out so she had a mostly dry return trip.

I'm in this too deep to get out now, she thought. *KC needs my help. What the hell am I thinking? I gotta find him.*

Suddenly mindful of the Russian commandos, she approached her car with care. She found the road deserted when she edged out from the safety of the rocks and vegetation.

On the way to KC's office, her cell phone rang. She checked the caller ID, hoping it was KC, and grimaced. She closed her eyes and pressed the answer button.

"Hi Benjamin. How's it going?"

"What's going on down there? I've been expecting updates on those coordinates you've been working on. We need them to complete writing the software," her boss said.

"Well, I'm a little behind, Benjamin."

"Then you better catch up."

Nikki hesitated for just a moment. "Sorry, I'm doing the best I can. You know how it is on these islands. The sense of time is not the same as in the States."

"No excuses, Nikki. We've got a deadline. I expect it to be met. The team is arriving in eight days. Be ready for them."

Nikki breathed in deeply. "Ok, Ben. I've had a little personal setback here that's thrown me for a loop. I understand it's not a good excuse, but I'm sorry."

Benjamin's voice rose to a near shout. "Your personal problems are not my problem, or the company's problem. I'm sorry you're having trouble, but your obligation to the company must come first. We've got a lot of money at risk with this project. You're treading on thin ice here, Nikki."

The line went dead.

CHAPTER 35

Oleander Restaurant, El Fortunato

Here's the problem, KC," Nikki said as she raised the iced tea to her lips. "My fiancé dumped me for another woman. Really wonderful for my ego, I can tell you. Here I am, just about to turn 30, and I'm already going downhill."

"I'm sorry, Nikki. Hey, you're far from going downhill in my opinion. Did you see it coming?"

Nikki's eyes narrowed. "No. Not at all. And there's more bad news. My boss is really pissed. I'm way behind and we've got a deadline to meet. The rest of our team is scheduled to arrive late next week."

"How crappy. I'll tell you what. Let's the two of us find the weapons for Colin, and then I'll help you with your job. At least I can help you with that aspect of your life. Okay?"

Nikki sipped her drink and wiggled her foot a little. "Well, okay, but I've got to get back to work real soon."

KC and Nikki sat at a table at Oleander Restaurant, perched high on a cliff overlooking the scenic El Fortunato marina. The docks were crowded with power boats of all sizes and descriptions. Tourists stood on the docks, pointing at some of the larger yachts. Crew members were hard at work polishing brass and scrubbing decks. The sea beyond was darker and choppier than usual, losing its luster to the pending storm. Surprisingly, the wind was still fairly calm. Nikki had called him back after leaving Cooper's Beach and agreed to get together for lunch and plan a strategy to find the weapons.

The day was clear, warm, and humid. Without needing to look at a menu, KC ordered the cracked conch and lemonade. Nikki needed more time and finally settled on conch salad and iced tea. They sat at the table looking at each other for a moment and then KC said, "You know that Colin can't send protection for us, but he's got his people working on the poem. They should figure it out for us, but we don't have a lot of time. The Russians are still out there somewhere. You have any ideas?"

"We don't even know who wrote it, or why," Nikki said.

"That's the strange thing about this. Jimmy Calhoun seemed to have knowledge of the weapons, but claimed someone had removed them before he explored the cave."

"Do you believe him?" Nikki asked.

KC took a bite of his conch and chewed for a minute. "I can't be sure, but I know something's not right. How did he know Lewis Michaelson had information about the scroll?"

"Hey, they're both old codgers. I'll bet the old hermit talks to Jimmy from time to time."

"I don't understand why Lewis hid the scroll in the cave. He doesn't seem the type to believe in a curse. He wanted to save the scroll, but why?"

Nikki looked over KC's shoulder and shook her head. "Lewis is a strange guy. But no matter. We need to decipher the poem. Right now."

"Ok, finish your food and we'll go to my place. I've got better security than Emma's bed and breakfast," KC said.

CHAPTER 36

The Aqua Palms motel, three blocks from the Secret Bay Beach,
El Fortunato

The Russians had rented a two-bedroom suite in the Aqua Palms motel, located about three blocks from the beach. Pavel Dubkov had taken one bedroom for himself and assigned the other to the two women. Fadey and Jasha slept on a rollaway bed and a sofa bed in the main room. A small kitchenette was tucked in one corner of the suite.

Pavel stood with hands on his hips and glared at his team. Except for Vilma Revnikova, they stood against the far wall and stared at him. She sat on the sofa and looked at the floor. Dubkov took a step forward.

"When we were in Cuba, I received word that Nikolai Chuikov was on route there. Apparently he did not trust our abilities. We don't know where he is, or if he is on his way here, to El Fortunato."

Vilma rose and tossed her long lustrous black hair and said, "We are professionals. The elite among our kind. We do not need Chuikov to tell us how to operate."

"What do we do with the weapons when we recover them?" Jasha asked.

"We will take the weapons to Cuba as arranged. Someone will meet us to transfer them to our buyers. We will be proclaimed heroes when the terrorists use nuclear weapons against the American President," Fadey Goguniv said.

"And we will be rich as well," smiled Vilma.

Alena Lukova stood quietly, apparently deep in thought staring at her fingernails.

Pavel whirled about and glared at Vilma with steady eyes. "Girl, for your information, money is of no consequence. Not today. You might have noticed the two Americans eluded our efforts to capture them. Time is running out, and we do not have the weapons. Lucky for us, neither do the Americans. Should we fail in this mission we will not be famous or rich. Instead we will be quite dead."

"I, for one, do not plan to die on this desolate island," muttered Fadey.

"I think the Americans are closer to finding the weapons than we are. Where did they go in the helicopter? Not to the airport. I checked. Remember, we must capture them alive. I will not tolerate any more reckless shooting. Keep your pistols loaded, but there will be no firing at anyone without my express orders. We know what type of vehicle they drive so it will be easier to locate them," he said, glaring at Jasha.

"I look forward to that moment," Alena said, her eyes boring into Pavel.

Dubkov stared at her in silence for a long moment before turning to the others. He took a deep breath.

"I have formulated a plan. Here is what we will do."

CHAPTER 37

Elsewhere on EL Fortunato

Jimmy Calhoun's cell phone chirped and he picked it up.

A familiar voice said, "If you tell anyone I've got one of these contraptions, I'll come over there and cut your nuts off."

Jimmy laughed loudly into the telephone and said "Don't worry, Lewis. Your secret is safe with me. As far as anybody knows, you communicate with a string tied between two tin cans. What's the latest?"

"They took the bait. Now all we gotta do is wait. But there's still a lot of risk. These people are unpredictable. Watch your six."

"Not to worry. We're past the point of no return, Lewis. The cat's out of the bag. There is only one good outcome." Jimmy replied.

"I know. And that's what scares me."

§ § §

At KC's house

After finishing lunch at Oleander Restaurant, KC and Nikki climbed in their respective vehicles and drove a short distance down the hill to his house. They didn't pass another car or person on the way. At KC's house, Nikki stared at the ocean while KC unlocked the side door. The wind had picked up and the bay was covered with whitecaps. They entered and KC reactivated the security monitors, poured two glasses of lemonade and settled on the sofa in his living room. Nikki withdrew to a comfortable chair next to a low coffee table.

The dynamics between KC and Nikki had subtly changed since she had revealed the news about her terminated engagement and her threatened job status. Nikki seemed more relaxed and had even laughed several times during their meal. Still, they chose separate chairs instead of sharing the sofa.

"Let's go through this poem line by line. I'm convinced that once we decipher the meaning, we'll learn the location of the Davy Crockett nuclear weapons," KC suggested, reading aloud.

Forty-five minutes later, after two glasses of lemonade, Nikki said, "I think we generally understand most of the poem, but the last two lines are crazy. I think they are the most important part."

"I agree, but let's review. The first line,

    'Oh, how they flew from wave to wave.'

Must mean someone came to the island on a fast boat or a helicopter."

"I'm inclined to go with a boat," said Nikki.

"Ok, good. The second line goes,

    'When the devil came to our blessed shores.'

Probably means men came ashore and did something evil. Remember in those days the island was sparsely populated and most of the natives lived in several small villages. There weren't any white people here. During the early 1800s European colonists converted many of the local population to Christianity. Religion is still a very important aspect of life here."

"Why did the Europeans leave?"

KC looked up from the scroll and said, "As I understand it, a violent hurricane wiped out the entire cotton industry and the white settlers left."

"Why call them devils?" asked Nikki.

"One of two reasons. First, most islanders had never seen a white person, or second, the men who came treated the natives badly, like the devil. Maybe both. OK, now on to line three.

    'And with smoke and fire defiled the cave.'"

"They used explosives to seal the cave, or threatened the natives with weapons. Either way, the local residents feared the intruders," Nikki said.

"Yes, and line four,

    'The abyss now bare, spears no more.'"

"We can infer that the nukes were taken by the time the poem was written. Taken from the cave at some point. By whom? Why? Where did they go?" Nikki asked.

KC rose to his feet and began pacing the tile floor. "I don't know. But here's what we know. Bad men came to the island, probably with the nuclear weapons, scared the natives, hid something in the cave, but now the weapons are hidden somewhere else on the island," KC said.

Nikki folded her arms and said, "I agree with all that, but what do the last two lines mean? Here, I'll read them once again,

    'They lie below her most sweet soul
    That, stabbed with seven sorrows.'"

KC sat down on the sofa with his elbows on his knees and rocked back and forth. Silence descended on the pair as they sat staring at the scroll. KC rubbed his forehead and Nikki bit the end of a pencil. Suddenly Nikki stood up, stretched, and checked the time.

She looked up at KC, licked her lips, and said, "Look at the time, KC. I gotta go. I'm having dinner with Emma at the Bed and Breakfast, and then I plan to go straight to bed. I'll get up early tomorrow and get a little work done before we get back to this. I hope we'll get an answer from Colin by then."

"Be careful. Lock your doors," KC said with concern in his voice.

Nikki rose and stood for a moment staring off into space while KC disabled the security system. Without a word she spun on her heels and strode out of the house. KC listened to her car door slam and her tires spin on the gravel driveway.

CHAPTER 38

Moscow, Russia—A few hours later

The Russian President sat at his mammoth mahogany desk as the elderly man swept into his office. The President's beady eyes bore into his visitor like twin laser beams. The man was dressed in a tailored gray woolen suit, light blue shirt, and striped necktie. His medium length blond hair was combed to the side with a little gray showing above his ears. As the President leaned back in his plush leather chair, his visitor noticed a nearly imperceptible twitch in his upper lip.

He approached the desk and waited for an invitation to sit in the stiff wooden chair. When it was not forthcoming, the tall man shrugged, eased into the chair and crossed his long legs.

"I bring news, Mr. President," he said.

"Tell me."

"Chuikov has been eliminated. Nikolai was a dangerous man, but he let his guard down and was fooled by Juan Diaz. Unfortunately Diaz met the same fate."

The President shook his head and said, "What about the weapons?"

"They are still missing. Several Americans have proved troublesome. They appear to be working for Colin Farthington. You know of him, the Seattle billionaire. A weapons collector. A crafty and worthy opponent."

"Yes, I know of him. He has business interests here in Moscow and is a very formidable man. But I doubt his people on the island are up to the task. What else?"

The elderly man frowned and wiggled a finger in his ear. "Chuikov's team eliminated the American soldiers as well. There are rumors the Americans were sent by the American Vice President. Dubkov is a resourceful man, even if he is misguided. You know that it was Nikolai Chuikov who turned him against us. Unfortunately we had an opportunity to take him out three years ago and failed."

"Yes. That's regrettable. But it's a good thing that Vice President Gordon's soldiers were eliminated. He could be more of a problem for us than Farthington. What can we expect next?" the President said.

"I control an asset on the ground in El Fortunato. We will obtain the nuclear weapons for Mother Russia. Dubkov and the others will be neutralized. Foreign elements will never get their hands on the Davy Crockett weapon system."

"What about the locals?"

"So far, only the two Americans appear to be involved. No one else we are aware of," the man said with a glance over the Russian President's shoulder.

"Let's hope you are correct."

"Don't worry. Not only will our bombers be stationed in Cuba, the American's own nuclear weapons will lead our parade. Perhaps you should attend as the Grand Marshall. We will enjoy watching the Americans squirm. How will they explain their own weapons in the hands of their old enemy?"

"What about your asset, Boris?"

"Capable and trustworthy beyond doubt. I can attest to it. Ruthless too, but absolutely loyal to me. I am confident of success, even if the mission is taking longer than anticipated," Boris replied.

"Russia will once again be respected as she deserves. And in the process, the Americans will look like fools when we march with their own weapons high over our heads. The current American administration is no match for us," the Russian President said, smiling broadly.

CHAPTER 39

El Fortunato

Shortly after ten o'clock the next morning Nikki kicked off her flip-flops and slumped onto a chair at KC's kitchen table. She was dressed in a blue sleeveless t-shirt and pale yellow shorts. Her toe nails were painted a soft red. A bead of sweat had settled on her upper lip. The stiff onshore breeze did nothing to ease the stifling humidity. KC eyed Nikki for a long moment then shifted his feet and poured two cups of black coffee.

"Any word from Colin?" she asked

"Nothing yet. Remember, the west coast is three hours behind us. But I found a clue."

Nikki's head snapped up. "Well, come on, tell me what you found."

"Ok, I Googled the words 'seven sorrows' and came up with some interesting hits. There's a Christian rock band with that name and a video game called *Gauntlet: Seven Sorrows.*"

Nikki rolled her blue eyes. "So? Are they important?"

"No. Both came into existence decades after the Cuban Missile Crisis and long after we think the scroll was written."

Nikki leaned forward, and said, "So you didn't find anything useful."

"Well, I think I did. I found a reference to the Seven Sorrows of The Blessed Virgin Mary," KC said.

"You've got to be kidding."

"No, look at the last two lines of the poem," KC said as he unrolled the old piece of paper.

Nikki read the first line aloud. *"They lie below her most sweet soul."* She stared at the floor and closed her eyes.

She scratched her cheek with a forefinger and said, "OK, I give up."

"I'm not a Catholic, but I learned that in some of their rituals the Virgin Mary is referred to as a *sweet soul.*"

"She lived two thousand years ago. And far from here. What's the connection?"

"Well listen to the last line. I think you'll understand. *'That, stabbed with seven sorrows'* is a reference to The Seven Sorrows of the Virgin Mary. Apparently there were seven important events in her life directly related to her son Jesus Christ. The Crucifixion is one of them, of course—His burial another. The Prophecy of Simeon, which confirmed that Jesus was the Messiah, is a third. There are four more."

Nikki hesitated, tapping a finger on her lip. "I'm not sure I understand. How does this fit in with the nuclear weapons?"

"I'm not sure. But I'm certain the beliefs of the Catholic Church are involved somehow. They celebrate the Seven Sorrows with some sort of ritual several times during the year."

Nikki rose, marched to KC's telephone table and opened his telephone book. She flipped through the yellow section, stopped on a page and traced her finger through the names.

"Only three Catholic churches on El Fortunato. One for each of the native villages. What do you think?" she said.

Before KC could answer, Nikki's cell phone rang.

"God, this better not be my boss," she said. She punched the accept icon and held the phone to her ear. KC studied the scroll and paid little attention to her. He certainly didn't want to eavesdrop on her private conversations and had to plan their next step. Should they go back and talk to Jimmy? Or should they visit the Catholic churches in hopes of finding more clues about the Seven Sorrows?

A shout interrupted his thoughts.

"Get the hell away, Emma! I told you there was some trouble going on, but I never thought you would become involved. Those are bad people, very bad. Get out of there as fast as you can. Now! Emma? Emma!" Nikki screamed.

"What the hell?" KC stuttered, looking up.

"I think they've got Emma. She said five people, three men and two women, drove up to my room, tore open the screen door, and marched in. The Russians for sure. How did they know where I'm staying? We gotta help Emma."

"Is she okay?" KC asked.

"Hell no, Jameson. Right before the connection was cut off a door slammed and Emma shouted at someone. They've got her. I'm positive. Remember they've got guns. We've got shit."

"Don't forget we have the scroll."

A shrill ringing jolted them both. Nikki answered her phone again and listened for a few seconds. She turned and handed it to KC.

"He wants to talk to you."

KC fingered the phone lightly, said "yes," and listened for a long minute without uttering a word. His eyes narrowed and his jaw clenched. Finally he said, "I'll call you back in five minutes—No, I said five minutes," and hung up.

"The Russians have kidnapped Emma. Their leader said they will kill her if we don't tell them what we know about the weapons. I don't think they're aware of the scroll, but they figure we know more than they do. Remember, we got to the cave first."

"You're sure they're Russian?"

"Must be. He said his name was Pavel Dubkov. Sounds Russian to me. Plus he's got an eastern European accent."

"Let's give them the scroll and get Emma back."

"It's not that simple. We don't need the scroll anymore. I think they want to permanently shut us up so they'll have a clear run at the nukes. There's too much risk for them if we stay alive."

"Okay smart boy. Now what do we do? Call in the CIA? The local police?"

"No way in hell. First, Colin doesn't trust the U.S. government and second, the locals would tie us up, maybe literally, for hours, if not days. We'll have to do this ourselves. You up for it?" KC said and began pacing the tiled floor of his living room. Hands behind his back, head down, he slowly circled the room.

"Three minutes to go," Nikki muttered without answering KC's question.

KC glanced up at Nikki briefly and stood with his hands on his hips.

"Two minutes."

KC pursed his lips and squinted at the floor. He raised his head and smiled.

"Yes!" he said and raced to the back of his house and rummaged around in a utility closet.

"One minute! Come on KC, we gotta save Emma!"

"Aha!" came a yell from the utility room. KC raced into the living room with a mischievous smile on his face. He grabbed the phone, checked the call record, and punched the connect button.

It was answered after the first ring. "Speak. And know this, Jameson, I am in no mood for games."

"OK, Dubkov, here's what we're going to do. We possess an old scroll with information about the merchandise you want. We will give it to you in exchange for Emma."

KC listened for thirty seconds.

"No, not at her bed and breakfast. I'm not an idiot, Dubkov. There's an outdoor market in the parking lot of the Roundy's grocery store up on the main highway. Not more than a mile up the hill from where you are. Emma can direct you there. An open public area with lots of people. Nobody gets hurt. In exactly one hour. I'm coming alone. I bring the scroll, you bring Emma. We trade, and you leave us alone. You can have the damn merchandise."

KC hung up a few seconds later and smiled.

Nikki's eyes were pinpoints of fire. "Screw you buster if you think you're going without me!" Nikki shrieked. "She's my friend, too. And what's this about letting them get the nukes? I didn't go through all this for nothing. I've almost lost my job because of you. I'm going with you."

KC smiled, then broke out into a short laugh. "Don't worry, Nikki, you won't be left out. I know what I'm doing. Follow me. I have a job for you. And it's more important than mine."

Thirty five minutes later KC loaded a cardboard box into the back of his truck and climbed into the driver's seat. He placed the scroll next to him as Nikki settled into the passenger seat.

"Jameson, you amaze me. First you figure out how to blow out a window using household cleaners and aluminum foil, and now these things in the back of the truck. Where did you learn to be such a delinquent?"

"Because I was a juvenile delinquent before Colin took me in. I grew up on the wrong side of the tracks in Seattle and got into petty thievery, vandalism, and gangs. I was a pretty angry guy and lashed out at the fine citizens of Seattle."

"What changed you?"

"My little sister. A drive-by shooter killed her late one night. She wasn't the target, but that didn't change the reality of her death. She was the only real family I had. We were very close. It was a real wake-up call for me. I'm not sure I'll ever get over it."

Nikki sat quietly as KC drove quickly toward the market, his vision blurred with tears. Nikki noticed and shifted her eyes.

"I'm sorry," was all she could say.

CHAPTER 40

The Outdoor Market, El Fortunato

KC and Nikki turned off the main highway several hundred yards before the entrance to the grocery store, meandered along a gravel road, until they reached a small housing development. KC edged over the side of the road and killed the engine.

"We've got about five minutes before you have to get in position. Here's the scoop: we finally got a really good grocery store here about ten years ago and it's very popular. It's got the best produce and the deli is excellent. Most of the ex-pats shop here, as do lots of locals, and many of them still use cash to buy their groceries. They had a real problem with crime about five years ago and hired several armed guards. Then, when the weekly farmers market opened a couple of years ago, they had to add another guard because most of the transactions were done with cash. You can't let anyone see you. It would ruin everything. Ok, time to go."

Nikki stepped out and grabbed a large bundle from the truck bed. "I understand," she said.

"Remember, Nikki, we don't want any innocent bystanders at the market to get hurt, so it's vitally important to aim carefully. Light it, count to three, and then get rid of the damn thing. I don't want you to lose a hand. All we need is a diversion."

"I understand, KC. Are you sure these will work?"

"Make sure they are lit before you throw them. They work. Trust me. Sneak around the far side of the store. The outdoor market is right around the corner of the building. Keep hidden and stay low," he said pointing the route to Nikki. "When this is over, blend into the crowd. You'll be safe."

"Got it. You can count on me," she said with a grin.

KC and Nikki had spent thirty minutes making ten sparkler bombs out of leftover fireworks an American couple had brought to his house for a Fourth of July party the year before. KC had shown Nikki how to wrap twenty colored sparklers with numerous layers of electrical tape. One sparkler stuck above the rest, acting as the fuse. The small bomb would spew sparks for five to ten seconds after lighting before exploding in a huge flash of light and a thunderous bang.

KC drove back to the main highway and turned toward the grocery store. Fifty eight minutes after his phone call with Dubkov, KC parked his truck in plain view, twenty five yards from the edge outdoor market, and a mere four yards from the low wooden fence where he hoped Nikki was hiding. Sixty minutes came and went, while KC waited in his idling truck. The scroll rested on the seat next to him. The outdoor market was busy, as usual. Children raced through the crowd squealing with laughter. There were booths for flowers and small cacti, original paintings, nature photographs, native trinkets, hats and baskets, as well as seashells and original creations that defied definition. Others sold ice cream, cold drinks, and sandwiches. The low buzz of shoppers haggling with vendors gave energy to the event. KC slouched low in the driver's seat and studied the crowd. He estimated there were at least 150 people there today and didn't want anyone to recognize him. The last thing he needed was someone to interfere with his plan.

He checked his watch.

Sixty four minutes.

The Russians were late.

Sixty eight minutes. He began to wonder if he had been set up, but couldn't think of a reason why the Russians wouldn't show up. Slowly he surveyed the area around his truck but didn't find anything suspicious. KC tapped the top of the steering wheel with three fingers. He looked more carefully into the vegetation that lined the parking lot. What are they up to?

Seventy one minutes.

A green sedan turned off the main highway and headed toward the market. KC relaxed just a little when he recognized Emma's car with four occupants sitting inside. Emma was in the back seat.

"Three bad guys accounted for, two missing," he said to himself and scanned the parking area. He didn't like the fact that he couldn't account for all the Russians. They didn't trust him any more than he trusted them, but he knew the territory and they did not. He casually glanced toward the fence and was relieved Nikki had moved several trashcans to give her more cover. She was out of sight.

He peered toward the two exits of the parking lot. A lone man leaned against a tall lamp post at the edge of the road. A woman stood at the other exit, surveying the activities below her. Not tourists, for sure. Definitely not natives.

KC smiled. "All five accounted for. Ambush avoided."

Emma's green sedan stopped on the asphalt ten feet in front of KC's truck. Nikki's cell phone rang.

"You're late," KC said

"The woman did not cooperate."

"Send her over and I'll throw out the scroll."

"No. First I need to know where you are hiding your woman friend." Dubkov said.

KC paused. "She didn't need to be here."

Dubkov stared at KC for several seconds. "Show us the scroll first then we will turn her over to you. If you don't follow our instructions, we will feed her to the sharks."

"How can I trust that you'll let her go?"

"You can't. But you have no choice."

KC resisted the urge to check his rear view mirror for Nikki.

"Let her get out and stand next to the car. I know you are armed. She won't run. Close the door and send your woman over to examine the scroll. I don't want anyone here to get hurt."

Pavel Dubkov cut the connection and stared at KC through the salt stained windshield. Dubkov turned his head and spoke to Emma. A minute later Emma stepped out of the back of the car and closed the door. She remained still, one hand resting on the door handle. The Russian in the back seat rolled down the window, never taking his eyes off Emma. KC assumed he had a gun pointed at her.

KC reached for the scroll, rolled down his window, and held the scroll out at arm's length. Vilma Revnikova got out of the vehicle and edged toward KC's truck.

Suddenly a figure emerged from the throng of shoppers and shouted "Hey KC!"

Vilma halted abruptly and jerked her head toward the voice. A woman came trotting from the market and stopped at KC's truck. She eyed the Russian woman, then turned and smiled at KC.

"Two-timing me, KC? Well I never!" she said and laughed.

"Oh, hi Melinda, no it's not like that. Just someone who's interested in some artwork I'm selling. Sorry I can't talk right now. We'll get together for a drink soon."

"I hope it's more than just a drink, KC," Melinda snorted with a raucous laugh. She spun about and skipped back to the market.

The Russian woman stared at Melinda as she melted into the crowd of shoppers at the outdoor market. Emma stood ramrod straight, staring at KC. She cocked her head slightly toward the throng of shoppers, and raised an eyebrow.

KC held her eyes and gave his head a quick shake.

"Come on Nikki, come on!" he whispered to himself. "Throw the damn thing before it's too late."

Vilma Revnikova stood half way between the two vehicles and kept her eyes on KC. Finally she stepped toward his outstretched hand. Out of the corner of his eye, KC detected a bright light sail through the sky, coming from the direction of the low fence.

Atta girl Nikki!

BOOM!

Several women in the market crowd shrieked, others ducked down and peered toward the noise. Vilma crouched down and held her position. Emma squatted out of sight of her guard in the back of the sedan.

BOOM!

Two loud blasts with bright flashes and lots of smoke. The smell of gunpowder filled the air. People in the crowd screamed and children began crying. A dog barked. Several men dropped to the pavement. Most ran away from the loud noises. Vilma fell to the pavement and scurried back to the cover of their car. At the same time Emma lunged toward KC's truck. KC reached over and opened the passenger door an instant before Emma grabbed the handle. She leaped into the cab and ducked below the dashboard.

BOOM!

A muffled blast came from underneath the front of Emma's car. Smoke immediately erupted from the engine compartment. Dubkov leaped out of the driver's seat and hurtled toward KC's truck. KC stiffened, jammed the gears into reverse, and backed rapidly towards the low fence.

Dubkov recoiled and ducked for cover when one of the sparkler bombs exploded only three feet in front of him. The two security guards came racing around the corner of the grocery store waiving their pistols high in the air. KC forced the gearshift into drive and pressed the accelerator to the floor. In the moment before the truck accelerated, he felt something bump the truck.

BOOM!

He ignored the thud and sped around the back of the building aiming toward one of the exits of the parking lot.

Jasha Kerensky had been standing along the edge of the road, guarding the east exit. Watching shoppers mill around the market bored him, and he'd become enamored with a group of school girls waiting at a nearby bus stop. The girls noticed his stares, giggled, and pointed at him. He gave a little wave, thinking that maybe this was his lucky day. Neither of the women on his team interested him—in fact, they frightened him. He feared a wrong word with any of them would result in a broken nose, or worse.

Several loud explosions abruptly interrupted his gawking. Drawing his gun from his pocket he ducked for cover behind a tall light pole. He watched the events below him unfold. Some in the crowd fell to the ground while others ran off in all directions. In the confusion Jasha lost track of Dubkov and the rest of the team.

Moments later KC's truck raced toward Kerensky.

KC checked the other exit and caught a glimpse of the Russian as she scrambled down the slope toward the parking lot. He ignored her and shifted his attention to the problem ahead.

"Keep down, Emma!" KC shouted as he approached the exit. "We gotta get past one more and we're home free."

"What about Nikki? Where is she?"

"Safe, I hope," he said.

Jasha raised his gun and aimed carefully at the truck. The schoolgirls reeled back instantly. Several fell to the ground while the rest screamed and scampered for cover behind the bus shelter. KC's truck barreled toward the exit without slowing down. Below him, the entire outdoor market had broken into pandemonium with hordes of people running in all directions. Men yelled, women screamed, and children cried. Even the dogs had run off, tails between their legs. The two security guards tried to restore order, but the crowd ignored them.

KC checked traffic on the main highway and realized that he would not be able merge with the oncoming traffic without crashing into an oncoming vehicle. Several delivery trucks streaked down the highway toward him. Jasha grinned.

A flash of light wiped the smile off his face.

BOOM!

A sparkler bomb exploded inches from Jasha Kerensky's head. He recoiled from the blast, twisted, and fell hard on the asphalt pavement. He landed with his full weight on his right knee. His pistol scattered into the middle of the busy highway and disappeared from view.

"Nikki!" Emma squealed with glee as KC accelerated and careened around the light pole and sped down the main highway. Emma squinted out the back window of the pick-up truck. Nikki grinned at her.

"OK, Jameson," Nikki shouted. "Step on it."

KC smiled with relief and put his foot to the floor. Nikki was safe.

Behind them Jasha struggled to get to his feet. His injured knee collapsed and he fell back to the pavement. He grabbed his leg and rolled to a grassy area next to the highway while KC's truck flew down the highway.

KC turned off the main highway at the next crossroad. He felt the back roads would be safer than the main highway. Several police cars flew past them, lights flashing and sirens screaming. None of them paid any attention to KC's truck.

He pulled the truck over to the side of the road and let Nikki hop into the back seat.

Nikki's blue eyes sparkled. "Holy crap, that was fun."

CHAPTER 41

Washington DC, later the same day

Vice President Sydney Gordon stared at his half empty glass of Woodford Reserve Bourbon and scowled. All the ice in the glass had melted. The President had shut him out of an important policy meeting again and instead sent him to Senator Martin's funeral. The old man had been a fixture in the Senate for nearly fifty years, dying last week at the age of ninety six. He'd been useless for at least a decade, but his presence on the floor of the Senate allowed President Alexander to maintain control of Congress.

Gordon paced on the plush carpeting in his office, his hands clasped behind him. He stopped at a narrow window and looked across the street to the majestic Executive Office Building. Some day, hopefully soon, he'd be looking out at the South Lawn from the Oval Office. His office.

Controlling the Davy Crockett nuclear warheads was crucial to his plan. They would be leverage for his climb to the Oval Office. In recent years, he'd picked up rumors that other small tactical weapons had gone missing, too. He thought these rumors to be baseless, but knew for a fact that the Russians had stolen the Davy Crockett nuclear weapons in the late 50's. The American soldiers in Germany who'd been on duty when the weapons were stolen were all dead, but there were still men and women in powerful positions, both in the government and the military, whose careers and reputations would be ruined if word got out that either Russian or Islamic terrorists had gotten their hands on American nuclear weapons. That they were small was irrelevant. Perception meant everything.

The Press would crucify those guilty of the long cover-up. The left wing would scream for impeachment and push for Congressional investigations. He'd take credit for keeping the weapons out of terrorist's hands and his party would rally around him. Once he got his party's nomination for President he'd campaign on a platform of strong national defense and a tough stance against terrorism.

Even so, President Alexander's treatment both humiliated and infuriated him. He'd show her, some day.

His private phone rang, interrupting his thoughts. He activated the scrambler button and picked up the receiver. "Yes?"

"Baker and his men are dead."

"I am aware of that, Ralph, what about their bodies?"

"Sealed in the cave, for now. Except for Garcia. He stood alone at the top of the Abyss when the Russians killed him. I think the Russians hid his body at the bottom of the pit."

"OK, and their helicopter?"

"Still on the salt flats."

"Get rid of it. Anything else?"

"No. Shouldn't be a problem. I haven't received word from Colonel Wilkerson or Sergeant Smith."

"Don't worry, they're not a factor anymore. What about the weapons?" Gordon said.

Ralph Dodge hesitated. "Still missing. Jameson and the woman created quite a scene today at an outdoor market. They damn near started a riot."

"Find them, eliminate them, and get the weapons."

"What about the others?"

Gordon took a sip of his drink and said, "Our Russian 'friends'? Arrange for an accident. We don't need any loose ends."

"Yes sir. Just like I've done for you before. You can count on me. Wire the money to the usual account."

Dodge hung up the telephone, pressed the "off" button on his digital recorder, and smiled. *Gotta look out for number one first.*

Back in Washington, Sydney Gordon smiled, confident his plan was coming together. It was a positive omen that Dodge recently decided to spend his semi-retirement on El Fortunato. The man was very good and had never failed him. Gordon hoped the situation would conclude soon. He poured himself another Bourbon, without water this time.

He stirred the ice slowly with his finger. His eyes became dark BBs and he pursed his lips. He'd used Dodge too many times and realized it was time to end the relationship. Permanently. Just as soon as the mission was over. Too bad— good men are hard to find.

But Dodge knew too much.

CHAPTER 42

KC's house, El Fortunato

I'm sorry I damaged Emma's car, but I didn't know what else to do. I didn't want them to chase us or run someone over. People were screaming and running all over the place," Nikki said.

"You were terrific, Nikki. The look on Dubkov's face was priceless."

"The sparkler bombs worked perfectly. Just like you said they would."

They'd returned to KC's house after dropping Emma off at the airport. Her niece lived on nearby Mango Cay and had graciously agreed to take her in for a few days. Emma kept the reason for her visit vague, and the young woman was delighted to have some company. Her family had been early settlers on the island and owned a modest home and five acres on a beautiful bay on a remote area of the island. KC had once considered moving there but realized he wouldn't fit in with the wealthy American actors and financiers who had built luxury homes on the Cay. As well, the laid-back pace there was even too slow for him.

"Hey, tell me about the girl who came up to your truck at the market? What did she mean about wanting more than a drink?"

KC stared at her and his mouth hung open. He wondered how she possibly could have heard Melinda. "Er—"

"Yea, I could hear it all. The wind blew just right and carried her voice to me." Nikki's eyes twinkled.

KC's face became hot. He turned away from Nikki. "She's only a friend. We've been on a few dates. That's all."

"Oh sure," Nikki said and nodded her head.

"Anyway, we can't stay here. They found Emma's house, so we have to assume they'll find my place soon. We'll hole up at my office."

Nikki wrinkled her nose. "Hey, I gotta get some clean clothes and a toothbrush. I look like a bum. Plus I stink."

"You look fine to me."

Nikki just glared.

"Ok, but we gotta be quick. The Russians might come back looking for you."

Nikki stared at KC then turned toward the door without uttering another word.

§ § §

KC's office, El Fortunato

KC's pulled up to a non-descript gray concrete building nestled into a hill high above the El Fortunato Marina. The low concrete building afforded a narrow view of the ocean and held a few of the conveniences found in the typical home. KC's office consisted of three rooms. A kitchenette with refrigerator, coffee maker, sink, propane stove, and a microwave oven neatly filled one wall of an outer office. A small wooden table and several straight-backed chairs occupied the center of the room. KC's own office, across a hallway, was a mess. Stacks of papers and manila file folders covered his desk and two chairs. A wastebasket overflowed with crumpled sheets of paper. A desktop computer and laser printer occupied a table next to his desk. A cabinet in the corner housed a combination scanner, fax, and copy machine.

But his lab in the third room was something else. A stainless steel countertop, with glass door cabinets above, ran the length of one wall. Test tubes, beakers, and an assortment of scientific equipment lined the shelves. A lab table stood near the counter. Microscopes and other apparatus stood in a neat row. Everything was spotless.

Near the far side of the room, a row of tall bookcases separated the lab from a small sitting area. A brown three cushion sofa, comfortable reclining chair, and television set occupied the area. A small window looked out over the marina.

Nikki ambled through the three rooms, glanced out the window and shrugged.

"Nice," she uttered without much enthusiasm.

"I'd say 'satisfactory.' I spent one hurricane in here when I first moved to El Fortunato. The power went out and I hunkered down here in the dark. I'll never forget the heat, humidity, and putrid smell of stale air and sweat. I had no idea what was going on outside. The raging wind nearly drove me crazy. After that experience I fixed up this place for the next big storm. Everything's got battery backup, even the air conditioning. So we should be comfortable, and safe, for a few days. Not many people even know this is my office. Addresses aren't listed in the phone book, so the Russians can't find us easily. You can sleep on the sofa bed. I'll string up a hammock. Tomorrow we'll make new plans."

"We need to end this, KC. Soon. I have to get back to work. I'm already in deep shit. Then I have to try to figure out what went wrong with my personal life."

"I know, Nikki. But you'll do nobody any good if you are dead. I'd have a real problem with that."

Nikki started to say something but instead stared at KC. She turned to the window, a hint of a smile on her lips. "Where's the bathroom?"

CHAPTER 43

Moscow, the next morning

Boris drove his Land Rover Discovery 4 into the parking lot at the Russian Academy of Sciences Botanical Gardens a dozen kilometers north of the Kremlin and parked near a pedestrian walkway. Few vehicles occupied the paved lot. He shut off the engine and stepped out of the vehicle. He loved the power and prestige of the luxury sport utility vehicle and actually enjoyed driving in the brutal Russian winter snow storms.

He trekked the hilly terrain for ten minutes following a narrow winding path. Though close to the center of a large bustling metropolis, the huge park was serene and quiet. Harried Moscow residents came to commune with nature, relax stream-side, and enjoy a colorful arrangement of flowers and shrubs.

He reached the top of a hill, lowered himself on a hard limestone bench, and looked at his watch. Glad to be ten minutes early, he used the time to breathe in the fresh air and gaze at a beautiful display of ornamental grasses. He listened to the birds chirping and the leaves rustling in the wind. Fluffy clouds eased across the sky high above him. Eight minutes later his phone rang, interrupting his study of a large yellow sunflower growing next to the bench. In an instant he sat up, forgot about flowers, and answered his phone.

"Report," he said and listened intently for several minutes.

When the caller stopped speaking, he said, "That Jameson is something else. However, he is not your immediate concern. You must eliminate Dubkov and the rest of his team as soon as you recover the weapons. We have a helicopter on standby ready to retrieve you and the weapons. Does anyone suspect you?" Boris said.

After listening for another minute he said, "Good work, honey, now find the weapons and clean up loose ends. You will be rewarded. And I will be very proud."

The tall man returned to his vehicle and started back to The Kremlin. The Russian President would be unhappy when he learned of the havoc created by Jameson and Colt. This mission was turning out to be much more difficult than either of them had anticipated. However, he was comfortable with the knowledge that success rested on the shoulders of a single double agent, one he had personally selected and trained. One he could trust without question.

With success his future would be secure. He didn't want to consider the consequences of failure.

CHAPTER 44

Blessed Sacrament Catholic Church, Blue Harbor, El Fortunato

Sister Mary Catherine finished reciting the Morning Prayer then rose to her feet. She crossed herself, pivoted, and trudged through a narrow door into the sacristy. She wore a veil on her head, but didn't wear the nun's traditional habit. That was reserved for Sunday. Father Andy Prescott was spending the week at Saint Anthony's Church Parish in the village of Williams Bay tending to the needs of the poor and the needy. El Fortunato had three Catholic churches, but only a single priest who rotated from one to the other on a weekly basis. Most of the responsibility for maintaining each church fell upon the shoulders of the few nuns on the island who were assisted by a handful of dedicated volunteers.

Sister Mary Catherine made her way to a small kitchen in an annex building and poured herself a cup of strong black coffee. She was alone in the church this morning and relished the solitude. She was responsible for greeting those who relied on the church for their needs, both material and spiritual, but today she welcomed the quiet. The last week had been a whirlwind of activity with Father Prescott ministering to the faithful here in Blue Harbor. Sister Mary Catherine had organized the feeding and the care of most of them, with help from only one volunteer. This week, she tended the church by herself. The needy still came, but not as often as when Father Prescott was on duty.

From her perch in the kitchen, she gazed across the road to the beautiful blue ocean beyond. In spite of the poor weather, the water always gave her a sense of peace. She finished her single cup of coffee, rinsed it in the old sink, and hurried out of the annex. She crossed the road, taking the narrow path past the cemetery to the beach. The morning sun was partially hidden behind gray clouds, and the humid morning air still retained its warmth from the evening before. Mary Catherine glanced up and down the beach, searching for movement. A lonely pelican glided along the leading edge of the incoming tide looking for its morning meal. Mary Catherine removed her shoes and socks, hid them behind a small bush, and strolled across the sand toward the water.

The soft sand, while cool, felt good sifting between her toes. The wind riffled her skirt, and the tall palm trees waved in the breeze. A small crab darted inches in from of her feet and disappeared into the safety of its sandy hole. Mary Catherine smiled at the wonder of life. Pelicans and crabs, tidal movements, billions of grains of sand. God's creation was surely a marvel.

Her eyes clouded over, her thoughts in conflict. While she loved the church, admired Father Prescott, and gave her full devotion to her Lord, she couldn't rid herself of a nagging doubt that she was not meant to be a nun.

A Catholic orphanage in Philadelphia had taken her in at age eleven after a drunk driver killed both her parents and her younger brother. She moved in with a foster family the following year, but she returned to the orphanage when she turned eighteen and spent two years in apprenticeship as a novice. When she turned twenty, she entered the Sisterhood and spent her time toiling at food banks and soup kitchens in the worst districts of Philadelphia. After that stint she spent a year in Haiti managing a program to provide clothing to children in dire need. High school students in the United States turned old worn out clothes into functional items and sent them to Haiti. Mary Catherine ensured that the clothes were properly and fairly distributed. When her year came to an end, the church posted her on El Fortunato. Helping the poor and the old gave her a wonderful sense of accomplishment and satisfaction.

In recent weeks she'd began to wonder if her life was as full as it should be. At 24 she had experienced more than many women much older but sensed she was missing something important.

But what? The church had been her whole life. What else could she do?

She had been so absorbed in her thoughts she had not seen the man approach from down the beach.

"Morning Sister. Perfect morning for a jog."

"Uh, yes," she stuttered.

As the jogger disappeared around a bend in the shore, she scanned up and down the beach, finding herself alone once again. She shuddered, hoping the Lord would forgive her for her innocent little pleasures of the flesh.

Mary Catherine spun on her heels, retrieved her shoes from behind the shrub, and hurried across the road in her bare feet. She crouched on the steps of the side entrance and hastily donned her shoes and socks.

Guilt prevented her from entering the chapel. Instead, she spent the rest of the morning in the hot hazy sun tending to her small vegetable garden behind the church.

CHAPTER 45

El Fortunato Golf Course

Ralph Dodge loved working a few days a week at the golf course. He didn't need to work full time and hoped to stay on after he finished the job for Vice President Gordon. Maybe he'd learn kiteboarding. He couldn't believe his luck when Jameson and Colt showed up at the club to meet with Jimmy Calhoun. Ralph didn't know their current location, but felt confident he would find the pair soon and take the weapons. Gordon wanted them killed, but Ralph wasn't sure killing them was the smartest thing for him. Jameson was well-respected on the island, and killing him might make it impossible for Ralph to remain on El Fortunato. The Russians presented a much bigger challenge, though. Five against one was not very good odds. He would bide his time, and when the opportunity presented itself, he would jump into action and finish the job. Ralph had no problem with the idea of killing the Russians.

He also had something to celebrate, but couldn't share his good fortune with anyone. It was another lucky break that Jameson and the woman returned the Eurocopter to the salt flats. When this operation ended he'd find a buyer for the helicopter. Probably get at least one hundred G's from a contact he had with a drug cartel in Mexico. Then he'd terminate his relationship with Sydney Gordon. The man was evil and couldn't be trusted.

"Nice having a job you can enjoy," he said to himself and went back to work cleaning dirty golf carts. He was amazed at the amount of litter left by the duffers. Beer bottles, empty golf ball boxes, and sandwich wrappers. Once he found a camera left behind by a careless golfer. He'd made a pretty penny off that one.

The Seven Sorrows

CHAPTER 46

Divine Mercy Parish, Queenstown, El Fortunato

KC and Nikki drove along the asphalt road, dodging huge potholes and doing their best to avoid wild dogs searching the roadside for scraps of garbage. These "potcakes" posed a big problem for people on the islands. Packs of inbred, flea infested, and emaciated dogs roamed the island freely upturning garbage cans in search of food. Many had grown so bold that residents feared the dogs would enter their homes or attack their children. The government tried to reduce the population, but funds for the project had run out. When adopted by a loving "parent" most potcakes adapted to domestic life and became fine pets, but there were just too many of them.

After KC parked his truck in a rusty metal shed near his office they hiked to the Marina and rented a minivan from a colorful entrepreneur named Motorcar Mike. The risk of discovery by the Russians was too great to continue driving his truck.

The small native village of Queenstown, located on the southernmost tip of the island, was strewn with empty bottles, half-filled garbage bags, and other litter. Garbage collection in the village was sporadic, at best, and few residents made the long trek to the dump at the east end of the island. Tiny concrete houses lined the street, junked cars littered the yards, and groups of men lounged on low stone walls glaring at the passing traffic as they played dominos. KC never felt welcome here and only passed through the village on his way to the local lobster market.

Divine Mercy Parish occupied a small concrete building, painted white, with a blue metal roof. A cross adorned the simple steeple that reached high above the front door. A single bell hung in the steeple, quiet today but waiting to call its flock on Sunday. The yard was immaculate.

"Are you familiar with the Catholic religion?" Nikki asked.

"Not much. Religion wasn't a fixture in our house, but some of my friends were devout Catholics. I would have been a terrible altar boy. How about you?" KC said with a chuckle.

"My parents are Methodists. I went to Sunday school until eighth grade, and then lost interest. I admire people of faith, but I never found a real need for it."

After parking the van, they stepped into the church through a set of large heavy wooden doors. The air inside the dark chapel was cool, a welcome relief from the rising temperatures outside. Seven rows of wooden pews flanked a center aisle that lead to a raised platform at the far end of the room. A small dais rose on one side of the platform, a small organ on the other side. A large table, draped with a yellow cloth sat in the middle, several candles sitting lifeless. A life-size painting of Christ on the Cross hung on the wall.

The room stood empty.

"What are we looking for?" Nikki asked.

"Clues," KC said, studying the walls on either side of the church.

"No shit, Sherlock. What kind of clues?"

KC frowned. "Sorry. The Virgin Mary. The Seven Sorrows. I don't have any idea. You read the poem. And watch your language. We're in a church."

They tiptoed around the perimeter of the chapel, studying several large paintings hanging at even intervals on the side walls.

"These aren't originals, are they? They're beautiful," Nikki said softly.

"Nope. All copies. Most of the originals are in Italy, probably Rome or Florence. I'm not much into art, but I remember some things from a trip I took to Italy with Colin. Here's one painted by Botticelli. Another by Lippi. I'm not familiar with the rest."

"Such beauty. They certainly did like their scantily clad women. But I don't see anything here that might lead us to the Seven Sorrows."

They walked toward a side door and opened it. The hinges squeaked and they hurried through. They found themselves in a small circular courtyard, perhaps ten feet across, surrounded by a neat white picket fence about three feet high. A wood bench sat beneath a shade tree at the far end of the garden offering a bit of respite from the hot sun. A small plaque that read 'Mary's Garden' hung on the tree.

KC and Nikki stopped and stared at the very center of the garden. Sitting on a low raised platform stood a statue. It was about two feet tall and faced the bench. The pair walked to the bench, turned, and studied the statue. It was definitely a woman, dressed in robes with both hands outstretched and palms facing upward.

"This has to be the Virgin Mary," KC said.

"Good. This has to be the place. Let's start digging."

KC turned slowly, studying every inch of the small garden. He shook his head.

"Wait a minute. We can't just start digging here. See any clues about the Seven Sorrows? I don't think this is the place. But let's check anyway."

They spent ten minutes searching the garden. KC lay on his back and peered under the bench. Nikki poked the soil around the base of the statue. Finally they stood, looked at each other, and shook their heads.

"Nothing here," Nikki said. "What about over there?"

On the other side of the courtyard a gate hung open on a single hinge, as if inviting the pair to explore the outbuilding on the other side of the fence. Nikki led the way, hesitating when she reached the small shed. She surveyed the area, found no one in sight and scooted in. KC waited outside, keeping watch. Two stray dogs trotted past, giving KC a short sniff before moving on.

Two minutes later, Nikki emerged and shook her head.

"Nothing but gardening tools," she said. "Let's try the next church on our list. Where to?"

"Williams Bay. It's not too far from your B&B. We'll be there in fifteen minutes"

Nikki stepped toward their van when her cell phone jingled. Her eyes rolled when she realized who was calling.

"Hi Benjamin," she said and listened for a few seconds. "OK, calm down. I've got a friend to help me. Won't cost us a cent. I'll get everything done on time. Don't worry."

She hung up and turned to KC.

"Now I'm really screwed."

CHAPTER 47

National Hurricane Center, Miami

Charlie Holly closed his eyes and sighed. When he applied for this job he thought the work would be exciting because hurricanes and tropical storms were fascinating creatures of nature: unpredictable, powerful, dangerous. Sally was a good boss, but he'd come to realize his job no longer interested him. Storms were not very exciting when watched on a computer monitor. Even more, hurricane season lasted only six months, leaving a full half year of tedium. When a hurricane or big storm did form, the excitement ended in a matter of days. Maybe it was time for him to consider a new line of work.

Even so, the latest storm, Hurricane Ida, had held his interest longer than usual. It roared across the Atlantic and then abruptly weakened when it passed Haiti. Curiously it had backtracked to a position over Haiti. The winds died to 40 mph but torrential rainfall had led to massive flooding. The Red Cross was mobilizing rescue teams to assist the stranded and homeless.

The storm was on the move again, inching on a northerly path toward El Fortunato Island.

"Hey Sally," Charlie said. "I think we have to issue another tropical storm warning for the southern Bahamas. This thing is still packing a lot of power and it's moving north again. Think it will become a hurricane again?"

"Very possible."

CHAPTER 48

D id you see Jimmy Calhoun driving off in that car?" Nikki asked as they stopped in front of St. Anthony's Catholic Church at the outskirts of the native village of Williams Bay. She'd seen a man wearing a straw hat slip into his car and speed away from the church. "I'm pretty sure it was him," she added.

"Didn't notice. Why would he be here? He sure didn't seem like a church-guy to me," KC said as he got out of the van.

KC and Nikki strolled to the shabby wooden church building. A small white cross hung on the outside wall above the entrance. The building lay only yards from the road. A store with posters in its dirty front window advertising a sale on fresh snapper occupied a small concrete building next to the church. Across the street several potcakes lay in the shade, tongues hanging from their drooling jowls. KC and Nikki followed a narrow stone path that led to the front door and entered.

The interior of the church had a similar layout to Divine Mercy Parish, but much smaller. A few uncomfortable looking wooden pews flanked a center aisle, a low platform with a lectern sat at the far end, and a huge wooden cross and statue of Jesus hung on the wall. A small piano occupied a corner of the room. Light filtered in from four windows that rose from the floor and extended nearly to the top of the side walls. A cathedral ceiling gave the illusion of a larger space. Heavy wood beams implied strength and durability. Peeling paint on the walls and brown stains on the floor told another story.

The walls were completely void of artwork.

A short man approached them.

"Hello. I'm Father Andy Prescott. May I help you?" Father Prescott was dressed in black slacks, a black short sleeved shirt, and traditional Catholic collar. He was a thin man with short graying hair and deep blue eyes. He had a friendly twinkle in his eye.

KC liked him instantly.

"Uh, hi Father. I hope you can," KC said.

Father Prescott clasped his hands and smiled warmly. "Well, tell me what I can do for you. You may know that St. Anthony, whom our church is named after, is the patron Saint of the lost, the poor, and travelers. I hope you're not lost. And you don't look poor."

"No, of course not. I live on the north shore, near the Marina. I'm KC Jameson, and this is my friend Nikki Colt. She'll be on the island for only a few more weeks. Say, by any chance was that Jimmy Calhoun who drove away a few minutes ago?"

Father Prescott shook his head and looked over KC's shoulder. "Uh, well, are you a friend of his? He brings things over once in a while. Lost and found clothes from the golf course. But no, he hasn't been here in a few weeks, at least. You must be mistaken."

"Could have sworn it was Jimmy with that straw hat of his. Oh well. Anyway, we're curious about religious art, paintings and such. I've been to Italy and visited some of the famous museums. I wanted to show my friend the works of some of the Master artists. We thought we'd find some examples here."

Father Prescott stared at KC for a moment, his perpetual smile fading. He sighed.

"Not in this church, I'm sorry to say. We've got the poorest parishioners here and any money we can scratch together goes to help them. Our congregation is rather small, but they are dedicated. You might visit the Blessed Sacrament Catholic Church in Blue Harbor, at the other end of the island. They've got the best pieces, mostly donated by a wealthy ex pat. One or two remind me of my travels to the Vatican. Ah, those were the days."

"Thanks, Father. We'll head up there tomorrow."

"I think you'll enjoy yourselves. The church is about a mile past the Conch Shell Restaurant, across the road from the beach. Sister Mary Catherine is on duty there. You'll like her. She'll be happy to assist you. Have a Blessed Day."

"I almost forgot, Father. You don't happen to have a statue of the Virgin Mary here, do you?"

Father Prescott frowned. "The Virgin Mary? No, we don't have any statues here."

KC and Nikki hurried outside, climbed in their minivan and pulled back onto the highway.

"Do you think he was lying about Jimmy?" Nikki asked.

"Well, I didn't see the guy drive away, but you seem pretty sure it was him."

"I'd swear it was him."

KC shrugged his shoulders and said, "That makes no sense. Why would a priest lie to us?"

"Something's going on here, and we don't know what it is. I can't imagine the nuclear weapons are part of this, can you?" Nikki said, tugging at her ear.

"Nothing would surprise me at this point," replied KC.

CHAPTER 49

In the Aqua Palms motel, El Fortunato

Vilma Revnikova bent over Jasha Kerensky and frowned. When the security guards at the outdoor market had arrived, Pavel Dubkov ordered his team to conceal their weapons and act like frightened tourists. Alena Lukova had seen the events unfold from her post at one of the parking lot exits. She had realized Emma's car was disabled and had run to the lot and stolen a car. In the confusion, nobody gave her a second glance. They all jumped in the car and sped back to the motel where Vilma, the only one with more than basic first aid knowledge, had patched up Jasha as best she could. Alena later ditched the stolen car on a nearby dead end lane half a mile from the motel.

"He won't be going anywhere soon," Vilma said. "The pain killers I gave him should keep him knocked out for a couple of hours. He tore or severely strained a bunch of ligaments in his knee. I put a splint on it. He'll be out of commission for a few weeks. Other than that, he's got some cuts and bruises. Nothing serious. But he'll be no use to us."

"No matter," Dubkov said. "We will proceed without him. Now get something to eat and then get some rest. We must find the two Americans. I look forward to renewing their acquaintance. I have a plan."

"I hope better than your other plans," Fadey Goguniv sneered. "This whole operation is turning into one big fuck up."

Pavel spun around. His face was bright red and his hands shook.

"That is enough from you, Goguniv. We've had one or two setbacks, yes. Make no mistake, we will prevail. We have eliminated the American soldiers. We know who has the scroll. I'm convinced it will lead us to the weapons. We are five against their two. Kerensky's injury brings us down to four now. Any more disrespect from you and we will be three."

Fadey's face turned red, but he held his tongue. He stomped across the room, grabbed his jacket and left, the door slamming shut behind him.

"Good," Dubkov muttered. "He needs to cool off before we finish this. None of you will question my authority again. Make sure Goguniv understands. Yes?"

Vilma glared at him for a brief moment, then lowered her eyes and nodded.

Alena remained quiet, as usual, and returned to her duties in the kitchenette preparing a light meal for the squad. Vilma considered cooking to be below her dignity, and the men were useless in a kitchen. Alena liked to cook and had taken it upon herself to learn the individual preferences of each person in the group. She had gained their trust. She smiled when she thought of what would happen to them when they found the weapons.

Well Fadey was right, it did go wrong, she thought. So much for Dubkov's planning. She had a plan of her own.

CHAPTER 50

El Fortunato Golf Course

Ralph Dodge paced back and forth and scowled at his watch. Fifteen minutes until quitting time. He was supposed to be on his day off, but the golf course manager had called him in when another employee called in sick. When he balked his boss threatened to fire him. *Yea sure*, he thought, *I bet the other guy is kiteboarding this very minute. What I need is a cold pint, and I'm not drinking here. Screw the employee discount.*

He'd spent the previous evening devising a plan to find KC Jameson and the woman. He knew where Jameson lived and had hoped to find them first thing in the morning. Now he had to wait until after work.

Twenty minutes later, he strolled into O'Shea's Irish Pub, perched himself on a bar stool, and ordered a pint of Harp Lager. Two other patrons sat on tall stools next to the bar. The clock on the wall read 4:00. In another hour, the sun would be low enough in the sky to force sun seekers off the beach and into the pubs.

He enjoyed his second pint while ogling several young women sitting at a nearby table laughing and drinking their sweet cocktails. They paid no attention to him.

The front door banged open and a lone male burst in. He stood for a moment while his eyes adjusted to the dim light. Finally he strode over to the far end of the bar and straddled a stool.

The bartender finished washing a beer glass and looked up. "What can I get you, sir?"

"Vodka. Straight, no ice," the man said in a firm voice.

Ralph nearly spit out his mouthful of Lager when he recognized the man's thick Russian accent. He calmed himself and eyed the Russian as he downed two shots of Vodka in rapid succession. Ralph finished his beer, threw some bills on the bar and slid off his stool.

"See ya around Art. Come on over and play a round," he said to the bartender.

"Thanks, laddie, I plan to. Just remember to put it in the back of the hole," Art chuckled as he glanced at the young women.

"You bet."

He strolled out of the Pub, scurried across the driveway and stepped into a narrow alley where he melted into the shelter of dark shadows.

Ten minutes later, the Russian lurched out the door and weaved his way along the sidewalk, unaware that Ralph Dodge was following him. When Fadey Goguniv entered a first floor room at the Aqua Palms Motel, Dodge smiled.

"You're mine, all mine," he said softly.

CHAPTER 51

KC's Office, El Fortunato

KC rolled out of his hammock and stretched. He'd slept hard after the stress and activity of the past few days. As usual the soft popping sound of the coffee maker woke him. He gazed at Nikki as she slept soundly.

KC shook his head. Their relationship had improved, but frustrated him in a way he was unable to describe. One moment she'd be diligent and helpful, eager to help him in his quest, and then the next she'd be unpleasant and short tempered. And now she was in a funk because her ex-fiancé dumped her and her job was in jeopardy. Not that he could blame her.

Yet Nikki intrigued him in a way he couldn't explain. He wasn't sure it was love, but it felt good to have her near him. Last evening he couldn't help but stare when Nikki came out of the bathroom and climbed into bed. She was a beautiful woman, didn't wear any make up, and didn't need it. KC longed for a meaningful relationship but didn't think Nikki was looking for one having just lost her fiancé. Hell, she hadn't shown any interest in him. Emma Cameroon had it right when she called Nikki a 'firecracker.' KC never knew when she would go off in a tirade or belittle him for the most minor thing.

"Stubborn woman," he muttered as he stared out the small window at the gray overcast sky.

"What did you say, Jameson?" Nikki said suddenly.

KC spun and gaped at her. She stood at the sofa bed wearing short sleeper shorts and a halter-top. She wasn't wearing a bra. His mouth hung limply open.

"Quit gawking. You look like you've never seen a woman get out of bed before. Please tell me the coffee is ready," Nikki said as she sashayed to the bathroom. She faced away from KC so he didn't notice the twinkle in her eyes. Nikki returned a few minutes later and slid her feet into flip flops. She poured a cup of coffee and eased into a chair across the table from KC.

They discussed their plans for the day over black coffee, fresh squeezed orange juice, and English muffins. Nikki suggested they visit the Blessed Sacrament Church and find the Seven Sorrows. It was their last hope.

KC wanted to talk to Jimmy Calhoun again. He believed Nikki when she said she spotted Jimmy Calhoun leaving St. Anthony's and didn't understand why Father Prescott had lied. KC picked up a butter knife and drummed it on the table.

"It's a loose end we should tie up before going to the church," he argued. "Maybe Father Prescott is part of all this, but I'd like to learn more before we stick our necks out again. There's something going on here we don't understand."

Nikki nibbled at her muffin and nodded her approval without comment.

CHAPTER 52

At the Aqua Palms motel, El Fortunato

As a dim daylight broke, Pavel Dubkov emerged alone from his bedroom and shook his head. Jasha dozed on the sofa with his injured leg propped up on a pillow. Fadey, sprawled on the rollaway bed they'd ordered from the motel staff, continued to snore. He was still fully dressed. Pavel nodded at Alena and Vilma as they stepped from the second bedroom.

Pavel paced with his hands behind his back, eyes raised. His squad was falling apart, and they were really no closer to obtaining the nuclear weapons than when they arrived on El Fortunato. He had to take immediate measures to get the situation under his control and to secure his authority. He spun to his left, strode to Fadey, reached down and, in one swift move, flipped both the mattress and Fadey upside down.

"Get up!" he shouted.

Fadey Goguniv groaned, surprised to find himself underneath his mattress. He closed his eyes, belched, and clutched his throbbing head. Pavel Dubkov's upper lip twitched, but he ignored the man lying at his feet.

"I have purchased disposable cell phones for each of you. Here is what we will do. First we need to find another boat. I don't want to bring attention to us by trying to free our boat from the sand bar on the other side of the island. Too many people might notice. The boat might be damaged as well. Goguniv, this is your assignment. Find a boat and steal it. Get us something similar to the one that brought us here. You will contact me for instructions after you complete your mission. Lukova and Revnikova, you will rent motor scooters and drive all the roads and locate Jameson and Colt. It is very likely that they have changed vehicles. Call me as soon as you do. We will continue without Kerensky."

"But—" Vilma mumbled.

"You have your orders. Don't come back here until you find them."

"What will you do?"

Pavel's face flushed. "Do not question me, girl. I will finalize plans for our escape with the weapons. Now move out."

CHAPTER 53

El Fortunato Golf Course

As had become their custom, KC and Nikki stuck to back roads and alleyways on their way to the golf course. The parking lot was nearly empty, a result of the muggy, overcast, and windy weather. The dark sky hinted at hard rain. They proceeded around the clubhouse, expecting to find Jimmy at the starters shack. Both the shack and the first tee were vacant, so KC and Nikki went into the pro shop and asked the woman behind the counter where they might find Jimmy Calhoun. Following her directions, they stepped up the stairs and into a bar.

Jimmy straddled a stool at the bar and was engaged in animated conversation with another man. There was no one else in the bar room.

As KC and Nikki approached him, he swiveled around and faced them. KC thought that for a brief moment Jimmy's eyes narrowed before opening widely when he realized that Nikki was trailing behind KC.

"Well, darlin'. I knew you couldn't keep away from old Jimmy. Come on over and sit right next to me," he said with a huge grin on his face.

Nikki blushed and said, "Nice to see you too, Jimmy."

KC started to laugh, but stopped when he remembered why they had come to talk with the man. He played with the top button of his polo shirt while Jimmy fawned over Nikki. The man who had been talking to Jimmy melted into the background, moving to a booth to nurse his mid-morning beer.

"To what do I owe the pleasure of another visit? It's not a good day for golf. Please don't tell me you want to talk about that ring business again," Jimmy said.

KC straddled a stool next to Jimmy and, in a low voice, summarized their activities since they had last seen him. News of the near riot at the outdoor market had spread across the island. Jimmy laughed when KC related how Nikki had thrown the sparkler bombs with perfect precision and assured their escape.

"So that ruckus at the market was all your doing? Impressive. But you haven't told me why you've come back. Just bragging, or did Lewis Michaelson cause you trouble?"

"No. Of course not. I assume you're aware of Michaelson's scroll and the poem. Well we found it. We think the poem might somehow be connected to the Catholic Church. You have any ideas about that?"

"Sorry, KC. I'm not much of a church man myself. More power to them, but religion's not for me." Jimmy glanced around the bar and frowned. He twirled a small golf pencil in his fingers, then made a few doodles on a bar napkin.

"But yesterday when we went to talk to Father Prescott at St. Anthony's Church we thought we recognized you driving away. The driver wore a hat exactly like the one right there," KC said as he pointed to the straw hat sitting on the bar directly in front of Jimmy.

Jimmy hesitated for a moment.

"What kind of car do you drive, Jimmy?"

"Wasn't me. Well, sorry sweetheart but I gotta go. My break is over. I've got responsibilities around here, you know. You can finish my beer, KC," Jimmy said as he got up and stared intently at his beer bottle for several seconds.

Nikki frowned as he ambled down the stairs. "That was strange. Why didn't he take his beer with him?" she said.

KC picked up the bottle, poured some of the amber liquid into a small glass, set it back on a napkin, and said "I don't know."

"KC," Nikki whispered.

KC didn't move.

"KC," she repeated. "Look. Pick up the bottle."

KC shook his head and scowled. He shrugged his shoulders, picked up the bottle, and studied the label.

"The napkin, you dope," Nikki hissed.

KC glanced down at the napkin. Several words were written in pencil.

"Watch your 6."

Nikki crumpled up the napkin and stuck it in her pocket.

"Come on KC, let's get out of here. Jimmy was no help," she said a little too loudly. She got to her feet and sidled toward the door. She stopped, turned around and stared at KC. She raised her eyebrows and glared at him.

"Oh, uh, right Nikki. No help at all," KC stuttered

Nikki nodded, pushed the door and stepped outside. KC caught up to her when she got to their van.

"Sorry I didn't catch on right away. But why did Jimmy write the warning on the napkin instead of telling us?" KC said.

"I think we have more than the Russians to worry about. Trouble is we have no clue who or what we're up against."

"Do you think Jimmy is in danger?"

"We all are."

CHAPTER 54

The Marina, El Fortunato

The El Fortunato Marina was a large natural lagoon on the north side of the island with a narrow channel leading to the ocean. The famous barrier reef lay several miles offshore. A narrow sandy peninsula on the north protected the harbor from wind and rough seas. Luxurious mansions, with views of both the marina and the open ocean, lined the peninsula. Three story condominiums stood on the east side of the peninsula; the remainder sported a mix of restaurants, shops, and a small motel. Most important, there were slips for 60 or 70 boats.

Fadey Goguniv lounged in a chair overlooking a maze of docks and piers nursing a beer. The smooth lager, combined with the four large pickles he'd managed to eat earlier in the morning, had taken the edge off his hangover, and he began to feel almost human again. He'd searched the docks looking for the perfect boat, but hadn't found one he thought Dubkov would approve of. He discovered a small pub that offered a good view of the docks and watched the feverish activity of the marina. Boats of all sizes and shapes chugged slowly through the marina. Some were rigged for SCUBA diving, others with towering flying bridges were equipped for deep-sea fishing. There was even a glass-bottomed boat used to show tourists the colorful coral reefs scattered in the shallow waters inside the long barrier reef.

He nearly missed it while ogling three barefoot young women wearing short shorts and tight tank tops. When the girls ignored his lecherous looks he turned away just in time to spot a luxury yacht cruising to a slip in front of one of the condominiums across the harbor. Perfect. Just like the boat they got in Cuba. Well, almost the same. He trusted Dubkov would approve.

Fadey paid for his beer and ambled along the wooden docks, smiling at people he passed until he came alongside the boat. It was a Sunseeker Manhattan 55, about the same length as the boat that brought them to El Fortunato. Fadey took in the high bridge and luxurious furnishings. He couldn't determine how many horsepower the inboard engine had, but the boat looked fast. The top and decks were painted pure white, while the sides sported a broad navy blue tapered stripe.

He peeked at the aft end of the boat and laughed. *Perfect for us*, he thought. The name printed on the rear was *Rebellion*, and registered in Palm Beach, Florida.

Fadey strolled over to a lounge chair, sat down and closed his eyes, acting like a lazy tourist soaking up some rays.

He listened to the chatter of the two men on the boat and learned the owner planned to leave the island on the afternoon plane to attend to some business in America. He'd be back in five days and told the boat Captain to take a few days off, but before leaving order the parts needed to repair the electronics. Fadey couldn't hear the rest as they stepped to the cockpit and continued their conversation.

Fadey smiled, got up, and strolled down the dock back to the pub for another beer. He absently patted his back pocket, feeling his lock picking set.

His assignment was nearly finished. He hoped Alena and Vilma met with success as well.

CHAPTER 55

El Fortunato

KC and Nikki motored along the busy main highway. He checked his rear and side view mirrors at regular intervals.

"I'm scared, KC," Nikki finally said. "What did Jimmy mean?"

"Damned if I know. I'm fairly certain he was at the church yesterday but couldn't tell us why. Did you notice anybody suspicious hanging out at the golf club?"

"Nope. Just the bartender and another guy who left as soon as we arrived. I think we should go to The Blessed Sacrament Church, right away. Let's get this over with."

KC slowed down to blend into the traffic flowing through the round-a-bout. He successfully negotiated his way through the busy traffic without noticing the woman on a motor scooter who'd came up closely behind him. When he cleared the round-a-bout, he checked his rear view mirror again, but only a delivery truck followed close behind him.

Alena Lukova dropped back and settled her scooter behind the truck, out of sight of the Americans. With one hand she flipped open her cell phone and called Pavel Dubkov.

"I found them. Heading west on the main highway. I will call again when I know where they are going. Don't worry, I won't let them spot me."

Ten minutes later KC and Nikki turned off the highway toward the northwest shore of El Fortunato. A minute later they came over the crest of a hill. Below them the village of Blue Harbor spread out along a narrow strip of beach. The bay was decorated with whitecaps, and far beyond it waves were breaking across the barrier reef. The village was home to several native-style restaurants, a scattering of native shops, and a few churches, including the Blessed Sacrament Catholic Church. The white sandy beaches matched the beauty of those at the other end of the island, but the real estate boom had yet to find Blue Harbor. The small harbor provided a sanctuary for native fishing boats, a few small yachts, and well-crafted sail boats. Rumors were rampant that a major hotel chain was negotiating to purchase a large tract of land with frontage on both the harbor and the beach.

KC and Nikki pulled their van into the parking lot of the Conch Shell restaurant, went in, and settled into a booth at the back of the room. Through the wide picture windows they had an impressive view of the wind whipped waters beyond the harbor. Only one or two boaters had dared to venture out into the rough seas.

They'd decided to grab some lunch and plan their strategy, feeling certain the Catholic church in the village held the answer to the mystery of the scroll. KC ordered the cracked conch and lemonade. Nikki nibbled on a grouper sandwich and sipped an iced tea.

"With Father Prescott on the other side of the island, I suggest we walk into the church through the front door and look around. There has to be a clue somewhere," Nikki said. "Didn't Father Prescott tell us that someone would be at the church?"

"Yes, Sister Mary Catherine should be there. But first I want to drive around the area a little to make sure we haven't been followed. Like Jimmy said, we gotta watch our back. Then we'll go in and find her." KC added.

Nikki folded her arms and said, "I haven't seen anybody suspicious."

"We can't be too careful. These guys are pros and mean business. They probably know how to tail someone without giving themselves away."

"Why don't you drop me off at the church and I'll scout around."

"I think we should stay together. Anyway it's starting to rain again."

"But—"

"Nikki!" KC hissed. "We'll do it my way."

She finished chewing and touched her mouth with her napkin and said nothing.

They finished their meal in silence as a large luxury yacht sped past, aiming for the protected harbor. A lone man, drinking a beer, stood at the helm.

KC pushed his plate away and stood up and stuck two ten dollar bills under his plate.

"Let's go. This may be our last chance. If we strike out this time we might have no choice but to call in the police."

KC drove slowly down the main road of the village, passed the church and turned around at the entrance to the harbor. The streets were nearly deserted, only a few men hauling sheets of plywood in preparation for the impending hurricane.

A white metal gate leading to a parking lot next to the church hung wide open. The lot was empty when KC and Nikki entered. He drove to the far corner and parked the minivan behind a low concrete planter. He didn't want to attract any undue attention.

The church was a sprawling complex of several buildings, all painted white, connected by covered passageways or shrub-lined walkways. A large three story structure that had the appearance of a school building loomed silent and empty at the back of the property. It, too, was connected to the main building by an enclosed passageway. KC and Nikki hurried across the parking lot and stepped through a massive wooden door. They found themselves alone in a large foyer and drifted to the center of the room, almost afraid to make noise. They stopped to get their bearings. To their left, two rooms appeared to be a library and a meeting hall. Several tables were lined up in a row, a few hard backed chairs placed among them. Small floral paintings decorated the walls. Another door hung open at the far end of the foyer. They crossed to the door and found themselves in a long hallway. About a third of the way down, a second hallway branched off to their right with a small sign indicating the way to the church offices.

"Don't you think we should we go find the Sister?"

"No. I'd rather search on our own first," KC whispered. "Our best bet is in the chapel. Straight ahead I think."

They strolled past photographs displaying a variety of church activities with smiling children and proud parents. Others displayed church elders and previous pastors and nuns participating in baptisms, weddings, and picnics. At the end of the hall they opened another wooden door and entered a large chapel where they found the familiar raised platform, this time with a pair of matching lecterns. Several pews, presumably for the choir, shared the platform. They reached the center of the room and noticed an organ above them on a small balcony overlooking the chapel. Stained glass windows lined the walls, offering a bit of light in spite of the rainy overcast day outside. Not a single painting was in sight.

KC and Nikki separated, each taking a different route to the altar on the raised platform. Along the way they searched for any clue of The Seven Sorrows of the Blessed Virgin.

"Maybe there's a clue engraved on the floor, or the ceiling," KC said. "Check every inch."

A thorough search turned up a few interesting artifacts, including a small reproduction of Michelangelo's "David," but nothing of the Seven Sorrows. After ten minutes, Nikki settled on a wooden pew and sighed.

"Nothing here, KC. Now what are we going to do?"

"Keep looking. This is a big complex. It's gotta be here somewhere. Let's check the hallways. Then find Sister Mary Catherine."

CHAPTER 56

Blue Harbor Village, El Fortunato

Fadey Goguniv's cell phone rang. He flipped it open and listened for a moment. "I'm tying up the boat now at the public dock in Blue Harbor. Right next to the parking area. Where are you?" he replied.

He listened for a minute longer, and nodded.

"Okay, I'll wait for you here. With this weather there aren't many people around. We should be able to load the weapons without any trouble. Call me when you're on the way."

He was happy to hear Jasha was joining the squad. He could still fire a weapon and help the team if needed. The pair had a common bond, one fueled by fear of Pavel Dubkov. The two women were capable, but he did not like their attitude. They showed no respect for the men and treated him, in particular, like a teenage boy. But, he admitted, he had to give Lukova credit for finding the Americans.

He hoped the operation would be over soon. He missed his native Russia.

§ § §

Sister Mary Catherine had hoped to finish her garden chores before the hurricane came. She'd been struggling with her crops for weeks and prayed that the coming rain would bring renewed growth to her weak vegetable plants. The church had a large cistern full of rainwater that supplied them with fresh water, but Mary Catherine was careful not to use too much for her garden. While the wind whipped about her, she tied several tomato plants to green bamboo stakes and grubbed out stubborn weeds with her three pronged hoe. The heat in the courtyard was oppressive. Sweat dripped off the end of her nose. She grabbed a small rag and wiped her brow. When she finished, she stepped to the small shed that contained her fertilizers and other tools.

Maybe I'll sit inside on my bench and take a breather, she thought. *Just for a few minutes.*

She sank on a small bench in the dark shade of the building and rested her head against the wooden wall and closed her eyes.

§ § §

Ralph Dodge parked his white Chevy S-10 pickup truck several blocks from the beach and made his way on foot meandering through backyards littered with debris and junked cars until he reached the rear of the old school building adjacent to the church. The wind had picked up and menacing dark clouds swirled high above him. He was glad he'd worn his rain slicker and golf hat. He found refuge in a small shelter at the corner of the building where he kept an eye on the Blessed Sacrament Church. Fortunately, the building appeared to be deserted. Following the Americans to Blue Harbor had been a simple task.

They hadn't seen him eavesdropping from the wrap-around deck at the golf course. They didn't expect anyone to follow them and left an easy trail. He drove past them when they'd stopped for lunch and circled around behind the church. Dodge bent over, unzipped a small duffel bag, and removed a Russian-made 9mm PP-2000 submachine gun. The weapon was only thirteen inches long with a short barrel. It wouldn't win any beauty contests, but its small size and light weight made it a perfect weapon for close quarter combat. He inserted a 20 round magazine and attached a second loaded 44 round magazine into the rear of the gun, using it as a stock. The weapon, with the stock attached, weighed a little over three pounds.

He had to admit he'd been surprised to find the Russian woman tailing Jameson and Colt. None of them were aware he was on their tail. In fact, no one even knew he was in the game. The odds definitely favored him. It would all be over before the Russians and the Americans had a chance to react. Dodge wasn't a natural born killer but had no qualms killing the Russian commandos. However, killing Jameson and Colt wasn't in his best interests. He'd figure a way to explain to Vice President Gordon why they survived.

Ralph spent a long minute rummaging through his duffel bag looking for a special piece of equipment. With a grunt of satisfaction, he withdrew an object from the bag. *Don't want to alert the neighbors*, he thought as he carefully attached the noise suppressing silencer into place on his submachine gun. Finally, he pulled a Walther PPK hand gun from the duffel, made sure it was locked and loaded with the safety on, and attached it to his belt.

When he finished his preparations he reviewed his plan. He'd keep hidden until the Americans found the Davy Crockett warheads. He guessed the Russians would show up about the same time. Then he'd step in and take care of the situation. With a little luck, he'd have all his adversaries together at the same time.

His ace in the hole was the element of surprise. It was all on his side.

CHAPTER 57

Blessed Sacrament Church, El Fortunato

KC and Nikki drifted back into the church's main hallway, taking their time to study the paintings. Failing to find a clue, they strolled towards the office complex. Oversized ornate rugs covered the wood floor in an almost haphazard fashion. The pair continued on, awed by the grandeur of the artwork, but beginning to worry they'd found yet another dead end. Cherubs dominated one ornate painting, Jesus on the Cross another.

Halfway down the hallway, Nikki stopped in front of a large painting. She knitted her brow and cocked her head. She leaned forward on tiptoes and studied the picture. It completely filled its thirty by thirty-six inch frame, and even Nikki could tell it wasn't an original oil. She took a step back and stood with hands on her hips. Her eyes grew wide and she turned to look for KC.

"KC!" she hissed. "Here."

KC jerked his head toward her, and then trotted to her side. "Is this it?" he said.

The pair stood in silence and stared at the artwork. Before them was the image of a woman, a blue shawl covering her head, with her hands folded together over her waist. A single tear trickled down her cheek. Suspended in front of her chest, seeming to float in thin air, hung a human heart with what appeared to be flames rising from its top. Seven small swords pierced the heart, three from the left and four from the right.

"Look, seven spears. This has to be it. The last part of the poem. Repeat it," Nikki urged.

KC repeated the last two lines from memory.

> *"They lie below her most sweet soul*
> *That, stabbed with seven sorrows."*

"This is it! The Virgin Mary is the 'most sweet soul' and her heart is 'stabbed with seven sorrows.' The swords represent sorrow. The seven pains she endured during her life."

"Well, then, where are the nukes?" asked Nikki.

KC shrugged and studied the walls of the hallway. Smooth concrete, painted white, glared back at him. The cathedral ceiling high above him failed to yield any clues. Still he stared upward, hoping for inspiration, or perhaps a sign. Outside, a shutter broke free from its latch and banged loudly against the window, startling KC. His trance broken, he sprang to the middle of the hallway.

Nikki reached up to take the painting off the wall.

KC grabbed her arm and said, "Wait. Here, help me move this large rug. Remember, the poem said 'they lie below her'."

They each grabbed a corner of the rug and pulled it to the other side of the hallway. KC lowered to his hands and knees and used his index finger to trace the grooves and grain of the wooden floor. Finally, he detected a slightly wider gap. He reached in his pocket for the knife he always carried and used it to clean out dust and grime that had built up in the grooves of the wood floor.

"I think we're on to something. Run and find something we can use to pry up these boards. My knife isn't strong enough."

Nikki returned a minute later with a heavy letter opener and a long screwdriver. KC was just finishing cleaning out the grooves. Now they easily saw a four foot by four foot section of the floor that was different than the surrounding area.

KC reached for the screwdriver and inserted it into the widest part of the gap. Nikki watched as he pushed and pried. Her eyes grew large again.

"My God, it's a trap door," she whispered.

KC worked the screwdriver and letter opener along the widest part of the gap until he was able to reach a finger through the opening. "Go see if you can find a flashlight."

Rusted hinges let out a loud screech as KC lifted the trap door and folded it all the way back to the floor. He peered into the opening and discovered a set of narrow steps descending into the darkness. He was about to take a step down when Nikki returned with several candles and a box of wooden matches.

KC lit one of the candles and led the way down the steep stone steps. They found themselves in a room about twelve feet long and eight feet wide. The ceiling was low, not more than five and a half feet above the floor. After lighting another candle and passing it to Nikki, KC hunched over and crept to the end of the room where a lone object sat on a low platform. The room was dry, but reeked of old stale air. A layer of dust covered everything, with no evidence of footprints on the floor.

They approached the end of the room together and stopped before the platform. Sweat dripped off KC's nose. His shirt clung to his back.

They stared at the platform. The candle flames stood erect in the still air and cast an eerie glow over a long wooden box.

"Is that a casket?" Nikki asked, and reached for KC's elbow.

"I hope not. What do you think?"

"We have to open the lid," Nikki said.

"What if there's a body inside?"

"Jameson, open it!" Nikki ordered.

"What if it's booby trapped?"

"Jameson, it's too hot in here to argue. Do I have to do all the dirty work?"

KC shrugged, handed his candle to Nikki, and began to pry open the top of the casket, hoping that he wasn't disturbing the dead. He half expected something to jump out at him or that poisoned darts would fly out of some secret compartment in the wall. Visions of his sister lying dead on her bedroom floor swirled in his head, blurring his vision. He stumbled back.

Nikki didn't say a word. She handed the candles to KC and grabbed the screwdriver, stepped forward and pried open the top of the casket. The lid creaked open and rested against the back wall. She dropped the screwdriver, reached for the candles and held them over the open casket.

"Come on KC, there isn't a vampire sleeping here, if that's what was worrying you."

KC recovered his balance and stepped close to Nikki. He smiled weakly, turned to Nikki, and gave her a little hug.

"Careful there, buster," Nikki said, but didn't pull away. "We're not done yet. Let's see what we've found."

KC reached into the casket and peeled a lace blanket off objects resting on the bottom.

There they were. Seven Davy Crockett tactical nuclear warheads. And the launcher used to shoot them.

"Beautiful, just beautiful," KC said and let out a long breath. "Let's get them out of here and back to my office. We'll lock them up and then lay low until Colin can transport them to Sinclair Island."

"OK. I found a side door down at the end of the hall. Outside is a small parking area."

"Excellent. Go retrieve the van and bring it around to the back of the church while I haul these upstairs. Be careful. Keep an eye out for anyone suspicious. We've got more than Russians to worry about."

"What do I do if I run into the Sister?"

"Wing it."

Nikki hurried off to get the van while KC started to haul the seventy-five pound weapons up the steep stairs. He found the door near the end of the hallway and stacked the weapons just inside. By the time he had hauled up the fifth weapon his back had begun to ache. Carrying the weapons out of the cramped hot cellar and up the stairs was taking its toll. He rested a moment wondering what was taking Nikki so long. Shrugging his shoulders, he gathered the energy to finish the task. Four minutes later KC set the last nuke on the pile and stepped outside, expecting to find Nikki and their vehicle.

The wind had picked up again, harder than ever. KC found himself in a small courtyard where the wind swirled and the rain blew around him in all directions. An unusual darkness descended upon the courtyard, as rivulets of water washed down the asphalt pavement. A vegetable garden at the edge of the parking area was flooding. He dashed back inside to wait for Nikki.

"Where the hell is she?"

Moments later, headlights flickered around the corner of the building.

"Finally," he muttered recognizing their van. He opened the door and stepped outside as a second vehicle careened around the corner and screeched to a halt only two feet behind Nikki. Only then did KC realize Nikki wasn't alone. A woman was seated next to her holding a gun to her head. A second woman and a man bolted from the trailing vehicle, a light blue pick-up truck. KC realized a third person was huddled under a tarp in the bed of the pickup.

Pavel Dubkov pointed his pistol at KC.

"Thank you Mr. Jameson," he said in a thick accent. "You have performed a great service for the world."

"We meet again, Dubkov. What do you mean?" KC said.

Dubkov raised the gun and waved it at Nikki as she emerged from the van. "You have given us the means to help bring down the imperialists in America. Now, Mr. Jameson, load the weapons into the back of our truck. Quickly or your woman will die."

Nikki held herself ramrod straight next to the van door. Vilma Revnikova stepped out and pointed a small pistol at Nikki. She gave KC a quick nod to let KC know she wasn't hurt and relaxed her shoulders.

As KC loaded the weapons on the truck, the other woman trotted into the church. A few minutes later she came out and spoke quietly with Dubkov.

"Very good, Lukova."

The storm eased a little, the rain nearly stopped, and the wind lost some of its intensity. The sky was still dark and the air humid. Water still poured from a corner downspout and ran in little rivulets toward the vegetable garden.

KC finished hauling the warheads. His mind was spinning. Moments earlier he'd been in a state of euphoria, but now he was truly frightened. KC leaned over, hands on his knees, and breathed hard. While bent over, he tilted his head toward the shed, hoping to find salvation or a means to free himself and Nikki. He saw nothing to relieve his fear. He stood up and stared at Dubkov.

"Thank you Mr. Jameson. Lukova here has given me some useful information. Soon you will return to the cellar where we will tie you up. If nobody finds you, well, too bad. We will take your woman, but if anyone interferes with us, we will kill her."

"No. Take me instead of her," KC pleaded.

"I am giving the orders here. Back into the building. Now!"

KC turned toward the door. The rain stopped and the wind eased just a bit more. An eerie light filled the small courtyard. KC's mind reeled in confusion. He didn't know what to do.

"But—"

Suddenly series of loud noises echoed in the courtyard.

Pop! Pop! Pop!

One of the Russian women screamed, "Take cover!"

KC snapped his head toward the noise. A man he'd never seen before stood next to the small shed holding a small pistol in his left hand. The man raised the firearm in the air and fired two more times.

"Nobody moves," he shouted and raised a small submachine gun with his right hand.

Pavel Dubkov ducked behind the truck and raised his own weapon. Ralph Dodge fired a short burst with his P-2000 submachine gun. Dubkov's pistol flew in the air and blood trickled from his hand. Nikki stood frozen while Vilma, standing next to her, crouched into a defensive position. Alena stepped forward, gun raised, and KC stepped toward the door leading back into the church.

"I said nobody moves!" Dodge said and fired another short burst inches above Dubkov's head. The bullets smashed into the wall behind him sending chunks of concrete in all directions. Everyone froze.

"Now that I've got your attention," Dodge said. KC detected an American accent, possibly from New England. "Thank you for coming together so nicely for me. You will all drop your weapons, line up, and face that wall. Get the man from the back of the truck. Keep your hands high."

The women dropped their guns while Jasha struggled out of the truck and hobbled toward the wall. Ralph Dodge sighed. It was unfortunate that he hadn't had a clear shot at the Russians, but he couldn't risk disabling the truck carrying the nuclear weapons. He had to be careful.

"Ok! Both hands on the wall. Raise 'em high. Now!" Dodge ordered.

CHAPTER 58

Blessed Sacrament Church, El Fortunato

Sister Mary Catherine, eyes snapping open at the sharp popping sounds, was wide awake in an instant. Confusion flooded her thoughts as she remained hidden in a dark corner of the shed. She started to rise when a man raised a rifle and fired it over the heads of a group of people in the courtyard. Then, when she observed the blood soaked sleeve of one of the men she realized that her own life was in danger.

The gunman, unaware of her presence behind him, gave his full attention to his captives, and ordered them away from the truck. Jasha's injured knee buckled and he fell to the ground with an agonized shout. Ralph Dodge hesitated, thinking that his actions were nothing more than a diversion. He stepped sideways and raised his assault rifle, his right forefinger on the trigger, still facing away from the shed.

"Keep both hands on the wall," he began.

At that instant, a huge limb from a nearby tree broke free and crashed to the ground. Everyone ducked. Mary Catherine used the opportunity to search the inside of the shed. When her eyes fell on one of her tools, she shuddered. With little hesitation she picked it up and crept toward the man with the rifle. Mary Catherine said a silent prayer, asking God to forgive her for the sin she was about to commit. She wielded her three pronged long-handled hoe with two hands like a baseball bat, raised it over her shoulder and stepped out of the shed. Not one of the Russians detected the movement behind Ralph Dodge as Mary Catherine stepped forward with her left foot and unleashed a mighty swing. The sharp prongs of the garden hoe dug deep into Dodge's right bicep.

Dodge shrieked in pain and stumbled. He fired off a short burst, but the bullets flew wildly and harmlessly. The submachine gun fell from his grasp and splashed into the growing puddle of water next to Mary Catherine's garden.

Pavel Dubkov rolled to his right, found his pistol, and fired at Dodge. Blood gushed from Dodge's scalp. He fell to the ground and remained motionless. Vilma Revnikova dove to her left and retrieved her gun. She rolled behind the truck keeping her weapon aimed at Nikki's head. Mary Catherine stationed herself over Dodge's body and glared at the intruders.

Time seemed to stop.

KC took advantage of the hesitation and confusion and raced toward the church door. He ducked through the door seconds before Vilma fired her pistol in his direction. Glass shattered and part of the wood door jamb splintered into small pieces. KC threw himself to the floor inside the hallway and crab crawled away from the half open door. Shards of glass gouged his palms, but he kept moving. Vilma Revnikova stepped quickly in his direction.

"Go, Revnikova. Take him out. Quickly. Before he calls the police. Then meet us at the marina," Dubkov shouted. "We have what we want. Goguniv has a boat waiting for us. Lukova, bring the woman."

Alena Lukova hustled Nikki into the truck. Jasha struggled but managed to pull himself into the bed of the truck. Pavel Dubkov studied Mary Catherine for a long moment. His injured hand hung limp at his side, blood dripping on the wet pavement. With his good hand, he bobbed his pistol several times in her direction and smiled. In a smooth move he spun to his right and fired two shots toward the ground. Mary Catherine didn't move a muscle but held her ground and glared back at the Russian leader. Ralph Dodge sprawled motionless, blood oozing into a small pool of water next to his head. Pavel Dubkov glanced at the man and then laughed out loud. He loved it when he won a battle.

"Thank you, Sister. You have been of service to the enemies of America."

He nodded. Then pivoted quickly, opened the driver's door, and stepped into the truck. The vehicle spun around in the small parking area and sped away.

CHAPTER 59

Blessed Sacrament Church, El Fortunato

KC raced down the hallway toward the church school's office complex. It was his only option. He didn't want to get caught in a long corridor or in the open chapel. Nor was the parking lot a safe choice. He turned the corner at the entrance to the office complex and glanced back toward the exit door. So far nobody had followed him, but he didn't believe they'd let him escape. He tried to open several doors, but found them locked. Far behind him a door slammed shut.

The sound of footsteps echoed down the hall as he grabbed at another door. KC had to hurry. This time it swung open. Inside he found a narrow set of stairs leading upward. He closed the door behind him and took the stairs two at a time. The staircase was deathly quiet, but his heart pounded in his ears. He had to find some sort of a weapon before the Russian caught up to him. He hesitated at the second floor landing catching his breath, unsure if he should continue up the stairs.

Vilma Revnikova smiled as she passed into the office complex. She enjoyed the hunt, especially with human prey. She'd trained hard, advancing in rank by defeating men twice her size. They were good, but none were as smart or as determined as she was. She was convinced this American was no different. She would be the cat stalking the mouse. Too bad she wouldn't have time to play with him before she killed him.

Revnikova enjoyed tracking the fleeing American. It made for a great game. The American's wet shoes left streaks on the dark tiled floor. She knew exactly where he'd stopped and tried to open doors and soon she discovered the narrow stairway. She slowed her pace, opened the door carefully and crept up to the second floor. She slowed her breathing and listened for any sound that might tell her where the American had gone, but the storm outside had intensified. Rain pelted the windows. At the second floor landing she paused to study both the floor and the closed door. She discovered a small spot of blood on the door handle and cautiously twisted it. She tensed as a sixth sense made her turn and once again study the floor behind her. She knelt down.

A small smear of water leading up the stairs to the third floor. Halfway up she found another trace of water.

"Nice try," Vilma said and chuckled.

KC closed the door behind him and raced down the third floor hall on his tiptoes, quiet as a scurrying mouse. He lurched past an open room without giving it more than a passing glance. He concentrated on a door at the far end of the hall, hoping to find his route to safety.

"Shit," he muttered when the door handle didn't turn. He pulled the handle hard, then reversed his momentum and rammed his shoulder into the middle of the door. It didn't budge.

KC retraced his steps trying each door as he passed, keeping an eye on the door to the stairway. He expected his pursuer to emerge at any moment. His heart pounded as fear began to bring on panic. Except for the one open door leading to a classroom, every door he was locked. He spun around trying to settle his thoughts. Finally he spied it. A small door almost hidden in a recess of the hallway. A moment later he slid into a tiny broom closet.

The closet was packed with mops, brooms, and pails, making it impossible for KC to fully shut the door. He held his breath when the woman pursuing him stepped into view. She eased from the staircase and crept along the hallway toward the closet where KC had taken refuge. She gripped her pistol in front of her face, ready to fire in an instant. She didn't see KC through the gap between the door and the jamb. KC didn't move and willed himself to breathe slowly. Sweat trickled down his nose.

"Silly boy," Vilma said to herself when she found KC's wet shoes sitting in the middle of the hallway.

She continued past KC's hiding place and reached an open classroom door on the opposite side of the hallway where KC was hiding and stood with her back against the wall. She scanned the area but didn't see him. KC's pounding heart echoed in his ears. Sweat trickled into his eyes, down his nose and onto the floor. Yet his mouth was dry. His racing pulse demanded his body into action.

With a sudden burst, Vilma raised her pistol and spun through the open doorway of the classroom. Without hesitation she fired several shots, then charged into the room and disappeared from view.

KC leaped from the broom closet and hurtled back down the hallway. He didn't have a weapon, but had grabbed a mop from the closet. He sped down the hallway and picked up his shoes by the laces. Halfway down the hall he reached the stairway when sudden gunfire blasted his ears. Splinters from the concrete wall flew past his head. He raced down the stairs three at a time.

Several bullets ricocheted around him, scattering more shards of concrete. Reaching the second floor landing KC jerked his head back up the staircase and caught sight of his hunter. His veins turned to ice when he took in her cold eyes and menacing grin. She laughed, held the pistol with two hands and took aim. Before she could get off a shot KC raced through the open door, found himself in the narrow second floor hallway, and slammed the door shut. The empty hallway, a carbon copy of the third floor, offered no hope of defense. In an act of desperation he opened the door a few inches, wedged the mop head between the steel door and the jamb, and shoved the door shut again. Breathing hard, sweat pouring freely, he stood next to the door with his back to the wall.

Vilma Revnikova pounded down the stairs and reached for the door handle but hesitated before opening the door. She was enjoying the hunt, but knew it was time to finish him off. She turned the knob and pushed the door. It didn't budge. Frowning, she searched around the edges of the door until she found strands of a mop head protruding to her side of the door. Realizing the door was wedged shut, she lowered her shoulder and gave the door a shove.

It still did not yield.

She rocked several times and slammed her shoulder against the door.

Nothing happened. She backed up two steps and fired one shot at the doorknob. Still it held tight. Once again, she rocked back and forth, and then heaved herself forward. The moment her shoulder hit the door it flew open and she lurched forward, unable to stop. Vilma stumbled, unable to keep her balance. KC leaped forward, grabbed her shirt by the back of the neck with both hands and used her forward momentum to run her head first into the solid concrete wall across the hallway.

KC heard bones crack as she hit the wall and slumped to the floor. Blood oozed from the top of her head. She lay still, eyes wide open, staring at nothing.

KC's hands trembled as he bent down and reluctantly picked up her pistol. When his sister had been killed, he'd sworn that he'd never pick up another gun. He'd kept his promise until now, but he had no choice. The Russians had Nikki. Still, the warm metal felt strange in his hand.

He gave the Russian one last look and sprinted down the stairs. He reached the hallway connecting the office complex to the church and halted. Sister Mary Catherine was bending over the man she had maimed with the garden hoe.

"Praise God, he is still breathing," she said.

"Tie him up, Sister. I'll come back, but don't call the police yet. I'm taking the van and going after Nikki. The Russian woman who chased me is on the second floor, dead. Don't touch her until I get back."

Mary Catherine nodded and crossed herself. "You can't take the car. The other man shot out the tires," she replied.

KC spun and tore out of the building. Rain pelted him and the wind tore at his clothes, but he paid no attention. All he could think of was getting to Nikki. He had to free her. The trees above his head danced wildly, leaves flying all about him. He ran toward the marina where he hoped he could stop the Russians before they escaped.

Saving Nikki was all that mattered.

CHAPTER 60

Blue Harbor Marina, El Fortunato

Fadey had the boat ready for them. Only two lines were strung to cleats on the dock and the engines purred like a contented tiger.

Jasha Kerensky hobbled below deck and into a tiny cabin where he collapsed on a small bed. Alena followed Nikki down the steps and shoved her on one of the plush seats in the main salon. From above, Pavel Dubkov finished taping a bandage around his injured hand and shouted instructions.

"Lukova, tie her up and lock her in one of the cabins. Then come up here and help us push off. Goguniv, you will help me load the weapons. Quickly."

Alena motioned with her gun for Nikki to move to the master bedroom at the front of the boat. When Nikki slumped on the bed, Alena rummaged through a storage bin until she found what she wanted.

"Hands behind your back. I will deal with you later, after we are out to sea."

"Up yours, bitch," Nikki said.

Alena bound Nikki's wrists and ankles with strong plastic cable clamps, then sidled close to Nikki and shoved her gun hard into Nikki's ribs. She rose up on her tiptoes, coming eye to eye with her captive. With a smirk on her face she smiled at Nikki.

"I am Alena Lukova and I will enjoy throwing you overboard. You and your boyfriend have caused us much trouble. In time he will get what he deserves as well."

She shoved Nikki on the bed and withdrew from the room, locking the door.

As she reached the bridge, Alena found that the nuclear weapons had been stowed aboard. When she approached the cockpit she picked up an argument between Dubkov and Goguniv.

"You idiot!" screamed Dubkov. "You steal a yacht without functioning electronics? In this weather? I should shoot you now. Imbecile!"

"I didn't know they were broken. This was the only boat I could steal!" Goguniv muttered.

Alena climbed up to the fly bridge, rain pelting her as she reached the open deck. The cover of the bridge above her was flapping in the fierce wind, but the voices of the men rose above the shrieking noise. She didn't care about either man. They were to be used for her higher purposes. It was coming together nicely. Soon she would be in sole control of the Davy Crockett weapons. Her father would be proud. Out of the corner of her eye she detected movement and turned her head toward the mainland.

"Dubkov, look!" she shouted and pointed toward a figure racing toward them.

Dubkov and Goguniv turned and squinted at the parking lot.

"The American. Hurry. Push off!" Dubkov shouted as he sprang to the dock and freed the aft line.

Fadey bolted forward and unhooked the line securing the bow. He took a look back and realized that KC was closing in on the boat.

"What about Vilma?" he yelled.

"Too late," Dubkov replied. "She's dead." It was the only reason Jameson was here.

Pavel vaulted back on the boat spun on his heels and stared at KC. He raised his uninjured hand and saluted KC with his middle finger.

KC watched in defeat as the boat drifted away. Rain pounded the pavement and wind blew straight into his face. He gasped for breath and stared at Dubkov who stared back in triumph and raised his arm a second time.

Alarm bells went off in KC's head. For a moment he was back in the rough neighborhoods of Seattle. He instinctively ducked and began to run in a zigzag pattern away from the dock. KC didn't hear the gunshots over the howling wind. When the pavement in front of him exploded as a bullet ricocheted he dodged to his right, rolled behind a lamp post and kept his head down. Moments later he raised his head and watched the boat pick up speed and plow through the waves toward the open sea.

KC slumped in defeat realizing that the Russians had won the battle for the nuclear weapons. He'd given it his all but had lost. He sat numbly on the wet pavement, raindrops stinging his face as waves pounded the dock. He closed his eyes, breathing hard, shoulders slumping in defeat. He'd failed another woman.

"Bullshit," he yelled, "not this time."

KC jumped up and started to run toward the dock. He'd steal a boat and chase the Russians. He nearly reached the entrance to the docks when a sloshing sound close behind him caught his attention. He spun around as a small pick-up truck barreled toward him. He stopped and stared as the truck veered sharply and spun to a stop not more than three feet from him. The driver's window rolled down.

"Get in sonny! No time to lose."

"Jimmy? What in hell are you doing here?"

"No time. Get in."

KC hesitated and turned toward the fleeing yacht. "No. I'm going after them."

"Not that way, boy. I've got a better idea. Come on. Get in. We don't have time to argue."

Confused, KC rushed around the truck and got into the passenger seat. Jimmy Calhoun pressed the accelerator to the floor and the truck tore off, tires spinning on the wet pavement.

"What the hell are you up to, Jimmy? They've got Nikki and the nukes. I gotta save her."

"Ah, my boy. I learned from Lewis that you can handle a helicopter pretty good. Figured you'd need my help."

"I've never flown in this kind of weather."

"You won't be able to say that after today. Got a better idea? Anyway, I think the wind has eased a little bit."

"No it hasn't."

Five minutes later they reached the Eurocopter after nearly stalling the truck on a flooded part of the road. The salt flats were somewhat protected from the violent storm raging around them. KC leaped into the pilot's seat as Lewis threw a large canvas duffel bag into the back of the helicopter. This time, KC lifted off smoothly and rose slowly before moving the cyclic forward. KC began to relax, as the calming effects of vertical flight settled in. The flight began without incident until they reached an altitude where the north shore of the island came into view. The wind whipped, spinning the helicopter nearly one hundred eighty degrees from their heading. Caught unprepared, KC overcompensated and the helicopter continued its spin.

"Easy there Captain," Jimmy chuckled.

The helicopter rocked and lost altitude. KC set his jaw, held the cyclic control lightly, and gently raised the collective. At the same time he pressed the right pedal forward, bringing the helicopter around into the wind. KC exhaled and began to relax. They cruised for several minutes at nearly 70 MPH, crossed the coastline not far from Blue Harbor and began their search for the cabin cruiser. They held at 100 feet of altitude and headed straight toward the barrier reef.

Jimmy reached in his canvas bag, drew out his binoculars, and scanned the horizon. "What kind of boat we looking for?"

"I think they have a Sunseeker Manhattan with a fly bridge. Fifty feet or so."

Thirty seconds later. "There! Eleven o'clock."

"Shit! They're heading straight for the reef. Don't they know where it is?"
"They can't really see it in this weather. Maybe they haven't turned on the GPS."

CHAPTER 61

The Sunseeker Manhattan "Rebellion"

Nikki sank onto the bed, her hands bound behind her back. The boat pounded through the waves, making it difficult for her to keep her balance. She'd been able to take stock of her situation while they'd remained in the relatively calm waters of the harbor. In their haste to push off, her captors hadn't paid much attention to the yacht's cabin layout and didn't notice the small porthole in the ceiling of the master bedroom. She thought that if she could free her hands, she'd be able to open it and squeeze through. Then play it by ear.

Nikki glanced out one of the portholes and froze. "Shit. Don't they know about the barrier reef?"

She had to hurry. She lowered herself to the floor and in sort of a crabwalk, slid her way into the bathroom.

§ § §

The helicopter cruised along 100 yards behind the Sunseeker and only fifty feet above the roiling waves. KC gripped the controls gingerly and kept a cautious eye on the whitecaps below.

"We gotta turn them before they crash into the reef!" he shouted into his radio.

"Not so loud, sonny. I ain't deaf," Jimmy replied.

"Take the gun. We'll try to lure them away. Hold on tight."

KC swung to the inland side of the boat and reduced his altitude. Spray flew up against the windshield, making navigation extremely difficult. He reduced altitude again, edging closer to the boat until he recognized several people in the lower cockpit. The Russians had abandoned the fly bridge after sailing from the harbor. Fifteen foot waves pounded the boat. They'd retreated to the relative safety below. A canopy was zipped tight, offering some relief from the driving rain and howling wind.

Someone moved behind the plastic canopy. Pavel Dubkov stuck his head out and grinned up at the helicopter. He extended his arm and aimed his pistol.

But he was unable to hold his aim for more than a second as the boat pounded over the huge waves. Raindrops and ocean spray sliced into his eyes, obscuring his view. He retreated into the relative safety of the bridge.

Slowly KC edged toward the shore, hoping the Russians would follow, but the cruiser didn't change course.

"Try the radio!" Jimmy yelled. "Or do you want me to shoot 'em?"

KC switched to the marine emergency band and called for the Sunseeker. Four times he tried to raise the boat and each time was rewarded with silence.

KC dropped the Eurocopter behind the stern and veered sharply to the outside of the cruiser, finally accelerating toward the front. He hoped to use the helicopter to steer the Russians away from the deadly reef. The two machines raced side by side toward the barrier reef. KC edged the helicopter closer. It was a risky move with the yacht moving at twenty five knots. One small mistake would sink them all. But the boat remained on course—straight for the reef.

"Hurry up, buddy. They'll be on the reef in two or three minutes." Jimmy urged. "I'm gonna shoot at them!"

They edged forward and KC detected movement at the bow. "Don't shoot! Wait. They're opening the forward hatch. That's crazy, they'll swamp the boat. What are they doing?"

They gaped in horror as two waves swept over the bow in rapid succession and into the open hatch.

At the cockpit, Fadey Goguniv gripped the steering wheel and held the throttle steady. The boat pounded on the waves so hard that he feared it would break up. But he dared not let up. He'd changed the angle enough so that they didn't head directly into the waves, thus reducing the impact on the bow. Still, it was a bone jarring struggle, made more difficult by the poor visibility.

All of a sudden, something moved on the bow deck. Someone opened the hatch! Dubkov spotted it moments after Goguniv and realized in an instant what was happening.

"Lukova! You stupid woman," Pavel screamed. "Look. She's opened the hatch. Go take care of her. Do it right this time."

CHAPTER 62

The Sunseeker Manhattan "Rebellion"

Following Alena's departure, Nikki got busy. She found a pair of scissors in a sewing kit in the bathroom and cut herself free. Then found a cane in the closet and wedged it under the door handle, hoping it would give her warning if Alena returned.

Finally free of the heavy plastic cable clamps, she stepped on the bed and unlatched the hatch located above the bed. As she squeezed through the small opening she heard banging on the cabin door. Alena! She continued her climb. The noise from the storm and the pounding of the cruiser on the rough waves were deafening. She was desperate to get off the boat. She'd rather drown in a hurricane than die at the hands of the cold-blooded Russian woman.

Nikki emerged onto the forward deck and lay as flat as possible, holding tight to the hatch cover. A wave crashed over the bow and nearly swept her off the deck. She slid to the bow railing and held fast. Glancing back to the hatch, she knew her options were limited. Jumping overboard meant certain death and a return to the cabin below was worse. With no real plan, she inched forward. Suddenly a new noise joined the scream of the storm. Confused, she looked up.

Nikki stared dumbfounded at the helicopter racing alongside the boat not more than twenty feet above her. She slid her butt across the open deck, reached the very front of the bow and clutched the railing with all her strength.

Jimmy climbed out of his co-pilot seat, squeezed into the back of the helicopter, and reached into his duffel bag. He found what he was looking for, yanked it out, and then he tied one end to one of the seats. Then he slid open the side door.

Rain and wind created their own mini-storm inside the helicopter. KC struggled with the controls to maintain his heading and altitude. But he was able to keep pace with the speeding boat. Slowly he edged closer to Nikki.

With one motion, Jimmy threw his rope ladder out the open door toward Nikki. Dubkov realized in an instant what was happening.

"Stop them! Kill her!" he yelled. He grabbed the wheel and spun hard to the right, then abruptly back in the opposite direction. "Keep going, rock her off the boat and don't let the helicopter get close," Dubkov ordered.

Below decks, Alena managed to break down the door and enter the master bedroom. The cabin was flooded with six inches of water. More continued to pour through the open hatch. She leaped on the bed and stuck her head through the opening. She drew a gun that she'd stuck in her belt and aimed at Nikki. But she was not tall enough to reach far enough through the hatch to take a good aim. She shoved the gun back into the waistband of her pants and vaulted through the hatch. The movement of the boat prevented her from standing up, so she did a military low-crawl toward Nikki. She wanted to get close enough to make a kill in one shot. She slid across the deck as Fadey wrenched the steering wheel back and forth.

Above her, Jimmy yelled, "Not more than thirty seconds to impact, KC. Hurry! My God. Look! They're after her."

Fadey realized that Alena was having trouble reaching the American woman. Instead of advancing toward the woman, Alena slid side to side. Fadey expected her to slide overboard at any moment. He decided that helping her was more important than following Dubkov's orders. In spite of his dislike for her, she was part of their team and he didn't want her to die. She was still a Russian. For a moment he turned the boat away from the waves. As he did, Alena reached behind her and grabbed her pistol. She rose to a knee and aimed at Nikki.

Dubkov felt the boat turn and realized what Fadey had done.

"Idiot! You'll swamp us. Turn back into the waves! Go and shoot down the helicopter."

He shoved Fadey aside, grabbed the wheel, and turned the boat back into the waves. The boat lost its momentum as another wave crashed over the cockpit.

Up on the foredeck, Alena wobbled on one knee and aimed her gun at Nikki. The yacht lurched into a wave, and Alena lost her balance and pitched head-first over onto the deck. She pulled the trigger of her pistol, but the bullet flew harmlessly into the sea. Fadey watched in horror as she slid across the deck on her back, her pistol sliding across the deck inches beyond her reach. Half her body hung over the side of the boat, but she grabbed a section of the railing and held fast.

Undeterred, Alena pulled herself onto the yacht, pushed off the railing, and slid toward Nikki, managing to grab her left boot. With the added weight pulling on her, Nikki lost her grip on the rail. The two women slid along the foredeck only inches from the edge. Nikki desperately clawed the deck surface, but couldn't slow their slide. As the boat lurched into another wave, one of the mooring lines flipped toward Nikki. She grabbed the line and held tight. At the same time she unleashed a mighty kick with her right foot to Alena's wrist. The Russian woman screamed, lost her grip on Nikki's boot, and slid over the side into the sea.

Then Nikki rose up, released the mooring line, and stretched for the dangling rope ladder. It swung mere inches beyond her reach. KC dropped the helicopter more and held his position to the moving yacht. Nikki lunged again for the ladder but Dubkov spun the wheel. Again, the bottom rung of the ladder hung inches from her outstretched fingertips. Nikki lost her balance, fell back to the deck and grabbed the railing.

Dubkov watched Nikki and failed to see that the boat was about to plow into a deep trough in the waves. The boat slid down the wave. Nikki looked up at a huge wave towering over her and held her breath.

The wave didn't pound over the bow, but lifted it straight up and over the top. The boat balanced for a moment on top of the wave and the propellers caught air. As the boat reached the apex of the wave, Nikki sprang up, grabbed the top of the chrome railing, and launched herself toward the ladder. She clutched the second rung and swung out over the roiling waves. KC pulled the helicopter up and headed toward the barrier reef.

"She got it! She's on," Jimmy shouted. "Hold her steady. Atta boy, they're following us. Lead 'em out to the reef," Jimmy screamed.

Pavel Dubkov was furious. He had the nuclear weapons, but wanted very much to kill these pesky Americans. Revnikova's death must be avenged. Dubkov turned the boat to follow the retreating helicopter.

"Shoot them you imbecile!" he yelled at Goguniv who had worked his way to a position near the aft end of the boat and had a direct line of fire to the helicopter. Fadey leaned far out, holding on the boat with one hand and fired at Nikki. A bullet nicked one of the vertical sections of the rope ladder. It began to unravel.

"Pull up, KC!" Jimmy hollered.

Dubkov gave full attention to catching up to the helicopter and the woman dangling from the rope ladder. He drove the boat like a man possessed, so focused on the helicopter he didn't realize they were heading directly for the reef.

Fadey Goguniv saw it first.

"Look out!" he yelled in panic. But his words were lost in the roar of the crashing waves.

Too late, Pavel Dubkov realized the imminent danger. In desperation he spun the wheel. The Sunseeker cabin cruiser smashed headlong into the coral reef. The bow splintered and plunged below the waves while the stern flew upward, completely out of the water. Fadey's head snapped forward, breaking his neck. He flew off the stern headfirst and disappeared. Dubkov slammed into the steering wheel and felt his ribs snap. The windshield shattered. He gasped for air and took in a lungful of salt water. Seawater poured through a large hole in the hull, flooding the interior of the yacht. The boat rolled on its side and sank below the pounding waves.

KC slowed the helicopter to a near hover and gently increased altitude as Nikki inched up the ladder. She'd almost lost her grip when Fadey's bullet hit the ladder, but the strong fingers she'd developed during years of rock climbing saved her. She grabbed onto a few strands of rope, and pulled herself up the ladder.

KC kept his eyes on the sea below, not wanting to make a mistake and take them all down. He searched the water below for movement or any sign of survivors, but there was only floating debris from the destroyed yacht. Nikki reached the top of the rope ladder. Jimmy grabbed her wrists, rolled her into the back of the helicopter and slammed the door shut. Nikki sprawled on the floor, gasping for breath. Finally she rose to one elbow, stared at KC and Jimmy and wiped seawater from her face.

"You guys are fuckin' crazy," she said with a huge grin.

CHAPTER 63

Seven days later, KC's beach house, El Fortunato

KC lounged at his breakfast table and sipped a cup of Blue Heeler coffee, black. He'd made it extra strong this morning, hoping for a jolt of energy before his morning swim. His laptop lay open, logged on to the Drudge Report website. He smiled at the huge headline screaming the news of Vice President Gordon's abrupt resignation. Long thought by many party faithful to be the logical successor to President Anderson, Gordon's announcement came as a complete surprise to most political pundits. Poor health was given as the official reason, but there were rumors of some sort of criminal investigation.

KC sat back in his chair and replayed in his mind, for at least the tenth time, the events of the last seven days. Even now, it seemed like a dream.

After the Russian's stolen yacht crashed on the reef, he'd piloted the Eurocopter to the parking lot at the Blue Harbor marina. Just as they touched down, the rain stopped but the wind still blew strongly.

KC and Nikki trotted back to the Blessed Sacrament Church and were shocked to find Lewis Michaelson sitting at a table sipping tea with Sister Mary Catherine. Ralph Dodge was sitting at the table too, his hands tied together. Bandages covered his upper arm and forehead. Luckily for him, Dubkov's aim was poor and the head wound was superficial.

Lewis Michaelson just grinned and pushed his teacup away. Jimmy arrived a minute later and gave Nikki a huge bear hug.

"Glad you're okay, darlin'," Jimmy said, breathing hard.

"Me too Jimmy, thanks to you," Nikki said and planted a kiss on his cheek.

Lewis laughed and Jimmy turned bright red. For once he was speechless. Nikki grinned, sat at the table, and wrapped a towel around her shoulders.

KC settled into a chair and leaned over toward Lewis.

"OK. Lewis, something tells me you're not just the simple hermit you claim to be. After all Nikki and I have been through I think we deserve an explanation. My guess is that you stole the nuclear weapons and hid them in the church. You wrote the poem, didn't you? But I don't understand why."

Lewis smiled and began his story. He'd been an agent for the CIA and had been posted to El Fortunato shortly after the Cuban Missile Crisis. Of course, his name wasn't Lewis Michaelson at that time. His task was to monitor communications to and from Cuba. He'd also been sent to Cuba to carry out covert missions for the CIA. Senior Cuban government officials had mysteriously disappeared and a man matching Lewis's description had been implicated. As a result, both the Russian and Cuban Communists had placed a price on his head. Dead or alive, but preferably dead. He had fallen in love with El Fortunato and decided to make it his permanent retirement home. He changed his name and appearance and assumed the identity of a cranky hermit.

Lewis maintained contact with old friends in the CIA and learned all about Vice President Sydney Gordon's suspected illegal activities. Gordon was crafty, and no one in the government was able to collect enough hard evidence to arrest him. When Colin Farthington became interested in recovering the Davy Crockett weapons, Lewis saw an opportunity to nail Gordon and to secure the Davy Crockett weapons in a safe place. Still, he had to stay undercover. He'd been warned that Gordon would stop at nothing to secure the nuclear weapons. The situation became more perilous when Dubkov and his commandos entered the picture. Then it became much more than a search and recover mission. But by then it was too late to change tactics.

Neither Communist assassins nor Ralph Dodge had been able to find him. However, Jimmy Calhoun, ever the scrounger, had stumbled on the truth about Lewis Michaelson and they became close friends. When Dodge began to ask curious questions at the golf course they turned the tables on him and had been covertly watching him for some time.

Once Dodge realized he could hang for his own crimes, he ratted on the Vice President in exchange for the promise of much reduced charges. Gordon's one mistake was relying too much on Ralph and not insulating himself from his operative. Dodge had dozens of tape recordings proving Gordon to be a ruthless killer who would stop at nothing to achieve power.

Dodge cooperated on the chance that he'd receive a Presidential pardon, with the condition he would testify against Gordon and then make El Fortunato his permanent home. He would keep quiet about the Davy Crockett nuclear warheads. President Alexander was officially undecided, but her inner circle had assured Dodge that she would agree.

Sister Mary Catherine had been an innocent bystander who was in the right place at the right time. Both Jimmy and Lewis felt certain that God would forgive her for her act of violence against Dodge. She said little, sipped her tea, and stared out the window.

Father Prescott, of course, had learned about the nuclear weapons, but could not tell anyone about them. He wasn't really sure if Jimmy Calhoun was Catholic, but when he had shown up at the confessional and told the priest everything, Father Prescott's lips were sealed.

A neighbor's dog barked at passing horseback riders, snapping KC back to the present. He took a sip of his now cold coffee and studied his computer screen. A final item on the Drudge Report caught KC's eye. Only one day before, a small jet plane had disappeared over Mongolia with all on board presumed dead. The only passenger was a member of the Russian President's inner circle by the name of Boris Lukova.

"Lukova? Russian President? Some pretty heavy hitters mixed up in this thing," KC muttered, remembering the Russian woman on Dubkov's team.

KC got to his feet, picked up his binoculars, and ambled outside. He remained at the edge of his porch and watched as a salvage barge chugged between two buoys, heading toward the barrier reef. Colin Farthington's people were on location. They'd recover the nukes and ship them to Colin's Puget Sound hideout.

KC had contacted Farthington and recapped the activities leading to the discovery of the weapons. Colin contacted President Anderson, and in spite of their political differences, had come to an understanding. Colin would keep the Davy Crockett weapon system in exchange for Dodge's testimony and for information about Lieutenant Baker and his missing squad. A Delta Force team would sneak on the island in the next day or two and recover the bodies of the five dead soldiers. The Eurocopter would be sold, at a price far below market value, to a local tour company.

KC listened to a roar overhead, leaned over the railing and gazed at the sky. An American Airlines Boeing 737 soared up on a steep trajectory, gaining acceleration for the ninety minute flight to Miami. A strange sadness came over him as he pictured Nikki sitting in a window seat gazing down on him. Had he made a mistake letting her go? Nikki's boss had recalled her to Boston. She'd strenuously objected, telling him she'd finish their project in less than a week. Her boss was not sympathetic and had ordered her to return immediately, giving Nikki the distinct impression that she'd be on the unemployment line within twenty four hours.

KC didn't see her during the first days after their ordeal, both needing the time alone to recover mentally and physically. They'd dined together the previous night but had talked little. Nikki spent most of the meal staring at her plate and pushing to food around with her fork. They'd been through such a whirlwind of activity that small talk seemed inappropriate. When the meal ended, Nikki told him she was leaving very early the next morning and doubted she'd ever return to El Fortunato.

On their way out of the restaurant, they passed a young woman walking up the steps from the parking lot. KC recognized her immediately.

"Sister?"

"Hi guys. Nice to see you under better circumstances. But I'm not a nun anymore, I'm afraid."

"What happened?" asked KC.

Mary Catherine smiled. "It's funny. Hurting someone made me realize my true mission in life. I'm thankful that Mr. Dodge will be OK. I love helping others, but I finally realized that being a nun didn't give me what I really wanted. I still love the Church, but I'm hoping to move to Olympia, Washington, and go to nursing school."

KC and Nikki congratulated her and thanked her again. Her bravery helped to save their lives. She turned to enter the restaurant unaware that KC had slipped a small card into her pocket.

Much later, after she'd had dinner, Mary Catherine found the card in her pocket. Written on the back were five words: *If you ever need help.* She flipped the card over and read the name followed by a phone number. *Colin Farthington. Sinclair Island, Washington*

KC escorted Nikki to her car. She opened the door, turned and looked at KC with moist eyes. Then she leaned over and gave KC a light hug and a quick peck on his cheek.

Then she was gone.

KC shook his head, returned to his dining table, and settled in front of the computer. He flinched and nearly spilled his coffee when the back door banged shut. He hadn't heard it open, and he wasn't expecting visitors. His nerves were still frazzled.

She waltzed in, wearing white shorts, a sleeveless pale green blouse, and flip flops. Toenails freshly painted a soft red. A silver necklace with a small whale charm hung from her neck.

She smiled, her blue eyes sparkling.

KC gawked.

"Nikki, what the—" he finally croaked.

"Jameson, don't be a dunce." She fiddled with her whale charm.

"But I thought you—"

"Oh shut up, please. It's time I took you up on your invitation."

"Invitation?"

"You've forgotten? On your beach. The first time we met." She stood with her hands on her hips and stared at him.

KC frowned and muttered, "What?"

Nikki smiled and tilted her head.

"Come on, let's go for a skinny dip," she said and reached for the top button of her blouse.

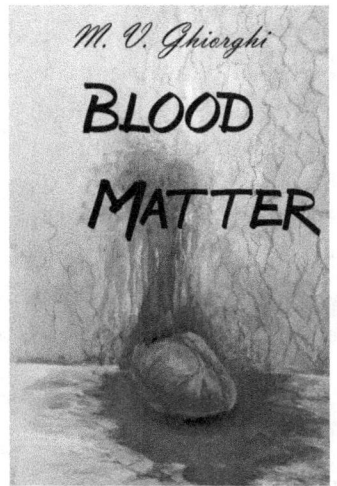

Blood Matter
by M.V. Ghiorghi

A broken hearted FBI Agent on the run from his demons...a sadistic genius with a penchant for vengeance...a beautiful forensic psychiatrist with a monstrous past...A doomed love triangle born of crime. Can Agent Vasquez survive the Blood Matter?

A Bother of Bodies
by A.J. Capper

Mabel Fuller and her brother are on the run because of Mabel's attempt to kill their mother fifteen years ago. But they're not worried about the law. Their main concern is the family that raised them, the McAllisters. Mabel and Dean manage to avoid the large Irish network with frequent moves and aliases. Or, so they thought. When dead bodies turn up in Dean's newly-purchased barn, the brother and sister fear the McAllisters have found them. Until they realize it's something worse...

The 8th Doll
by Chris Rakunas

When the body of geologist Charlie Landry is found beheaded beside the cenote at Dzibilchaltun, Skips Kane calls his old friend Professor Alex Guidry. Their only clue turns out to be a small doll with the number "8" written in Charlie's own blood. The mystery of the 8th doll will take Kane and Guidry down the winding paths of the Yucatan where they will discover the answer to the age old question: what will happen when the Mayan calendar ends?

Fugo: Terror From the Sky
by Elizabeth Young

In November, 1944, the Japanese began launching 9,300 unmanned bomb-carrying balloons (Fugo) that were carried east over the Pacific Ocean by the jet stream. Now, almost 70 years later, a group of terrorists using modern technology will try and succeed where the Japanese failed. It will be up to an unlikely group to find a way to stop one of the deadliest terrorist attacks on US soil.

www.ingramcontent.com/pod-product-compliance
Lightning Source LLC
Chambersburg PA
CBHW071331250626
47159CB00004B/1564